Praise for Subimal Misra

"When I read him for the first time, I saw that his stories rebelled against dominant literary conventions. His stories were anti-stories, a violent mix of fragmentary narratives and essays, even statistics, juxtaposed together to deliver a shocking statement."
—Amitava Kumar

"Misra leaps and alights from branch to bough in a cosmic garden of characters. . . . These two anti-novels are an invitation to engage with discomfort, through purposeful silence, jump cuts, and ferocious prose."—Percy Bharucha, *Hindustan Times*

"Misra's stories are not seductive; their power lies in their subversion. They look straight into the dark heart of the middle class and use an array of startling techniques to undercut the pretensions and hypocrisies by which we live."—Jerry Pinto

"The book is a *Guernica* of sorts in printed letters and words—stark, chaotic, gut-wrenching, and confounding in its immensity of interpretations."—Nabina Das, *Dhaka Tribune*

"Misra's anti-novels are as much a reinvention of the novel, that has been congealed and commodified into a methodised, stationary, inert 'cultural object,' as a critique of the bhadrolok, the bourgeoisie, whose totalitarian impulses have alienated and antagonised the rest in Bengal."
—Rohit Chakraborty, *Open Magazine*

"What was Subimal Misra thinking? Why can his stories catch your attention despite them not having a linear plot, a simple thing to tell? Who knows? They're worth reading and, if your imagination works, you could hear his laughter at the very end."—Luis A Gómez, *National Herald India*

ALSO BY SUBIMAL MISRA

This Could Have Become Ramayan Chamar's
Tale: Two Anti-Novels

WILD ANIMALS PROHIBITED

SUBIMAL MISRA

TRANSLATED FROM THE BENGALI
BY V. RAMASWAMY

OPEN LETTER
LITERARY TRANSLATIONS FROM THE UNIVERSITY OF ROCHESTER

First edition, 2021

Library of Congress Cataloging-in-Publication Data: Available.
ISBN-13: 978-1-948830-35-5 / ISBN-10: 1-948830-35-3

This project is supported in part by an award from the New York State Council on the Arts with the support of Governor Andrew M. Cuomo and the New York State Legislature

Printed on acid-free paper in the United States of America.

Design: Anthony Blake

Open Letter is the University of Rochester's nonprofit, literary translation press:
Dewey Hall 1-219, Box 278968, Rochester, NY 14627

www.openletterbooks.org

Contents

Thinking is the greatest pleasure known to mankind.
—*Bertolt Brecht*

Translator's Note

V. Ramaswamy

The first collection of Subimal Misra's stories in English translation, *The Golden Gandhi Statue from America*, was published in 2010. The response to this, by reviewers as well as readers I was in touch with, has been positive. That has been encouraging.

This collection grew out of work begun during the Sangam House writing residency, in early 2011. That was followed by considerable study, thinking, consultation, rethinking, selection, and reselection. I was aware that I carried a serious responsibility, of presenting and representing Misra's writing, and so I was alive to the importance of making a meaningful and substantive selection. A manuscript consisting of twenty-two stories, written by Misra over the period 1972–98, was completed and submitted in 2012. But I revised the collection in late 2013, limiting it to stories written during the 1970s and 1980s. I included, for instance, "Calcutta Dateline," which

I had translated during the Ledig House writing residency earlier in the year, as well as "Come, See India," both of which are among Misra's own favorites.

The first book was undertaken without much thinking. But it was while working on the present volume that I really began to enter the depths of Subimal Misra's writing. In 2006, shortly after I began translating Misra, my Aunt Revathy had shared with me an essay by Michael Hofmann, the translator of the Austrian writer Joseph Roth. That had planted seeds in my mind toward dedicating myself to a project of translating Misra. It was in the course of working on this volume and observing my own growth as a translator of Misra's writing, as well as zest in the work, that I implicitly decided to devote myself seriously to a long-term, multi-volume project of translating a fair representation of his short fiction.

The present collection is very different. The first volume was like a quick introduction to Misra's early short fiction, taking some of his more accessible and translatable stories. In his preface to the book, Misra used the metaphor of a staircase, to refer to readers climbing it to approach his subsequent work. This volume represents the next level of Misra's writing. It breaks new ground. It demands much more of the reader, it is more challenging.

Underlying the selection was my own urge to understand Misra's body of work, to learn about and find significant stories, and know their significance, even as I was translating. Hence my role has been akin to that of a—barefoot—scholar, sociologist or anthropologist, editor, compiler, and literary craftsman, besides being the translator. I felt rigor in selection was vitally important, I could not afford to be random or arbitrary in my choice of stories. I have tried to be as fastidious as possible. Growth is essential and vital for me, to be able to satisfactorily represent Misra.

Nilotpal Roy, a literature scholar, teacher, and writer has put together a list of eleven stories of Subimal Misra, arranged in a specific sequence, which he considers his best stories. According to him, this selection would give an idea about the kind of writer Misra is. He told me, "They show experimentation in narrative technique and departure from narrative, defying all conventions. There is also a thematic variation across these stories. They carry to fullest expression the various significances or characteristic aspects of Misra's work. These stories are also extremely challenging to transcreate in another language." Roy has also prepared another list of twenty-four Misra stories for a sequel volume to *Thirty-Six Years' Scuffles* (which brings together fifty-five of Misra's stories from across thirty-six years of his literary life). For my selection, I have benefited immensely from Roy's lists.

While the stories in the first collection were taken from *Anti-Stories Collection* and *Thirty-Six Years' Scuffles*, the stories in the present collection have been taken from these books as well as *Babbi* and *Anti-Novels Collection*.

Misra has told me that since he departs from the narrative form, the emphasis is on language. My eagerness and enthusiasm had to repeatedly contend with the impossibility and futility of meaningfully translating various significant stories. Hence, with dismay, several had to be left out, for not being amenable to translation. For instance, I had actually worked a lot on "Blue Phosphorus" (1977), an important and thought-provoking story. Discussing this, Misra told me that the translation should not be logical, but dreamy, like Lorca and Borges. He wanted indirect words, not direct ones. He wanted me to ingest Pablo Neruda and Paul Éluard. But finally, on his advice, the story was dropped. Nevertheless, I did include, say, "How a Horse . . ." and ". . . Who's Responsible?," both of which are also very much about language.

But I must admit that it is very frustrating and dismaying that one simply cannot really translate dialects or accents, or voices/language forms. The reader of the English translation—unknowingly—entirely misses so much more that the original Bengali has. I hope this eventually works as a creative challenge for the translator.

∽

In Bengali, a book is called "boi," and a film, which is called "chhobi," or picture, is also often referred to as boi, because films used to be based on popular or famous novels or books. Subimal Misra, however, calls his stories films, or chhobi. The film aspect, that is to say the language of cinema, of Eisenstein and Godard, for instance, and the attempt to render a film effect, is very evident. In *Thirty-Six Years' Scuffles*, Misra writes: ". . . I make collages. I cut. The way in which the camera treats a situated object. The object is already situated, the camera draws it out. From where it is situated. It gives it distinction.

"It creates. I too prepare writing. I do it in the manner of holding a camera. I cut from the writing. I create. Something new from what existed. A new kind of creation. A new presentation. A new point of view. A new measure . . ." At another level, to my mind Misra also anticipates Pedro Almodóvar.

Here I might mention that just like successive sentences or paragraphs by Misra, bearing visual quality, form a montage, Misra readers know that he also plays with text and font in the pages of his book. He forcibly enters the reading process too, with an actual visual intervention involving text, font size, arrangement, layout, and so on. A recent chance encounter with Anna Lena von Helldorff, a graphic designer from Leipzig, lead to my mentioning this aspect of Misra's writing to her. She was very interested. Nilanjan Bhattacharya, documentary filmmaker and Misra buff, has also been interested in this aspect. I am excited about this because I urged Anna and Nilanjan to initiate some kind of project that looks at this visual intervention, and it looks like it's happening.

A number of themes appear in this collection. A significant one is the Naxalite uprising. "Meat was Bartered," "Thirty-Six Feet Toward Revolution," "From the Morgue on Bhawani Dutta Lane," "Come, See India," and "The Road to the Mill Jetty," refer to events of 1970–71. Several stories in *The Golden Gandhi Statue from America* had also referred to Naxalism. Misra told me that some of his stories were also of a Naxalite bent or worldview.

I was ten or eleven years old in 1970–71, when Kolkata lived through those turbulent times. Although I was somewhat aware of what was happening around me, I was too young to understand anything. I began educating myself in the early 1980s, and thus began to know more, and understand something of the Naxalite uprising and movement. I entered social action in Kolkata in the mid-1980s, and became acquainted and associated with several former Naxalites in this work, who were active in the public domain after their release from prison in 1977. While they spoke to me about many things, I do not recall their having said very much about their own Naxalite experience, or about that time. I began translating Subimal Misra in 2005. Hence, out of my own interest, as well as to aid my translation work, I was eager to know more about the events of this time. I had read books and articles giving political accounts and analyses of the Naxalite movement, and had seen some films as well. But I wanted to know the nitty-gritty, of what it was like to live through that time. The slogans used in rallies and meetings, the writing on the walls, the names of places where murders and mass murders took place, and so on, all of which occupied and formed the vocabulary and consciousness of thinking folk then. I came upon Debashis Bhattacharya's *Shottorer Dinguli* at the Convention of Marginal People organized by Nagarik Mancha, in April 2011, in Subodh Mullick Square, Kolkata. It was among the books on sale in one of the bookstalls near the entrance. I flicked through the book, and bought it at once. Skimming through parts of the book in the following months, I thought it merited translation. The author, a journalist, was a former Naxalite activist, and the book brings together a series of articles he wrote about his experience. I saw it as an informative document about a significant period in the life of Kolkata and West Bengal, especially in a time when public memory is fading. Reading and then translating *Shottorer Dinguli* (under a Sarai fellowship), I was better able to understand allusions in Subimal Misra's stories. My translation is titled *Those Days*. It is almost like a companion volume to Misra's stories.

But equally, Misra's writing too provides a kind of lens through which one can view and understand that turbulent period, and the events that took place, which was formative in so many ways for an entire generation.

In the stories in this collection, there are facets of West Bengal during the late-1960s, '70s, and '80s; there is satire; the sexual morality of the Bengali middle-class is looked at, as is poverty and political degeneration. There are samples of different kinds of writing, pieces about what are essentially eternal problems, very ordinary and mundane, yet very real. Some of the stories are time specific, they help us to understand a particular time. There are some very short pieces—the term "flash fiction" is now in currency—like "From the Morgue on Bhawani Dutta Lane" and "The Road to the Mill Jetty." And there are longer ones, such as "Radioactive Waste" (which Misra calls a "novelette") and "Calcutta Dateline." Stories like "Come, See India" and "In a Deserted Spot Measuring a Foot and a Half" are prose poems. "Heramba Naskar . . ." is like newspaper reportage. And there is sex, which this collection deals with fearlessly—and heretically—holding up a mirror to Bengali middle-class society. Sonagachi, Calcutta's famed red-light district (adjacent to which Misra worked for many years as a schoolteacher), is the setting for "A Perfect Picture of This Social System—Who's Responsible?."

Misra had told me that he has a kind of Gandhi fixation. The title and a few stories in *The Golden Gandhi Statue from America* refer to Gandhi, and he makes an appearance in this collection as well, in "Mohandas and Cut-Ball." The reader may wonder whether Gandhi and Naxalism form two poles in Misra's writing!

Through it all, Misra chronicles the unceasing, relentless descent through the two decades, from the turbulent, violent early '70s, through years of collapse and stagnation, to the all-around, moral, and political bank-ruptcy and corruption in Calcutta and West Bengal of the late 1980s, under CPI(M) rule. It is like showing the other face of Bengali "enlightenment." Misra, an iconic and unequalled "underground" figure in the Bengali literary firmament, searches unremittingly for a form and a means to express and convey the reality of the ruinous putrefac-tion and mass debasement he lives within. Subimal Misra has constantly evolved as a writer. Moving on, and leaving behind what he did earlier, has been a conscious aspect of his writing practice. Through these stories, one can also observe the evolution of Misra's writing over the years, in terms of both form and content.

❧

Misra had spoken to me about being influenced by the Ben-gali writer Kamalkumar Majumdar. He said Majumdar knew French better than English, and actually preferred French. He liked Marcel Proust's long sentences a lot. His sentences are as if originally written in French, and hence they become long in Bengali. "Come, See India," one of Misra's favorite stories, bears the Majumdar stamp. The language is *sadhu bhasha*, i.e., close to Sanskrit, with *tat-samyo* or Sanskrit-like words. Eisenstein's montage also appears here. The story also exhibits the "cut-up" method, inspired by Burroughs and then given effect to by Misra in his own way. Misra said it is like cutting up a scene into tiny bits.

This was very interesting for me as a translator. It was as if I had to move back and view the text from a dis-tance, both visually and conceptually, to try and discern characteristic features, and then re-render this into English, thus restructuring the original and creating something new, with new punctuation. It was akin to a process of sculpting, to produce text art anew. I may have departed from the original in the course of processing the text in order to aid reading in English.

It is pertinent here to also mention something about the story, "How a Horse Becomes a Donkey . . ." In Sanskrit, one can create a compound word by stringing together one word after another. Thus, for example, in Sankaracharya's *Soundaryalahari*, we have the word *sukham-akhilam-aatma-arpana-drisha* (without hyphens), which means something like "with the sight of voluntarily offering up all pleasures." In "How a Horse . . ." Misra too creates compounds, like what I translated as "pervasive–boy–metaphor–rage–adorned" (without hyphens) and "massive shoulders–speedy–young son-in-law–lolling in adulation" (hyphenated). He told me that he had come across the former term in the Sanskrit text, *Harshacharitra*, about king Harshavardhana (seventh century AD).

"Calcutta Dateline" is among Misra's ten favorite stories. Here is an extract from the story:

> A dark-skinned adivasi, his wavy hair flowing down to his shoulders, plays a dhamsa like a crazed man—who knows how long he has been playing? The dhamsa was about six or seven feet long, as tall as a person and a half, made of ancient buffalo hide. It had been carried on people's weary shoulders. Dark-skinned, muscular, and bare-bodied, he kept assaulting the dhamsa in drunken intoxication with two saal sticks, and with the assault awakens Sing Bonga, the clan god . . .

Kudchi flowers, kudchi flowers
Bloom in bunches everywhere
A tiger ate the landlord in the forest

Translating this, I recalled a painting of an adivasi woman by Jamini Roy, which, when I gazed at it at an exhibition, had seemed to me to become like a hologram of the woman's movements and chatter. Similarly, Misra's use of this subversive adivasi song brought alive to me, anew, that it is adivasi society that teaches us and renews our civilizational and ecological values, as well as protest and resistance. The image, sound, beat, and cadence sprang forth from the page. Like the protagonist, Somprakash, who searches for "pure experience," I too, in the course of translation, slipped into the characters, I sang and danced, and I tried to translate in that mood and cadence.

The final stage of translation for this collection was an almost magical experience, each day carrying me to a new high of aesthetic, socio-political, and sensory awareness and craftsmanship.

With my son Rituraj training to be a chef, I had occasion to think of the body of work of a writer being akin to the work of a master chef, with the stories, essays, novels and so on forming different parts of a grand feast. In this vein, I had thought of my translation too as akin to a culinary craft, the book being like assorted hors d'oeuvres, or various cuts of meat with choice of garnishing. Craft presumes art. It leads to an artifact. Subimal Misra produces textual artifacts.

Misra holds that his conception of a novel is very different from the European one. He says that it boils down to whether one preserves or destroys the storyline. And so that determines how the writing will be read.

What does one make of a collection like the present one?

In "Babbi," which appears in this volume, Misra writes:

> All these disjointed narratives, coming in succession, produce a reaction in readers' minds. To extend their influence onto feeling and then go beyond that—to poison. That is what shock treatment is all about. Their mental balance wilts. The insensitive calculus of reason is shaken. Everything animate and inanimate, here and now, becomes mired in blood.

Janam Mukherjee, historian of the Bengal famine, sent me this comment about the story "Radioactive Waste" in a personal communication:

> Subimal writes about the persistent uncertainty, misapprehension, and trauma of human existence, juxtaposing the absurdities of desire, disappointment, and fear that characterize modern life against the mute indifference of dispassionate nature and the moral rectitude of myth. Man flounders, in Misra's prose, seeking to "pluck flowers of beauty," while wallowing in the muck. In this sense, it might be said, Subimal Misra is the Beckett of Bengal, with a keen and withering eye as devastatingly bleak as Beckett's, and a humor as dark and sublime. In "Radioactive Waste," goatish Ajoy's lust for fat and matronly Sushma is continually interrupted by the bomb blasts

that characterized 1970s Calcutta, as well as by the claustrophobia of middle-class life, and the blood-stains of the self-inflicted wounds of existential doubt. Such stains, Misra warns us, "are not easy to remove, they accrue, like a debt, over a long time." Tied to this wheel of unrelenting and unrealized desire and violence—both within and without—Ajoy remains human—all too human—and "not for once did the idea of snapping the rope and escaping enter his mind." Like the rest of us, imprisoned by fear, he watches idly while the undoing of the natural world continues apace, and the waste that we have created out of the natural order of things—in this case radioactive trans-uranium—threatens to drown us all, whole and alive.

Reading Subimal Misra is a process, in which one has to first learn to read his writing. A grounding or preparation is needed, so that one can start discerning and appreciating the quality of the work, and especially his later writing.

Misra has a mischievous and pungently vicious eye. Here are some examples: ". . . his freshly fornicated wife" ("Wild Animals Prohibited"); "The death-seed assumed labor pains . . ." ("In a Deserted Spot . . ."); "When the shameless god comes around dawn, hobbling on his crutch . . ." ("Calcutta Dateline"); ". . . the colorful slough of ply-wood, fabricated over thirty years, which people at every turn call democracy" ("The Cow . . .").

As a translator, it became only too clear to me that he pays minute attention to everything around him, all the things which people habitually disregard and take for granted. And he describes this environment, an effort akin to meticulous crochet work, depicting a vast scenery rendered with merely a needle and thread. To find words for this as a translator is not at all easy. One can write, express, and describe with ease all kinds of things. And yet be stuck at conveying the simplest things. Misra is a wordsmith of humble things.

In keeping with the objective of his writing practice, Subimal adds one or more blank pages at the end of his books, sometimes—as in the anti-novel, *When Color is a Warning Sign*—with the following note to the reader:

> As you read the book, write at once whatever comes to mind, whenever, here, on this blank page. Thereafter, copy that and send it to the publisher's address. In return, you can buy any of the writer's books at a 25% discount. Write whatever comes to mind, without inhibition. Bear in mind that the writer accords far greater importance to your opinion than to reviews in commercial papers, he accords your opinion respect and thinks about it. We would be especially grateful if you kindly include in your letter your name, address, age, occupation, which books and whose books you love to read, and a brief description of your point of view regarding the cultural world. If we receive your letter, we can send you a card that will serve as an acknowledgement.

Similarly, at the end of *Thirty-Six Years' Scuffles*:

> Write down your reaction to the reading in the blank pages, whatever came to mind while reading. The book will be complete when the writer's text and the reader's opinion come together. Subimal's books have never been completed, and won't, without the

active participation of the reader, without the reader's reaction.

Misra expects the reader to engage actively with the text, the reading being a form of activism, matching the activist writing he himself engages in.

∽

Some of Subimal Misra's images come up again and again. A magician performing tricks in the Maidan. A beggar woman on the street. The pages of an old calendar fluttering in the breeze. Lumpen youth sitting on newspapers under a street lamp, playing cards. Garbage, excreta, and corpses on the riverbank. A dog standing over a dead body, tearing out and eating the flesh. The henpecked Bengali husband. Ruffian youth affecting sartorial and coiffured style. The stench of death pervading the city. A woman standing in knee-deep water, collecting wild spinach.

Through the very words and terms of speech communicated by him, a reader of Misra's Bengali original discerns how much Bengal is essentially a rural land, of rural and predominantly poor folk. Misra's writing is full of the dialect of South 24 Parganas district. The sensitivity and empathy with which he represents humble, laboring folk is untranslatable. And simultaneously, by also looking at the juxtapositions regarding the urbane, cultured class, we can see how power plays out in the society in all its ugliness.

The treatment of women in Misra's stories could be a possible subject for study by an activist scholar. Only in the Bengali original would the full context and nuance of each word be accessible. Take, for example, the stories "The

Golden Gandhi Statue from America," "Money Tree," "The Naked Knife," and "Fairy Girl," from *The Golden Gandhi Statue from America*. Or "Here's How We Wring a Quarter of Lime," "Thirty-Six Feet Toward Revolution," "Heramba Naskar . . ." "Come, See India," "Spot Eczematous," "Calcutta Dateline," and ". . . Aparna," in the present collection. The women can be sexually promiscuous and uninhibited. They are feisty, practical, cynical. They are clearly superior to the men, whom they make fun of and use. There is the vile, uncouth, iconoclastic, and yet sentimental madam in ". . . Who's Responsible?." The typical aspirations of the middle-class girl-woman is portrayed in "Radioactive Waste." Reduced to prostitution by mill closure, in "The Road to the Mill Jetty." Vulnerable, raped, and murdered in "In a Deserted Spot . . ." and "Secret Vrindavan." I hope the translation prods someone to think and work on this subject.

A translator's take on the writing is perhaps quite different from anyone else's. Reading the original so many times, and so minutely, leads to another kind of sensibility. As mentioned, several stories could not be translated, and this translator can only vaguely glimpse the character and range of Misra's work, emerging from rooted literary genius.

~

I hope the publication of translations of Misra's short fiction is a means to greater and growing awareness and readership of his work, in Bengal, across India, and around the world, wherever literature is cherished and flourishes, despite all odds. Misra is not a writer whom any and every reader will like to or even want to read. That is natural and Misra knows that very well. But there will always be some readers who would. And taken together, from across the world, that would not be such an insignificant number. That readership keeps literature alive, irrespective of everything else. I know Misra would be happy that he reaches this readership, and so I hope this book is a means for that to start happening.

I also hope there is translation of more of Misra's considerable body of writing, and translation into several languages. I would personally like to see translations into Hindi, Marathi, Malayalam, Farsi, Japanese, French, Spanish, German, Italian, and Portuguese. I am happy that *The Golden Gandhi Statue from America* is now being translated into Malayalam, by Cecily Joyce, and into Farsi, by Mustafa Raziee. But the mediation of the English version can only lead to loss in translation, which a direct translation from Bengali to other Indian languages, can substantially remedy. Hence I will be working with Cecily and also hopefully with Mustafa, to attempt to bridge the translation gap.

I discovered Art Spiegelman's *Maus* in 1995 and over the last ten years or so I have been a collector and devourer of graphic literature. Almost from the time I began translating Misra, I have wanted to see graphic versions of his stories—although, perhaps because of his unfamiliarity with the developments in this medium over the last few decades, Misra himself remains skeptical about whether his writing can be represented graphically. I had thought about a graphic collection of some Misra stories set in Calcutta. In 2009, I discovered the work of the manga artist, Yoshihiro Tatsumi, and was overwhelmed. I saw Tatsumi as the Japanese Misra in graphic form, or Misra as the Bengali Tatsumi in textual form. I remain hopeful that Misra's stories will find graphic representation and would be happy to join hands with artists toward that end.

∽

This translation project has been a significant experience for me, a process of learning and personal growth. That is very satisfying. As someone who has lived and grown with books from childhood, I was very happy to formally enter the world of literature as a translator of a writer like Subimal Misra. On a recent visit to Brazil, I was fortunate to learn the name of the great writer of that nation, Graciliano Ramos, thanks to my friend João Carrascoza, the writer, who gifted me a copy of *Barren Lives*. Reading this, I could also see in perspective Misra's art, work and place in the world of literature. As this book went to press, I discovered the monumental book, *The Corpse Exhibition and Other Stories of Iraq*, by Hassan Blasim, translated from Arabic by Jonathan Wright. The title of the book and the cover design immediately brought Subimal Misra to mind. Once again, reading this helped me see Misra in perspective in world literature.

I read an interview with Michael F. Moore, the American translator from Italian to English. In it, he said: "The authors I translate are like houseguests. I don't let them sleep with me: they get the sofa bed." In my case, it is as if I am a willing conscript to the project of translating Subimal Misra.

There are many writers, but there are very few translators. And yet, without translators, the world of literature would dry up and die. Literature is about reading, but it is also about sharing. The American writer, Paul Auster, has said: "Translators are the shadow heroes of literature." And Göran Malmqvist, the well-known translator of Chinese literary works into Swedish, said in a recent interview: "World literature is translation and translation is world literature—without translation there is no world literature, and that is true."

Translation is a magnificent and powerful vocation. Just as a writer must and will write, some people must translate. It is a peculiar temperament, an aesthetic, a pleasure, and a passion. A translator may choose a writer, but a translator may also get chosen. That happened in my case. Being a "chosen one" is satisfying but also difficult.

Subimal Misra is a not just another writer, but a different kind of writer. Similarly, he is not just another person, but a different kind of person. Hence it is only natural and inevitable that working with him is also a different kind of experience. I am fortunate and glad that my translation venture did bear fruit in the form of books. It has been a valuable apprenticeship in the practice of literature. I hope I shall continue to learn and grow through the Misra translation project.

—V. Ramaswamy

In Lieu of a Preface

I am distanced from these stories because of the passage of time, and so I am unable to say anything about them. There is a great distance, because of time. Besides, I have objections regarding the selection of stories as well as the title of the collection.

I want to write so as to disturb the reader, and that has been my practice so far. I am not sure whether the stories collected here do that, whether they make the reader throw away the book in disgust and rage.

Every story carries the mark of a particular time. I don't know whether the story has an appeal outside of that time. Unless the story is very powerful, it may seem dated.

Several of the stories are from the Naxalite period, and are written with a Naxalite bent, for instance, of doing away with everything.

I don't expect much. It depends on the readers how they will take these stories. Each reader is different. Whether at all the stories will appeal to them, and if so how—I don't know. My writing does not conform to the kind of reading that has gained currency. Readers would definitely be dismayed. There is so much work with language, so much of destruction, which would challenge readers. It is difficult to bring this out in translation.

Breaking narrative—that is what I seek to do. So the emphasis is on language, and not on the story. The emphasis is not on what I say, but how I say it.

This kind of writing is hardly seen in world literature. After writers like Dostoevsky, Tolstoy, and Thomas Mann, the narrative tradition is saturated. There can't be any more. And so I ventured in another direction, departing from narrative. A major reason why I never wrote a voluminous novel was because I would not be able to have it published. I preferred short writing, in the style of Kafka and Camus.

Everyone wants to be a big writer. I don't want to be a big writer at all. I want to be a completely different kind of writer. When I am read, it should not seem like writing at all. I would be most happy if I am not counted among writers.

Subimal Misra was unwell and hence unable to write a preface for this collection. However, he agreed to make a few comments that could be used in lieu of a preface—Trs.

WILD ANIMALS
PROHIBITED

Wild Animals Prohibited

Any person bringing, keeping, or raising in urban areas categories of animal or animals notified as dangerous vide government gazette notification, in contravention of regulations promulgated by the government, or in violation of the rules and conditions of the license, shall be fined an amount not exceeding rupees two thousand.

—Clause 71 (a) of the Bengal Law no. 4 of 1966

When Jodu arrived with his wife in the evening, we got started. Ram and Shyam had come by late afternoon and were sitting around, making conversation every now and then. Every once in a while they said: "We're gonna have a helluva time today!" At three thirty, when it was time for the daily water supply, my wife entered the bathroom with a loosely draped sari around her and a towel and soap case in hand. When she emerged an hour later, her body exuded the fragrance of sandalwood soap. I often feel like biting her exposed shoulder but don't, thinking it would be improper. But as soon as Amala emerged and my old maidservant went into the bathroom with a pile of unwashed plates and utensils, I took advantage of the privacy to fondle my wife a little. But Amala was largely preoccupied with getting dressed or doing up her face, she didn't give me much time. Yet I took the opportunity to lick and lap up as much as I could. Ram and Shyam called out from the next room a couple of times, "There are some squeaky sounds coming from your room, what are you up to, Madhu?" Making no bones about it, I replied, "I'm kissing." They got excited and said, "We wanna kiss too." In response, I tried to explain the situation to them. I counseled them to wait: "Gently into the night."

And thus the evening advanced. Ram and Shyam looked at their watches, they were getting impatient and restless. They knew things couldn't begin before Jodu and his wife arrived. In the other room, Amala daubed color thickly on her cheeks and face. The old maidservant shuffled back after washing the dishes. I shouted at her: "What's with you, you whore, you take so long to wash the dishes—come on now, hurry up and pour the liquor into the glasses." The old woman was afraid of me. She quickly busied herself with fetching the liquor from the cupboard. In whispers, I indicated to the others the authority I wielded in my house.

The evening grew darker and the lights were turned on. Sipping our drinks, we waited in silence for Jodu and his wife. They arrived after a while, sat down, had a drink. I closely observed Jodu's wife, Kamli—how she sat, how she spoke, the way she laughed animatedly at every turn, almost to the point of keeling over. My wife Amala joined us after a while. She brimmed over with laughter at every word, her entire torso from waist to shoulder swaying lustily, the anchal of her sari slipping off time and again to expose her breasts. We carried on talking while we drank.

Ram asked: "Is the revolution advancing?"

Shyam replied: "I don't know."

Jodu asked: "How many salary increments did you get?" I replied: "Three."

"What are those people doing?"

"They keep playing cards, sitting beneath the mezzanine verandah upon newspapers spread out under the tube light."

"What do they do?"

"Sometimes when we are rapt in pleasure, they climb the stairs and knock on the door, they look here and there suspiciously and with angry expressions they ask, 'What's happening here?'"

In the midst of such talk the flower seller's cry could be heard: "Bel, buy belflowers!" Hearing the word "bel," the women got excited. I called the flower seller upstairs and bargained with him. Then I bought two strings and we fixed it on the women's hair, me on Jodu's wife's, Jodu on my wife's. They were beside themselves with joy and let us kiss them right there in front of the flower seller.

After sending off the flower seller, while some of us were kissing—were getting ready to, rather—standing at the door was the young beggar girl from the bottom of the stairs, dressed in dirty rags, holding in her arms a rickety baby just a few months old. She wailed: "Ma, a roti for me, ma!" And I don't know why but I thought of the people sitting beneath the mezzanine verandah on spread-out newspapers, silently playing cards under the tube light. Sometimes my wife gave her a roti or half a roti and sent her off before her incessant wailing began to get on our nerves. But most days she got nothing and she stood at the door for a long time, pestering us. Sometimes we teased her: "Hey girl, wanna come and drink some booze?" She stared at us with wide eyes as we fondled each other. Sometimes one of us got up in exasperation and twisted her arm. She would turn blue in pain and her eyes saw only darkness as she tried to protect her now withered young breasts as well as her baby. Sometimes we chucked whatever we could find at her—pieces of stone, for instance. We even spat at her. Some days my wife took the situation into her own hands. When the water in the kettle boiled she splashed it on the girl's body, and when the girl and the baby screamed at the sudden attack, we enjoyed it.

The disturbance of the flower seller and beggar having passed, the night advanced. We kept waiting, kept getting ready. There were bits of stray conversation. We talked about how the number of our female members could be increased with the addition of at least two more persons, and our wives protested loudly at the suggestion. They said, "Getting more girls is not permitted. How are we inadequate in any way?" We laughed, and through our laughter we enjoyed their talk. "Compared to other countries, we simply haven't become civilized"—we talked about all that too, about social norms and taboos on sexuality being a sign of backwardness, and we talked about the many countries in the world that had left these behind long ago. Our women expressed their views on how outrageous the ban on the import of foreign lipsticks into the country was. Sometimes it was "contraceptives need to be more reliable." They talked about things like that. Ram and Shyam wanted to talk about those four people, the ones beneath the mezzanine verandah, who kept playing cards silently under the neon light, sitting on spread-out newspapers. We knew very little about them, and consequently our discussion lacked substance. Jodu said, "Those people are extremely unsocial, they don't say anything even when we walk past them." My wife said, "They're men, after all, the day you bring them under control they'll talk your head off."

The night progressed. We couldn't stand any more useless chatter. I said, "Let the real thing begin now. What's the use of sitting around any more?" Hearing me, everyone sat up. Everyone wondered what today's item would be. After some discussion, the day's program was decided upon. Given that there were four men and only two women, there was some argument and bargaining and laying down of conditions. But eventually everyone was reassured that they would get their share in the next session, and the matter was more or less resolved for the day. But on some days, there was a toss, and those who won the toss got the chance to get the women. Then the bright lights were turned off and a dim blue low-watt bulb was lit, because if anyone outside found out or suspected anything, it could be dangerous. I had locked the old maidservant up in the tiny store room. I had told her, "Sit quietly, you old woman, don't you dare shout and scream!" Each time I locked her up like this, I inevitably felt a surge of emotion, and in that agitated state, I felt like landing two blows on her face. Damn her, how long would she oppress us like this?

And so, taking care of everything in this way, we got ready.

We took the time we needed because if one was not well-prepared, if the chase was not undertaken, the whole thing got diluted. It became unappetizing. For instance, we always kept in mind the fact that there were four guys here and only two women, so when it came to taking off the women's clothes and all that, we never had them do it themselves. After all, even a tiny bit of excitement is achieved with a lot of trial and effort, so how could it be wasted just like that! Take those who didn't win the toss, or those who wouldn't get a chance that day. We gave them the chance to do a little bit in the beginning of the session, so they too got some crumbs of pleasure. And thus did we advance and become advanced in our quest for pleasure. The door to the house remained closed, we were shut out from the world outside, engrossed only in ourselves.

Sometimes there were hindrances in our work: those four people, the ones beneath the mezzanine verandah, who keep playing cards, sitting silently on spread-out newspapers under the neon light. They come upstairs with an air of enquiry. When I open the door, they come near and, wearing a grave face, want to know, "What are you people doing?" We are busy, and I say so, and not getting any cue from us they make their grave faces graver still and descend the stairs. Sometimes there's the sound of many feet arriving together and halting in front of the locked door, and in our languid embrace we wait in the dark with thumping hearts. But there is no knock and the moment passes. We suspect someone found out about the whole affair, that they spread the story in the entire neighborhood. But there was no reaction, no one came to apprehend us. We had been frightened in vain. No one in the neighborhood suspected anything about us. Those four grave-faced people who kept playing cards under the neon light did not suspect anything yet.

But sometimes, late in the night, after we have finished our business, when, on tired legs, I go down to see off our guests, I see the beggar girl in rags, lying in the dingy darkness on the last step of the staircase, holding the baby in her arms to her breast. Seeing her, my words suddenly choke in my throat. I feel a peculiar uneasiness rising within me, I can't make any parting talk. As quietly as possible, without waking them up, I run upstairs, my chest heaving in fear. As I climb the stairs, I feel the clutch of the desolate midnight in my heart. Observing my fear, my freshly fornicated wife says testily, "Just forget about it. I'll pour a pot of hot water on them tomorrow and the whole lot will be set right at once." It is this statement of my wife's that I am unable to rely on. I get scared, and on such nights I continue to feel scared. I go to the bathroom and splash water on my face and eyes to drive out the fear; I try to forget the whole scene. But try as I might, I can't. Fear roams through the recesses of my heart. Hearing the sudden screech of brakes of a speeding car in the desolate midnight, I sense that same fear awakening once more in my heart.

_____

Maratmok Jontu Aana Rakha Ebong Poshar Opor Bidhinished, 1972

By the Roots

One had to miss half a day's work to get from Madan's village to the post office. In order to reach the black tarred road where the motor bus plied, the village folk set out before daylight, packing some muri into the folds of their clothes. It would be close to noon by the time they arrived. In between lay a narrow creek, a tidal one. It didn't permit boats and boatmen all the time. During the rainy season the creek surged up. It brimmed over so much it reached the paddy fields on either side which stretched out as far as the eye could see. At such times, people reposed all their faith on the upland palm grove.

Steering a dugout through a half-submerged clump of babla, Madan took out the beedi tucked behind his ear, stubbed out earlier after two puffs. He asked for a light from the people in the dugout beside him. He closed his eyes and puffed, the borrowed light seeing the beedi through past the green, hand-spun string at its base—most of the time.

One day, as evening descended after a very hot day, a man from outside arrived in Madan's village. Bunches of bare-bodied people crowded around and gaped at the saffron punjabi he wore. There wasn't a single person in the village as soft-cheeked as him. He took out a sheet of paper printed in three colors and stuck it carefully on the trunk of the banyan tree. Rubbing his glistening, well-oiled cheek with a finger, he said: You lot get me all the votes in the village and I'll get you jobs for the village boys.

The word "job" was a joyful one. They had heard of this gold zari-bordered word before. Two people from the village worked in the district headquarters. When they came to the village on various occasions, the skin on their well-oiled cheeks also glistened like this.

The villagers were rapt. They thought about it. As they thought, they gazed at those cheeks upon which even flies slipped.

So it's settled then. You lot will give all the votes and I'll give the jobs.

What could they do! When a man from a distant land muddied his feet and came so far and asked fervently for votes, could anyone refuse? Wouldn't that be sacrilege? Give it, give it, give all the votes only to this babu. There was no dearth of people who could convince them otherwise, yet they gave it, gave all the votes to him, for they greatly feared sacrilege. On his part, the man did not betray them. He selected three or four stout, well-built boys and took them along with him, at his own expense. Going to the tar road, they climbed onto a motor bus. The next day a sheet of paper was handed to each of them. They were going to get jobs in the police. Apparently there was a training period for some time. After that, a full-fledged job!

Even though it was a bit difficult at first, in a few days Madan got used to the ways and ethos of the police. He made friends. When he donned the uniform and strapped on a weapon to his waist, a completely different person seemed to occupy his body. He could feel a unique enthusiasm within himself. He was a soldier now, protecting the nation's law and order. The muddy roads of his village, Shampa Raypur . . . steering dugouts during the rainy season . . . setting out for farm work before dawn along the narrow paths, clad only in a gamchha tied at the waist . . . the sensation of going with a group of friends to watch a jatra all night long—it all seemed like a dream now.

Lighting a cheap cigarette, he gustily blew out smoke. Having gotten half a day's leave, his friends came and said, Come on, boy, there's a new Hindi movie running in the city, with lots of fighting and action, let's go see it. He gazed at the poster of a barely clad dancing girl standing with her hips stuck out before he entered the hall, shoulder to shoulder with his friends. He still wasn't used to emitting whistles, but when his companions whistled during the movie's fighting scenes, even he couldn't help feeling boisterous.

Thereafter, there was a steady improvement in Madan's life. He understood that if people like him smoked beedis openly they lost their prestige. Not wearing underpants beneath trousers was uncivilized; wearing shoes without socks was terribly rustic—he learned practical things like that. He discovered quickly that to the police, ordinary peasant folk were no more than inconsequential members of the public, they had to be spoken to contemptuously.

Besides, the villagers were too unsophisticated, they lacked culture—he became aware of things like that. When he went to the village, he steered clear of the cowshed. It stank too much. And being bare-bodied was now unthinkable. After getting the job, he had returned to the village only twice. Smartly attired, in crisp police uniform, with the bearing of a soldier, his boots shining, an urbane, clean-shaven face. He went to his house, walking with his chest thrust out, observing everything with an air of contempt. Before reaching his home, he remarked, Oh, what muddy roads, how on earth do people live in villages!

As soon as the training was over, he was sent to a small police station in a mofussil town. It was early December. The dew on paddy fields full of golden stalks of grain glistened like tiny pieces of glass. There was a dispute between sharecroppers and the landlord regarding cutting the grain. Madan and a few others had to go into the village, walking some three miles or so, rifles slung across their shoulders. A lot of people had gathered. All the peasants stood on one side, cleavers in hand, and on the other side a man with sideburns, accompanied by a bunch of toughs armed with staffs—one of them also carried a gun—the landlord's gang. All the arrangements had been made in advance at the police station. The landlord's men had come at night and settled everything. As many as two whole chickens had been gifted, in addition to everything else. The landlord's gang would arrive first. Brandishing their staffs, they would start cutting the base of the paddy stalks. The police wouldn't be there then. They would arrive after the paddy had been cut; they'd catch a few innocent peasants and bring them to the police lockup on the charge of creating a disturbance. And that's exactly what happened. When they arrived, the landlord's paddy had already been cut. Some people had their heads broken. The atmosphere was tense. Madan and his group apprehended two meek peasants. As soon as Madan's eyes fell on one of them, he felt a blow inside his chest. The man looked like his eldest uncle—bare-bodied, a shabby gamchha slung over his shoulder, a salt-and-pepper beard of bristles on his long-unshaved face. Seeing the police, he muttered an abuse and spat out in hatred. Criminal charges had to be made against him. Madan brushed aside his reservations. One couldn't do one's job in the police with this mentality. The officer in charge had explained things threadbare.

Another time Madan had a different kind of experience. There was a pavement-clearing operation going on in Calcutta. Madan had been transferred to the Tollygunge police station so he had to participate in the operation. It was really strange. The shelters of those who slung gunny sacks and torn tarpaulin sheets to somehow be able to lay their heads on the pavement had to be demolished. All the clay utensils they possessed had to be dragged out and crushed. They were the refuse of the city; if they were not removed, the city—what was it they said—Calcutta could not become a Cleopatra of a city. He gazed long at them—torn, patched clothes, emaciated faces, bare feet, skinny children in their arms and on their shoulders. Here too, he received a jolt—the man who looked like his uncle had reached this place as well. Looking wide-eyed at them, wringing his hands, he said: You tell us where we should go when you drive us away like this. Madan saw a woman his mother's age lift a torn gunny sack to her head with sick, bony arms, a baby in the crook of her arm and another one at her shoulder. He didn't look too long—if he did he wouldn't be able to perform his duties. He had come on orders, so it was best to follow the instructions blindly.

Madan's third experience was when he had gone to combat striking workers of a jute mill in Howrah. The millworkers had begun an agitation demanding their rightful wages. As soon as the police squad reached the place, they dragged the workers out of their homes and arrested them. Apparently they had resorted to violence, attacking the owners with iron rods. Here too was a man who looked like his uncle. He wore a torn lungi and stood arguing with the police:

— The mill owners have stolen the money from the rightful wages for our labor and amassed piles of money, so we . . .
— Since you know so well what's good for you, get into the black van, quickly.

Each one of them had a rifle barrel pointed at his chest. No one spoke further, but their faces were like quarried stone. The man who looked like his uncle climbed in too. A police lathi had landed on his head by now and he was bleeding. Madan suppressed a deep sigh. The officer-in-charge had told them not to get embroiled in political complications under any circumstances. They were to remain neutral at all times, for they were soldiers follow-ing orders. Otherwise, they would lose their jobs at once. The law-and-order machinery of a sovereign nation had to be extremely strict.

Our Madan grew through a string of such experiences. If he was in a rural locality, the relevant people brought chickens and ducks. When he walked down the street, people automatically made way, even strangers offered salutes. Influential people established a good rapport with him in advance, just in case they needed police help some day. If he was based in the city, send-ups were obtained regularly. Naturally, the share of the collection from shops and pavement vendors was fixed. Those who sold soda and lemonade during the day and booze at night sent across special offerings from time to time—even women. By now he was well-versed in the pleasures of a police job. His neighbors' eyes danced when they saw his foreign watch and foreign transistor radio. But he knew that in this job, fetching even tiger's milk was not impossible.

Madan was married now; he had three children. He had built a house near Garia. But he hadn't severed his links with the village. He had expanded his paddy fields by a few acres. He went to the village at least twice a year, at the time of planting and during the harvest. His wife was a city girl. She disliked the village. But Madan could not sever his attachment to the rural soil. In the beginning, he went donning his police uniform, swaggering along, puffing a cigarette. Now he was getting older. People from twenty or twenty-five neighboring villages knew him well. When he visited he wore a ghee-colored terrycloth punjabi over a dhuti, with shiny gold buttons. He didn't even mind smoking beedis in public now. Rather, he always lit a beedi to go with his tea, though he was well aware that smoking was harmful. Seated in the ramshackle village teashop, he talked about the existing rural situation and prevailing conditions. He discussed politics. He spoke about unemployment. There was almost nobody in the village who had not sought his help for a son or brother or some relative. He would say politely: Do jobs come easy? Times are difficult . . . But despite his disavowals, he had managed to place quite a few people here and there. He had brought Dinabandhu Maity's widowed sister to live with him. She cooked, cleaned, and looked after the children and received a salary of ten rupees. Who else in the village, apart from him, had the means to help others like that?

For a while now he had been nurturing a fond wish in his heart. He wore four rings on four fingers, to harness the powers of all the planets for his personal advancement. Looking absentmindedly at his fingers, he recalled the famous astrologer telling him: Success in politics is clearly visible in your hand! The statement had struck him to the core of his heart. He would retire soon—his two daughters had been married off, his son had gotten a job at a bank. Shouldn't he try to get into politics now? What was the harm in trying it out when it was written in his hand?

But he couldn't tell anyone about his heart's desire. The nation's politics was deteriorating by the day. The Naxalite movement had touched him too. The country's youth were becoming wilder. And he felt he too ought to set aside everything else and do something for the country's poor folk. Or else who would think about the people of this region—who else had the means? And if he got the votes once, he would be able to get all the unemployed youth of this region some work or the other—come to think of it, after a lifetime in the police force, he didn't lack resourceful contacts.

When a meeting was convened regarding the proposal to upgrade the village's eighth standard school into a high school and he was elected to chair the meeting, he decided to air his proposal. When the business of the meeting was concluded, he said with an air of humility—in the same way that politicians delivered speeches, he placed the matter artfully before the assembled people: Brothers, I say, in the coming elections, if you people fetch me the votes, I'll get jobs for all of you—that's it, isn't it. Yes! Yes! Yes! The response came from beyond the span of the lantern's light, where a bunch of adolescent youths stood leaning against a bicycle like a forbidden bundle, from where they shot forward, trembling.

Shekhodshuddhu, 1977

Only God's Alive Now

The credo of the French Revolution was *liberty, equality, fraternity.* Three powerful words. I plucked these words from the dictionary and popped them into my shirt pocket. And thus my journey commenced. I had amazing strength of mind, waves of zeal surged from every pore of my body. But before I could advance even a little, I had to stop. A taro forest lay ahead. A huge taro forest. The road was covered in jungle. Giant-sized taros had borne fruit. The way ahead was completely blocked.

I found a relatively clean taro tree and sat under it. I sat down and began to think. The taro tree had fairly large leaves, so with the sunlight blocked the place was nice and shady. Lounging in that shade, I began to ponder.

I didn't have to think too long. Thoughts began to enter my head very smoothly, by themselves. They had to come. Because I had as many as three fresh words in my pocket. And they were considered the most progressive words of this age. By attaching these three words to any legal or illegal act, I could forage a pocketful of acclaim, I could obtain many clinking coins. After that, who could catch me! I thought:

In this country, when something's for free
Even for donkey's shit, a stampede there'll be
So hey, what's a taro forest!

And so I issued a call. I did that on behalf of the unfed and the homeless.

People came in droves. The peasant came, plow in hand (or perhaps it was a sickle in his hand). The clerk came with pen in hand. One or two people came on scooters, their wives riding pillion, tummy, midriff, and armpits exposed, who, in order to keep the outward glitter intact, were barely able to feed themselves. They came and ate. Ate and shat. Ate, shat, and filled that black-as-death taro forest. Within a few minutes the taro forest had vanished. There was only shit, it was full of shit. Let there be shit, at least the taro forest was gone. The shit didn't affect me. I plucked a taro fruit from the tree. Like a performer, I juggled with it for a while. And thus with the French Revolution's—what do they call it?—profound three words in one pocket and a taro fruit in the other, kerchief held to nose, I crossed the shit and journeyed toward the wide world.

As I walked along the path, I met a frog. Frog-baba went cock-a-doodle-doo, and calling out to me, he said:

Where are you going, my child, what's that in your
pocket I see?

I replied, matching his tune:

I've filled my pocket with liberty, equality, and fraternity.

The frog said: What are those? Insects of some kind? Can one eat them to one's fill?

Oh, what a stupid idiot—don't you know *liberty, equality, and fraternity*? What a waste that you were born on this earth!

I passed by the frog. It was not to the lot of frogs and such to grasp the significance of these things. That required awareness. It needed brains, knowledge. Traveling through mountains and forests, I came across a savage, a wild bird's feather stuck in his hair, animal skin on his hip, bow and arrows slung across his back. He brought me liquor in a bamboo mug. He roasted a wild boar he had hunted and set it down before me. At night he sent his wife to me, asking her to serve the guest. His conduct made me very happy. I took out the three words from my pocket and showed them to him. He toyed with them for a while. Holding them to his nose, he examined whether they had any smell. He knocked them against stone to see if they broke. He tried to melt them by putting them inside the wood stove. Then, not knowing what to do with them, he returned them to me. I grew thoughtful. The unfortunate savages could not really understand the value of these three words.

I came away in sadness. When my back itched, I scratched my back. When I was thirsty I gulped and drank water. There were no limits and frontiers to my grief. In such a state of mind, I came across Hitler. Yes, Hitler. He was running around organizing an anti-fascist movement.

This Hitler was unrecognizable. Moustache removed, he was well attired in dhuti-khaddar worn over the military garb. He had managed to get Mussolini with him. He was conducting public meetings all over India as part of an anti-fascist movement. Oh, the way he spoke—what magnificent gestures! He explained, clear as water, that Subhas Bose was no patriot but in fact a fascist stooge.

I stopped. Netaji Subhas Chandra a fascist stooge! I was amazed. Seeing me, he smiled mischievously. He said: You're puzzled to hear all this, aren't you? But don't worry. To each age its rites. Even I must be anti-fascist. I have to survive, don't I? Looking at my pocket, he asked: What's that in your pocket, bulging like a camel's hump?

Yes sir, that's the slogan from the French Revolution. I set out with that in my pocket.

Hitler was extremely pleased to hear this:

The French Revolution, my boy, is a mighty fine thing.
Superb its color and its finish just makes you sing.

Give me a couple of slogans, I'll put them on the anti-fascist festoons. In a trice he took the three words and stuck them on his red longcloth banner. The words swayed on the red longcloth like a skinned goat hangs in a butcher shop, its tongue sticking out. The whole thing looked very sexy. The red longcloth fluttered in the breeze. The words almost quacked out loud! Shaking his head, Hitler suddenly said: Here's an idea—you've come from India, why don't you add the word ahimsa to this? It would be fantastic. And of all the saffron-colored words, ahimsa is the most nonviolent one.

Without waiting for a reply, he fetched the word himself and put it on his banner. The word's faded saffron color almost seemed to sputter amid all the red. This was a miraculous connection. The slogans of the French Revolution on the anti-fascist movement's red longcloth, together with ahimsa's saffron. My mind danced in heavenly bliss. Oh, stupid life, what more do you want! So what if it was Hitler, hadn't he accorded the words adequate honor? In this marketplace of a world, how many could do that? How many had the heart? So what if he made Subhas Bose a fascist stooge? If he wished, he could prove that Lenin, Stalin, and Mao Tse-tung were all fascists. But what would come of it? Those were just words.

But the mental unease did not cease.

This boy, Hitler, was terribly clever. He could grasp things. Tucking the end of his dhuti pleat with native deftness into the pocket of his punjabi, he said: Hey, you're looking worried, my lad. It seems you don't like it?

It's not that.

Got it! I know what's on your mind.

He looked somewhat absentminded. He scratched his long sideburns noisily a couple of times. Then he said: All right. There is something you can do. I'll introduce you to a genuine person. Try to talk to her.

He signaled to a woman with his eye.

Do you see her?

Yes, I do.

This is a fallen woman. Feeds herself by—what do they say?—compromising her dignity. If you want to help her by offering some money, she'll refuse it. But be her customer, pay her for her services and she will accept. She wants to be honest, from her own perspective.

As soon as I saw the woman, she caught my fancy. Why not spend a night with her? What was wrong with that? It was useless to think of morality and sin right now. Later, at an appropriate time, with a puja offering of five shiki in Kalighat, all my sins would be wiped out, and so—

So I went with the woman to her room. Hitler whispered: You're going with the woman, that's all right, but your real work is to try to employ the words. Don't forget.

I did as he said. When she removed her sari, I took the words out of my pocket. I rang them like bells. Turning them around like a prism, I filled them with rays of light. I said proudly: These are real words! Their meaning is so wonderful. They're extremely useful. At one time these three words had turned human thought upside down. You'll never ever find anything like them!

Even if she earned her bread by selling her body or whatever, the woman was shrewd. Toying with the words for a while before pushing them away, she replied brazenly: I got all that. But of what use are these to me? I mean, can one buy rice with words, no matter how fine the words might be?

My spine tingled. I had never met such a brave woman in my life. She looked at me with fluttering eyes. My heart skipped a beat. But I had paid her cash and had to get my money's worth—whether she accorded value to the words or not. Now I could see clearly that the words would soon be weighed against the power to purchase bread. I didn't want any of that. I stood up. I couldn't look her in the eye. I had come for my bodily needs, so I would engage in the commerce of bodies—and then leave. What was there to be afraid of, that too with a prostitute like her?

I finished my business quickly. Sitting up, I saw something astounding. Who would have thought this thing could be put to such use? The girl had weighed down the sari and the chemise she had just shed with those words. And the words, each one like a colored paperweight, lay, somewhat like our ahimsic Ashokan wheel, on the sari and petticoat shed by the whore, gasping for life.

Ekhon Ishwori Ekmatro Jeebito Achhen, 1975

Meat Was Bartered

[Remembering Saroj Dutta's death]

The phantom-like figures said: We are policemen, from the CID, we are going to search your house.

Show me your identity cards. Show me the search warrant.

They said: We are from the CID. We don't need search warrants.

At that very moment, the chairman of the mayor's advisory council in the Calcutta Municipal Corporation declared that the number of people coming down with ailments of the blood from consuming rotten meat was growing by the day. Meat was being sold illegally throughout the city—stale, rotten offal, full of disease-causing germs. A lot of people were falling sick after eating the meat of sick cows, buffaloes, goats, and pigs.

In the dead of night, two guards entered the police lockup and once again pulled out Taera Master. The CID officer, Prabhat-babu, put his legs up on the table; he was lounging in the chair. As the guards brought Taera Master and made him stand in front of the table, he wasn't able to stand: a baton had been pushed up his rectum that evening. Prabhat-babu said:

I'm sorry, Taera Master, I am unable to move my feet away from your face. I am tired. We can talk.

Prabhat-babu sat thus for a few minutes with his feet in front of Taera Master's face. Taera Master could barely stand straight. He tried somehow, clutching the chair in front of him. There was silence. He was unable to hold himself upright. Seeing his condition, Prabhat-babu said, slowly, as if he were chewing his words: Tell me, Taera Master, what do you have to say?

Taera Master managed to say: Kindly tell me what you want me to say. I shall cooperate.

Complaints had been received about the condition of the slaughterhouses in Calcutta. Some citizens opined: The abattoirs are unhygienic. Entrails of dead animals everywhere. Diseases are spreading. This three-hundred-year-old abattoir has been transformed into an antisocials' paradise.

Some people barged into the room noisily—one of them brandished a revolver.

Taera Master said: Who are you? Who are you looking for?

We are searching for Taera Master.

I am Taera Master. Tell me what you have to say.

Come with us, the jeep is waiting outside.

But who are you?

Who are we—Hooch Gopal, explain who we are. One of them prodded another. His hands fidgeted.

What's the proof that you are policemen? Show me your identity card.

You want to see the identity card, bokachoda—Hooch Gopal landed a kick to his stomach—here's our identity . . .

Taera Master collapsed to the floor, his hands clutching his stomach. A thin line emerged at the right corner of his mouth, blood . . .

An officer of the municipal corporation said they were able to inspect only a small part of the meat sold in the city. About 350 cows and buffaloes and 400 smaller animals were slaughtered daily in the municipal abattoirs. They claimed these were in no way harmful to one's health. Their meat was stamped. They did not know how safe the huge quantity of all the other meat sold in the city was. That meat was not stamped.

Why are you taking me? Where will you take me? What's the charge? Have I committed an offense? If I have then you have to inform me of the charges against me before you arrest me.

One of the men, who wore a police uniform and whose face still bore the mark of a bhadralok, pointed a revolver at Taera Master's chest and said in a threatening voice: We don't have time to argue with you. As he spoke, he grabbed Taera Master's collar and dragged him outside.

There were several complaints against Calcutta's abattoirs. They had not been washed clean in a hundred years. Bones, intestines, and bits of skin belonging to the meek creatures had accumulated in various corners, there was hair strewn all over the place. Thirty thousand gallons of water a day were required. About ten gallons were available. In the hope of getting bits of meat and intestines from the heaps of garbage nearby, the poor folk gathered at dawn. They waited for hours, dreaming of a piece of fresh bone or a handful of offal. Earlier they used to fight among themselves for this at the slightest pretext. But they no longer do that. They single-mindedly scour the garbage. This has now become their method of fetching food, their only option. They frequently fall sick and die. But for every person who dies, five more take his place. Some of the employees of the municipal abattoir and the local mastaans are most enthusiastic about these hapless folk, they regularly take collections.

Taera Master was taken in a jeep and made to wait till 2 P.M. outside Alipore Court. No one knew he was there. At two in the afternoon, they announced that there was no lawyer and an order should be issued to keep him in police custody. And so an order was issued for Taera Master to be held in police custody for ten days. The sun set.

The municipal corporation's chief health officer announced that Calcutta's abattoirs had not been repaired for many years. He admitted that sanitation arrangements, water supply, and inspection facilities were abysmal now. But he added, on a hopeful note, that recently they had gotten down to getting rid of these problems. Whatever was of critical importance was being repaired. Licenses might be issued to some companies to oversee the business of slaughtering cows and buffaloes in accordance with the rules and regulations. All meat would henceforth be stamped.

—Are you in a political party?

—I believe in scientific materialism. I don't support any political party of India.

—Do you support the Naxalite movement?

—If a movement wants to do something positive to change the rotten system, even if it takes the wrong path, I will still support the dedication of those who do it. I have no doubt that there was no shortage of dedicated boys among the Naxalites.

—The path of parliamentary democracy or the way of the barrel of a gun—by which process do you think a change in the political structure is possible?

—Social change never came through the parliamentary process.

After that no more was asked. Taera Master was taken inside under special police watch.

There were no leftover body parts of cows and buffaloes. The talk of their being stolen was not correct. Skin, horns, hooves, offal, everything—everything was sold. That was why the complaint that diseases were spreading from the rotten body parts of dead animals was baseless. Every year the abattoir pays money to the municipal corporation on this account. The Calcutta abattoir was never an antisocial's paradise. All that was hearsay.

When questioned, the state health minister responded: It is the municipal corporation's responsibility to monitor matters pertaining to the abattoir and the sale of meat. If there is clear evidence of health hazards, the state government will investigate the matter. Why cry hoarse before that?

There is no further information about Taera Master.

Mangsho Binimoy Holo, 1986

Thirty-Six Feet Toward Revolution

1

Suddenly this morning, at exactly nine thirty, Subhendu, like a fool, got shot on the curb at the crossing. After being shot he gazed vacantly in all directions and saw no one anywhere. Only the wayward bullet from the pipe-gun that had lodged itself inside his chest. As he tried to fix the long lead pipe with his hands, he thought, This was not supposed to happen. For some reason he couldn't fix it. Raising his arm toward a young woman walking briskly along the pavement ahead, he called out: "Excuse me, I've been shot." The woman looked exasperated and stopped. "What the hell is wrong with you lot can't you see I'm going for love?" As she spoke she stared fixedly at Subhendu's eyes and—who knows what she saw—paused for a moment. "All right, come along." It was office time. People were moving very fast all around Subhendu. The wind blew on his face. The young woman lifted his bullet-pierced body to her chest, and like an expert mother, without any sign of weariness, crossed the road and put him down beside the lake, where the decapitated statue of a tonsured pandit stood. Just a few days ago, someone had broken the head of the statue in the darkness of the night. Blood gushed out from the hole in Subhendu's chest and wet the base of the headless statue. Subhendu was about to sink into terror. He saw rain descend, illuminating his surroundings. The rain poured down and in it his wounded self, the young woman, the waters of the lake, and the beheaded statue in dhuti-chadar and Taltala-slippers—everything got wet. It got flooded quickly. The pavement was flooded, so was the road, and every nook and corner between the buildings. Securing her clothes around herself, the young woman just about managed to salvage her modesty. The wind blew, a cold wind. Subhendu shivered and forgot about his bullet-ridden chest as the floodwater rose all around him. In front of his eyes the statue of the headless pandit was starting to go under. He made to scream to warn the girl, but she was busy protecting her life and dignity from the lashing rain. She didn't hear him. He lay there, bullet-pierced. After a while he saw the headless statue getting submerged in the water. It all happened so quickly and so easily. Subhendu's mental anguish was so terrible it made him want to cry. He saw a boy, naked, float a paper boat on the water. Pushed on by the wind, the boat floated over the headless statue. It seemed no one knew, except Subhendu, that the tonsured pandit's headless statue was submerged in the floodwater and that the paper boat set down by the little boy had just floated over it. The girl was still managing her clothes. The whole of Calcutta got soaked in the rain.

2

After a while, Subhendu found himself on a stretcher in front of the emergency block of a hospital, being carried inside. A crowd had gathered on the lawn to see him. The stretcher was taken into a lift and he was brought to the first floor. When he was taken off the stretcher and laid on a bed, he reckoned he was going to be operated upon and prepared himself accordingly. He wanted to turn his neck this way and that to see if there was anyone nearby. But as soon as he moved his head a little, a nurse appeared and scolded him, "What are you doing—you mustn't move, just lie still!" Subhendu was not used to being scolded. For a moment he thought of protesting in some fashion but for some reason he did not say anything. All he wanted was to know whether the girl from this morning was anywhere nearby. But he couldn't turn his head. Subhendu lay silently. As he lay he thought. They were doing all this only for his well-being. If these people did dig out the bullet that had been lodged in a corner on the left side of his chest this morning at half past nine, that was undoubtedly good for him. He patted his chest and could hear the bullet rattling inside. He placed his left hand over the spot. That would be convenient, he could show it for the operation. The light in front of his eyes kept getting brighter. It dazzled and then exploded right under his nose. For a long time a fly buzzed within that bright light. All around he could hear the shuffle of people moving about. The clinking of knives and scissors. A gloved hand appeared at his chest. A body covered in white cloth bent toward him. Subhendu lay still, as if under a spell. The place was enveloped in white light. He thought it must be like that even inside his chest. Within the whiteness a dot-like black fly buzzed and hovered, buzz-buzz. Why was there a black fly here in this white light? Subhendu tried to think about that. But he didn't get much of an opportunity to think. He saw a headless person clad in dhuti-chadar, his hands in gloves, about to cut open his chest with a surgical knife. Subhendu began to think that he knew this headless trunk but couldn't recall exactly where he had seen him. The person wore an ordinary white khaddar dhuti that ended at his knees, and a chadar wrapped around his bare chest. The Taltala-slippers on his feet looked extremely famil-iar. But there was no head. It wasn't easy to recognize a man without a head. He began to think about where he had seen him before, and how. The man did not hesitate. He extended his gloved hand toward Subhendu. "Where's your bullet hole, Subhendu Mohan?" At first Subhendu was assailed by doubt, and then, lifting his hand, he showed him the left side of his chest. The man examined the spot with his hand, knocking at it with his finger a couple of times, then he said in a grave voice: "Very bad place—I hope we don't have to cut out and remove the heart itself." At the mention of the word "heart," Sub-hendu's chest shuddered. He wondered what would remain once that was gone. His face turned pale. "Can't you retain it and do something?" In response, the man smiled. "Why do you worry so much, young man!" He knocked the wrong end of the knife on his chest. Subhendu saw that there was nothing to be gained from objecting now. With no option left, he lay with his limbs sprawled, and right in front of his eyes, the dhuti-chadar clad, short, headless trunk pulled out his heart, including the lodged bullet, and dangled it above the tip of his nose. Subhendu lay as if under a spell. He was so scared he could hardly breathe. Could a man survive once his heart was removed? As he thought about this he was astonished: he certainly was alive, wasn't he? It was above his nose that the heart dangled, this blackish-red lump of flesh. Subhendu had to concede that the man was indeed heroic.

3

When Subhendu was discharged from the hospital, his heart, packed in a paper box, was given over to him. Stepping outside, he saw the evening's wan light everywhere, and within it stood the girl. She stepped forward with a smiling face. "My god, was I scared!" Then, pointing at the paper box, she asked, "What's that?" Like someone who has suffered a great loss, his face pale, as if all the blood had drained away, Subhendu said, "My heart. They operated on me and removed it." The girl laughed heartily. "That's hilarious!" Subhendu did not laugh. He kept staring at the girl's face. What was he to do with the box now? The girl said, "Come, let's go and sit in a bar. I like you a lot." "But that lover of yours . . ." Subhendu muttered dejectedly. The girl laughed. "Oh, he was my lover at half past nine this morning, it's been six and a half hours since then. Now you are my lover." Saying so, the girl took Subhendu's hand. But despite it being a lovely evening, Subhendu could not summon the enthusiasm to hold the hand of this pretty woman with pointy breasts. He felt terribly confused. He simply couldn't figure out what to do with the paper box in his hands. Looking at his face, the girl perhaps read his mind. "Thinking about the box are you? Throw it in the street!" Subhendu felt an ache somewhere inside. "My heart, my own . . . how can I throw it away like that?" "You're a complete idiot you get nothing from hearts and suchlike nowadays. No one bothers about all that!" As she said that, the girl dipped her hand inside her handbag. She took out a brownish thing wrapped in cellophane paper and dangled it in front of his eyes. "Here, see my heart. I had an operation and took it out. I put it in again every now and then, as and when necessary. But nowadays I don't really need to have it in. Nor do I think I'll ever need it in the future!" Subhendu saw how the girl held her own heart in her hand, pressed between two fingers, dangling it before him like a pendulum. Perhaps he should do the same. But Subhendu couldn't find the courage. As if to console him, the girl said: "In the beginning it feels a bit strange. After that everything will be fine, just watch." Seeing Subhendu still staring, she said indifferently: "It's all right, you needn't throw it away, put it under your arm and come along." Saying so, she pulled him by the hand. Subhendu saw that he couldn't avoid going with her. This girl, who had had an operation and gotten her heart removed, who had wrapped it in cellophane paper and placed it in her handbag and used it from time to time whenever required—here she was, pulling him along, pinching his cheeks. He had to go. Subhendu began walking with the girl. The paper box was held under his arm. With his heart inside. For a moment he thought, What's the point in keeping this, it's best to throw it away. Then he thought, Let it be. After all, one couldn't get it back once it was thrown away. Walking together, they arrived at a bar. A dim blue light burned in the room, waiters in white uniforms and white caps hovered around, there were men and women seated, with food and drink spread out in front of them. In the back, music played to a fast beat. A girl wearing a satin brassiere swayed her hips and danced to the beat of the music. His girl pointed. "How do you like it?" Subhendu saw the satin-veiled buttocks and the flesh of the ample breasts of the dancing girl swaying animatedly. He thought the bright red of her lips would leap out and fill the room. He gently put the paper box down on the table and took a deep breath. No one understood his grief. He was about to pat the box for comfort when the girl pushed his shoulder. "What happened? Why are you sitting like an asshole?" Turning his face, Subhendu looked at his companion's breasts and saw her cleavage spilling out from the junction between her blouse and sari. Sipping from his glass, he forgot about all that had happened and took everything in. As he looked, the old sphere of light returned. That zone of white light dazzled the eyes and a dot-like black fly hovered around within it. Subhendu tried to think. Why was there a black fly in the dazzling white light? He couldn't figure it out. He saw: under the terrifying rain a statue of a dhuti-clad pandit erected in front of a huge building; it was sinking. It was submerged before his eyes. Little boys floated a paper boat, the boat floated away rapidly over the statue's head. Subhendu wanted to cry. But he didn't, thinking it would not be proper to cry as he was with the girl. He was perspiring profusely now. He wanted to run away. He wanted to run away and go some-where and be able to heave a sigh of relief. He stood up to get away, box in hand. The girl pulled him back and sat him down. "Where do you think you are going, leaving me behind?" Subhendu had no option but to sit down and keep looking at the wall, at the pictures of nude nymphs in the blue light. The musical ensemble kept playing to a fast beat, the swaying hips of the girl clad in the satin panty more animated now. Lacking recourse, Subhendu said plaintively, "I must go." The girl stared at his face. "Fine, let's go. Settle the bill." Subhendu suddenly came to his senses. He realized he had nothing more than some loose change in his pocket. When he looked at the girl's face and tried to explain his pathetic situation, the girl retorted angrily, "If you don't have money why didn't you say so earlier? Do you think you can make love for free in this market? Pawn your watch or something, or whatever, just do something!" Subhendu couldn't figure out what to do. The girl suddenly stood up and removed the watch from his wrist. She began to tug at his shirt. In front of Subhendu's eyes, the sphere of white light exploded in a thousand streams and the black dot-like fly hovered inside it. He stepped out of the bar—he was bare-bodied, no watch on his wrist. He began to walk slowly, the paper box under this arm pressed to his side. He didn't have the slightest inclination to turn back and look. Evening had descended on the city. There were crowds of people everywhere. And among them Subhendu alone, like a lost soul, started walking with his heart tucked under his arm. So he was all alone in this world—there was no one anywhere near him. All around him were people, shops and establishments, light as well as darkness. People streamed out of the cinema hall after a show. Yet he was alone, impossibly alone. He walked along like this, and after a while he had left everything behind. On the wall to the right he read, "Power flows out of the barrel of a gun." On the wall to the left he read, "Bokachoda masses, so many revolutionary opportunities, yet you didn't revolt—get rammed by the police now, bastards!" He heard Rabindrasangeet playing from a paan shop. A gray-colored tram passed by and on it was written in yellow: "Destruction is senseless—disavow violence." He read "Baba Naam Kevalam" written in letters of tar on the house in front, and right above that, the faded broken lines of the stenciled sketch of Chairman Mao. On any other day, he would have stopped, he would have thought about it. But today he just didn't have the inclination. Walking on and on in a world full of people, walking under the light, he reached the huge building and the bank of the lake. There were fewer people here. The dazzle of neon lights was absent. Although it was night, there were a few people bathing in the water. On an enclosed podium sat an enlightened elder with a shaven head, holding forth on the Mahabharata. Around him were a few elderly men and women. A man lay stretched out on a bench in one corner. A youth in blue trousers stood behind the screen of bushes, gushing out a stream of piss. Two boys went past, whistling at a girl in a frock. He raised his head and saw the massive university building standing tall across the road. A tram trundled down the road, making a clanging noise. As he gazed at all this, Subhendu's eyes fell upon the statue—like an image of a poor man amid immense wealth, it stood facing the huge building, abandoned amid a dense thicket. Earlier, crows shat on his tonsured head, recently the head had been broken. As soon as he saw the image it occurred to him that it was this man who had operated on him in the hospital and removed his heart. He recalled he had been laid down under this statue after he was wounded in the morning. In amazement and disbelief, Subhendu began to wonder why he had not been able to recognize him earlier. His eyes almost popped out. The sphere of white light was breaking up in front of his eyes. The black dot of a fly was hovering around inside that sphere. Just a tiny black spot on an immense white canvas. Subhendu couldn't remain standing any more. All his emotions surged out from inside him. Bending, he saw that the statue had been submerged in the floodwater after the morning's rain. After some time the water had receded and the headless body had emerged. As he peered down, Subhendu could still see beneath it the stain of congealed blood from his pierced chest. He could no longer remain standing. Trembling with emotion, he put the paper box down under the statue. He wanted to run for his life and escape from that obscene place to save himself.

Biplober Dike 36 Foot, 1972

Historic Descent

One Saturday afternoon in the month of May, a bus was about to depart from the terminus of bus No. 4. All the seats on the bus were occupied except for a double seat in the front where a middle-aged man sat, the seat beside him vacant. He had a few strands of gray hair on his head and wore a home-washed, white punjabi with a prominent blue print that gave it a bright, bluish hue. When the bus began to move, the three boys standing outside smoking took a couple of quick, deep puffs on their cigarettes and sprang up on the footboard.

Hey, come here, there's an empty seat—one of them advanced toward the vacant seat. He sat down and made some space—Come on, you lot, we'll manage. He took out a blue comb and began to fine-comb his hair, which was slicked back and dripping with oil, the front propped up artfully, reminiscent of a famous film star.

The second boy, wearing a bright-red vest over black trousers, sat down next to him. The third, who was dressed in a brand new, crisply starched punjabi and a pair of blue trousers, said: Mayiri, won't I get to sit?

Why not—come, sit on my lap. The third boy placed his rear on the second one's lap and sat with his thighs splayed at an angle of forty-five degrees.

With four persons seated thus on a two-person seat, the middle-aged gentleman got more and more squeezed into the corner. In some consternation he said: What's going on?

Oh, nothing at all, just forcibly occupying a seat.

Is this any way to sit?

Hey, Dadu's really dangerous!

What did you say, chhokra?

Baap re baap. Dadu's really angry!

Dadu? Whose dadu? The gentleman's voice was agitated.

Why, aren't you our dadu? Don't you recognize us? Oh Dadu, dear Dadu, where are you off to this hot afternoon, Dadu? To the race course?

The gentleman seemed to be burning with rage. But no words escaped his mouth . . .

To the race course? Is that true, darling Dadu? Why don't you come with us instead, let's stand in the queue for *Jahan Pyaar Miley*.

With great difficulty, the gentleman controlled himself and looked out of the bus window.

Baap re baap, Dadu's angry!

Why don't you ask him if he's really angry?

Dadu darling, are you really ve-rr-y, ve-rr-y angry?

The gentleman did not say anything. With all his will he stared outside the window.

Dadu darling doesn't say whether he's angry or not, he doesn't say anything at all.

You're a donkey!

How's that?

Don't you know silence is a sign of wisdom?

So our dadu's angry . . .

And so we must stand up on the bench . . .

The third person stood up.

Dadu darling, look, I've gotten up. Don't be angry now, Dadu.

What's Dadu going to do? Dadu doesn't speak! Dadu's become dumb!

Oh my god, our dadu's been struck dumb! What will become of us now?

Really, what's to become of us now!

The bus conductor came toward them on his round to collect fares. The third boy made to sit down as before. He said: Hey partner, our dadu's become dumb—what'll happen to us now?

Oh Baba Tarakeshwar, do cure Dadu, Baba!

The conductor asked for the fare.

They pointed to the man and said: Dadu darling will pay. We're with Dadu.

The conductor stared at the gentleman and then at the three boys. He didn't say anything.

Just you watch, now Dadu darling's going to get very angry and he's going to get off.

Not because he's angry. He's getting off at the Tolly-gunge police post. He's going to stand in the line for the sixty-five-paisa tickets at Dipti cinema.

They kept talking like this among themselves. The other party did not respond at all, he stubbornly kept his eyes fixed outside the window. The boys were silent for a few minutes. They signaled one another with their eyes:

Hey, what's one word for someone with sweaty armpits?

I don't know, why not ask our darling dadu?

The region around the armpit of the gentleman's punjabi was wet with perspiration.

Dadu, what's one word for someone with sweaty armpits?

Dadu darling, won't you tell us?

There's a limit to jesting . . . ! The gentleman was understandably enraged, his face flushed in anger and humiliation.

Baap re baap! Words flowing from Dadu darling's lips, that means Dadu darling hasn't become dumb . . . Oh Baba Tarakeshwar!

Hey, Dadu said something awesome . . .

Dadu really knows some fine talk. Dadu, write a book and we'll read it.

But he didn't tell us the word for someone with sweaty armpits . . . Dadu doesn't know, but I know. Shall I tell you? It's side-sweater!

Side-sweater! Baap re baap, you're awesome . . . side-sweater . . . side-sweater (the three of them sang in tune to a matching beat) . . . side-sweater, side-sweater, side-sweater, side-sweater . . .

Some of the people in the bus were listening to the entire conversation with great interest. Hearing the side-sweater chorus and beat, many opened their mouths wide and started laughing. The gentleman could not sit still any longer. He stood up.

Dadu, are you getting off? Are you really going to stand in the line for the sixty-five-paisa tickets at Dipti?

The gentleman's eyes and face were contorted, although one couldn't tell whether in fury or torment. He moved away and stood with his back turned to the boy, holding onto a rod.

Dadu darling's angry, that's why he got up.

Hell no, he's not angry—he's made a place for us!

We should thank him.

Do that.

Mr. Dadu, for doing us the favor of making a place for us, th-aa-nk yo-oou!

Ha ha ha, Mr. Dadu, do you hear us . . . ? Hey, Dadu hasn't heard us.

Dadu's really angry with us.

Are you really angry, Dadu darling?

Right then! Come with us to the cinema, we'll see a Dev Anand picture, *Pyar Mohabbat*—what a film!

Dadu's getting very angry.

Dadu looks like Ashok Kumar when he's angry!

Hey, don't talk rubbish man, isn't he our dadu? You should always uphold the prestige of respected elders . . . Tsk-tsk . . .

Oh no, I made a mistake—do forgive me, Dadu (pinching his own ears and nose), I'll never do that again . . .

The gentleman tried to shift farther away but there wasn't much space to stand. The bus was getting crowded so he couldn't go very far, he had to remain near the jeering boys.

Dadu darling, why don't you dye your hair?

What the hell do you think you're saying, isn't he a respected elder?

So what, there's nothing's wrong with dyeing your hair.

You trash, the gentleman muttered.

Dadu's abused us!

You should sing him a song too.

Shall I?

Do that, man!

. Then listen, listen—a lovely song—"*Bol radha, bol sangam hoga ki nahi . . .*"

The three of them began to sing tunefully. The people in the bus were listening attentively. Seeing their amused faces, one could infer they were enjoying the proceedings. The few serious folk in the bus kept their faces turned away. One could gather from their conduct that they had no desire to poke their noses into such futile, extraneous matters, thereby merely destroying their own self-respect. The gentleman couldn't take any more. Enraged, he shouted out: Sing the song to your fathers! Did you hear that—to your fathers!

Hey, he just insulted our fathers—one of them stood up with a start. He gripped the gentleman's punjabi and snarled: We bore it all this while . . . you think you can fuck with us . . . Take it back!

Another person stood up and landed a slap on the gentleman's face. Take it back, sala randi ka bachha . . . take it back!

The gentleman trembled in rage, grief, and humiliation. The bag in his hand fell down. The five kilograms or so of rice bought from outside the cordoned area lay scattered on the floor of the bus.

The gentleman tried to bend down to gather the rice. But the boy clutched his punjabi and shook him.

So you're secretly gobbling stolen rice . . . you fucking thief!

Helpless, the gentleman couldn't even bend down. He gazed at the passengers in the bus with pleading eyes.

He probably sells rice in the black market—some people whispered. Those of a serious nature, of a decent mien, having decided not to interfere, kept their eyes fixed steadfastly outside the bus window.

Seeing the commotion, the bus conductor came forward. Why do you make a scene? Let him go.

I'll let him go, but he has to apologize for abusing our fathers.

That's enough, let him go now . . . he's an old man.

The conductor freed the gentleman almost by force. Get off here—the conductor rang the bell.

When the bus stopped, he almost pushed the gentleman out. Before getting off, the gentleman reached for something—perhaps his bag. The conductor shouted at him: Get off, I say!

One man got off from the busload of people.

Everyone craned their necks to see the man getting off.

Oitihashik Obotoron, 1974

From the Morgue on
Bhawani Dutta Lane

As they dance face to face, holding one another close, "*I am
naked beneath my clothes*," in front of that, leaning forward
a little, two arms raised and flexed on two sides, fingers drawing whistles from lips,
Hips sway, swaying, gyrating, "*I am naked
beneath my clothes*"—
The lunatic woman sits . . .
Her whole earthly frame, from head to toe, terribly dirty,
bathed in sweat, an impassive face,   in her own thoughts
knotting, unknotting the strip of cloth she wears . . .
Past the steel cupboard, grazing Rumi's dressing
table the long rectangular shadow gathers and thickens.
Rumi doesn't know, not yet—
The final remnants of
the enormous red-blue crystal chandelier
spanning the hall in the deserted zamindar's house—
Cobwebs . . . only cobwebs everywhere—

A deserted, haunted house   very damp . . . the shuffle
and flutter
of owls . . . in that faraway darkness
Granular houses, g r a n u l a r h o u s e s
v i s i b l e—
The heat of late February bears down . . . a cuckoo calls
from the neem tree . . . at the rail line nearby, quite often
there are incidents of suicide . . . in the evening,
after her bath, Rumi puts a string of bel flowers
in her hair.   From the morgue on Bhawani Dutta Lane,
a monstrous purple
light streams out, without letup—
from where, about a month ago, rats had chewed on
a few dead bodies

Their night turned eleven then. The national anthem played
over someone's radio. And
lying over that national anthem
they fuck one another madly,
successively, continuously, o n   a n d   o n

———————————
Bhabanidutta Lane-er Morgue Theke, 1975

Come, See India

[In homage to Kamalkumar Majumdar]

As the girl offers her withered breast to the emaciated, lifeless baby with skinny arms and legs, which by all appearances looked like a mouse from afar, and boils vegetable peels in an earthen pot chipped at the edges, the other child, every one of whose ribs is visible and can be counted one-two-three, sits near the stove like a prodigal son, eyes and face fixed on the pot with singular attention, his nose exploding as he takes in the aroma of the cooking, the entire day's hunger in his belly like a raging fire, eyes too lying in wait for the pot to be set down, then, right then, a drop of rain falls on the Mongolian-style moustache of a bhadralok in freshly laundered clothes, who has a James Bondesque attaché case and wears a multicolored shirt with a floral design, and the man, in the artful composure becoming his big-babu bearing, casts his eyes once toward the sky and, in search of safe shelter, arrives at that very spot on the pavement, underneath the mezzanine verandah. The girl is a beggar, a few broken pots, a bundle wrapped in a rag and two skinny children comprise her world, which is here, in this deserted spot under the mezzanine verandah, now in disarray. At the sound of loud knocking on the door, all four persons inside the room are startled at once. Putting out the kerosene stove in a single blow, the young boy manages to squeeze himself under the taktaposh, where torn kanthas, broken tin cans, and so on are piled up. There is the sound of a staff banging on the door. The old door trembles ominously. As the old father, whose eyes have lost their sight and sequence, rises slowly and holds opens the door, four or five ruffians barge into the room. The one with the revolver in his hand screams out: "Where's Gour, the fucking son of a pig!" Now a dusty gale has begun. Dark swollen clouds gather in the sky. The rain is about to descend. The girl, with a child on either side, is busy as usual with boiling vegetable peels where her corner of domestic bliss used to be. She was once a young wife. She wears her favorite green sari (which isn't at all grand and yet very dear). Her arms are full of red and blue glass bangles, a broad streak of sindoor fills the parting of her forehead. Three or four iron bangles on the left arm (gifted to her when she was pregnant). Long black hair flows like waves down both sides of the parting. At this moment the mass of hair is tousled over her back, very wet, she has just bathed . . . Hussain Ali performs acrobatics before the assembled crowd. He hops onto the makeshift stage for the magic show, his lungi billows and flutters in the wind. From a pocket in his flowing robe he takes out three Japanese dolls, from another pocket, a revolver. He arranges the dolls one by one on the table, and pointing the revolver at the crowd, he starts to explain, with accompanying gestures and gesticulations: "Just watch, people, see how an enemy ought to be punished." As he speaks, Hussain Ali dangles and twirls the pistol under their noses, he keeps twirling it, and after a while he aims and fires. The dolls' chests are pierced and when drops of fresh blood pour out, the rapt public claps in amazement and delight as they learn with greedy eyes the trick to punishing an enemy. A boy and girl run up, they are still laughing gleefully as they enter the spot beneath the mezzanine verandah. On both sides of them, there are people who have taken shelter from the rain. They gape at the ripening young girl, at her gleeful laugh—they see everything. But they, the girl and the boy, don't pay any attention. The girl says: "How I love to get wet in the rain. Come on, darling, let's get wet again." As she speaks, she grabs the boy's shirt at the chest and brings her eyes near his face. Outside, the rain grows heavier. The tram lines become submerged. More people cram into the narrow shade under the mezzanine verandah where the beggar girl, two kids, and her beloved domestic world are. Hussain Ali performs the skull trick now. He is in his element. Placing a huge skull atop a shining brass plate, he explains to the assembled populace: "Babus, take a look, witness this, the skull speaks in the voice of a living man and answers questions." After the announcement he ceremoniously salaams the public and chants out the questions:

—Oh skull, are you human?

—By the grace of the compassionate Lord.

—Why are you here?

—The will of the compassionate Lord brought me.

—Why was your head severed?

—Everything in the universe is by the will of the compassionate Lord

—Who do you have in the world—father, mother, brother, friend?

—No one but the compassionate Lord.

The rain grows even fiercer. The streets get flooded. The shade beneath the mezzanine verandah fills up. It is crammed with people—a tie-clad, shiny office-babu with sparkling spectacles; a bald-headed, middle-aged, sad-faced government clerk, umbrella in hand; a dandy ruffian with long sideburns and long hair coiffured like the hero of *Bobby*; a peanut seller with a basket on his head; a ghugni-wallah with ghugni heaped on a huge platter over a lit kerosene stove. The beggar girl's cooking is now totally disrupted. Her world is wet with the spray of rain. Somehow she manages to crouch in a corner, watching over her worldly possessions—the bundle wrapped in rags, a couple of broken earthen pots, a battered metal tumbler, and two children. Here, in this locality on the fringes of the city, there is only empty desolation. On one side of the narrow potholed road are large tin sheds, the rear ends of factories. On the other side a vast wetland of segmented water-bodies hidden beneath water hyacinths, with their purple flowers blooming in all their fragrance, and a veritable jungle overgrown with clumps of kaalke-sunda, assheoda, and wild kalomi. Every now and then a cyclerickshaw goes past with a clanging sound. Trucks drive by noisily, raising a storm of dust. On one side of the deserted wetland lies Gour's corpse, cut into pieces and stuffed into a gunny sack, dirty with mud and slime. It lies there, rotting away. Just a hand sticking out of a tear in the sack; the liquefying hand, its fist clenched tight, guarded by two dogs and three vultures. The city is inundated with rain. The people crammed together in the spot beneath the mezzanine verandah are wet with the spray blown in by the wind. "Beggars even here," some of them remark. "They're making Calcutta unfit for habitation day by day." "Why don't you drive them away—here people are unable to stand and she sits regally with her household sprawled out!" The girl finally snaps testily, "Where will I go?" "A beggar by race and feisty too—a bloody nawab's daughter!" "They've occupied all the roads and pavements, as if it's their bloody father's property." A pretty-faced woman, her left hand still holding a pair of folded go-go goggles, can't find a place to stand. Her low-cut blouse and exposed back get drenched in the spray from the wind. The *Bobby*-haired boy with long sideburns moves up to the beggar girl, "Hey, you whore—get up from here, make place for the bhadramahila to stand." "Where will I go?" "Throw her out, mister, these shits don't heed straight talk." Gour's arms, legs, head, and torso, cut into pieces and stuffed into a sack, rot beside the desolate wetland, guarded by two dogs and three vultures. The body rots away. The clenched fist rots and poisons the atmosphere. The whole city becomes poisoned. Stench pervades the air. Hussain Ali stands atop a table and performs tricks—the trick of punishing the enemy by piercing him with bullets, and the skull trick. The girl refuses to vacate her space. Nonetheless, she is pulled out and dragged away. Now she is knee-deep in water, on her left side the baby in her bosom, the other boy's hand held tight in her right hand, the cloth bundle of her world on her head. The rain pours down lustily, over her, over her children, over her world placed on her head. The flood of water flows like a river.

All the roads are submerged. Directionless in the pouring rain and raging flood, with a child on either side and her world on her head, she looks on.

Then
The colors of the poster printed with the hammer
and sickle are washed away in the rain . . .
Robi Thakur's song plays on the radio:
You nurture me with tender care in your abode
Glory be to you, O Lord
Glory be to you, O Lord
And
Gour's cut-up corpse stuffed into a sack rots beside
the desolate wetland
Hussain Ali's magic show comes into its own
brilliantly featuring the skull   the punishment
of enemies

Ashun, Bharat-borsho Dekhe Jaan, 1975

The Road to the Mill Jetty

3 July 1978, remembering the first anniversary
of Gambhiraprasad Shaw's martyrdom

"Those who eat their fill speak to the hungry
of wonderful times to come."

—Bertolt Brecht

The third month was almost over, yet out of laziness the old calendar with Ma Durga's image hadn't been removed from the wall.

It's still as good as new, do you say? Hey, why won't you smoke a cigarette?

I've quit.

Or are you trying to save money? That's wonderful, only people like you can retain two pennies. We've puffed everything away . . .

The neon lights on the station platform had been lit. The 6:20 local train was about to leave.

The signal.

Bright green. A person dressed in blue walked alongside the train. At the entrance to the party office, a dusty picture of Lenin occupied the wall. It had hung merely as a picture for half a century. The train left the platform.

The station building, the ticket office, and tea stalls were left behind rapidly. By the time it went past the control room, the brilliance of the bleached-white neon lights on either side suddenly died like counterfeit revolutionaries. A procession of the hungry marched to the block development office. Vehicles came to a standstill. The curious public thronged both sides of the road.

Met Babulal's wife yesterday. Soliciting at the Bowbazar crossing, wearing a cheap silk sari and lipstick. Do you remember Babulal? The one who . . . at the time of the lockout . . . at the gate on the road to the mill jetty . . . the owner's hoodlums . . .

Comrades, shout the slogans out loud! Everyone call out together!

The procession concluded at the block development office. The road beside led to the mill jetty. Why are you on strike? Because we haven't gotten our bonus. What are your demands? Dearness allowance must be paid at central government rates. And you, Gambhiraprasad of East Champaran, do you too want only bonus and dearness allowance at central rates? No! I want my state! We shall till all the land in the country. We shall run all the factories. We shall carry out all kinds of production. And all the fruit . . . we ourselves shall . . . The minister with the picture of Lenin hanging above his head turned grave. A careful watch must be kept over the situation. The law in their own hands . . . No one, not any more.

Mill-er Jettir Diker Rasta, 1978

Spot Eczematous

Reader, the eczema on your vital spot
Whose itch at any and every time
You discern, and which does not form pus or
Bleed, just—scratch, scratch, scratch, scratch
Oh, what joy, what joy—
Don't go trying to heal it by applying
Ointments and such, for modern medical scientists
Believe this is a kind of bodily disease
Whose origins lie in the mind;
It's only what we think,
Not an itch of the skin.

Once there was a bad man and his soul was small and soft,
but fleshy. He put it in a paper bag and shoved it under
a pillow. A crafty girl stole it one day and, not knowing
what the fleshy thing was, threw it beside a drain. There
was a sly crow there. It picked up the paper bag in its beak
and flew off in search of a secure place. When it sat on
the branch of a peepal tree on the bank of Gobarjhuri lake

and pecked at it, the paper bag slipped off its beak, soul and all. And incredible as it sounds, under the peepal tree was a cow grazing. Thinking it was edible, it swallowed the bag in a trice. The cow belonged to a farmer in the village. After a few days, the farmer sold the cow. Astute readers should bear in mind that the farmer was not that poor and had not sold the cow even when he was in need—which would have been the formula for a market-able leftist story, in keeping with the pattern handed down by the masters. The trader saw that the cow was old and hobbling, it wouldn't live very long, he didn't think anyone would want to buy it. He straightaway gave it over to the slaughterhouse. This story begins where a beef roll—the present form of the cow—was sold, and taking a bite of it was—

Of course, the story can be narrated in another way too. Anindya was an independent citizen of this indepen-dent country. He was twenty-two years old. **Anindya was not quite unemployed, like most of the revolution-by-rote boys in our country, he was more or less well off. His father was a middle-ranking officer, his brother worked in a bank, they lived in a flat in Ballygunge, they liked Worcestershire sauce, his sister's marriage to an England-returned engineer was almost fixed, etc., etc.** One day, at three minutes to twelve, as he sat in a shop in Chandni Chowk eating a beef roll—which was the cheapest meat in the market and could satisfy one's hunger yet cost only a little money—a tin-gling ache began inside his stomach after a few bites, which suddenly increased and became so bad he began to see everything—this very world—upside down. He saw the girl with whom he played love-and-lovers in the darkness of the lake—who liked to be fondled to satisfy her urges—standing in the balcony, hastily plucking out lice from her hair, crushing them between two fingernails before popping them into her mouth. Seeing him, she said with a laugh, Who knew lice was so fine to eat! Anindya was worried when he saw this. A nineteen- or twenty-year-old, half-aristocratic, beautiful girl plucking and eating lice in broad daylight and in full public view. He thumped his head to try and clear his thoughts, rubbed his head, and trained his eyes on her once more to be sure he was not hallucinating. But he saw the same thing—gazing at him with a smiling face, the girl in bell-bottoms sank her nails into her hair, pulled out lice, and put them inside her mouth, her eyes brimming over with whoops of joy. Anindya couldn't figure out what he ought to do. Eventually, scratching his head, he said: Don't you get any other food to eat in this free country, beautiful? Why are you eating lice? The girl was unruffled. She said: Do you know what I once saw? A beggar on the pavement searched for and pulled out lice from his matted hair and popped them into his mouth. It struck me right then that lice has great potential to become the food of the proletariat. I tried eating it myself. It was fine! I want to introduce this dish to society. If those people can eat lice and survive, why can't we? We too are humans like them—what do you say? And the girl pulled Anindya close to her bosom. Ever since he ate that beef roll, it was as if everything inside Anindya's stomach was topsy-turvy. But how was he to know that a bad man's soul had entered his system and caused him to see and feel as he did? He brought his face close to the girl's. She said, You'll see, after a few days I'll be speaking on the radio about lice-fried rice. I'll be writing in newspapers. In about six months, I'm hopeful that I'll be able to get lice-based dishes introduced in restaurants as the food of the proletariat. As soon as Anindya heard this, he began to feel queasy. So far he had been trying to keep it down, but he could no longer control it, and *Owack! Owack!*—he retched out a mouthful of vomit on the girl. In this planet of ours, of the 2,850,000,000 inhabitants, only 1,600,000 get an adequate quantity of food—which means that the number of people in the world who go to sleep every night on an empty stomach is double the population of India. The vomit trickled down the girl's bell-bots, tummy, buttocks, and thighs. It had a sour, wet smell, and the most surprising thing of all was that he saw himself—yes, he, Anindya—bending down and licking up that foul stuff from her tummy and buttocks with his tongue, without any hesitation, just like a cow licks its newborn calf. Anindya watched himself in amazement, he observed how quickly and effortlessly he licked up his own vomit, with his own tongue, from the fleshy buttocks. He applied himself to the jiggling, bouncy, bell-bottomed buttocks with an easy, adept, yet casual posture. The girl did not mind such trifling matters, she knew that boys, after all, did do these things. In fact, there were many who wanted to put their hands in the lower parts after a mere five-minute acquaintance. She pulled Anindya by the hair and kissed him: Do you know, nowadays I teach sex to kids—oriental-style sex education. It is a matter of great sadness that this heroine of ours does not half-lie in bed with a pillow pressed to her chest, writing love letters on sky-blue letter paper, that she does not tell the hero in a nasal tone, Hey, don't be naughty—I'm ticklish! Anindya felt as if his life was about to come to an end. He was unable to say anything, try as he might. He went into the room with the girl. He tried to look around and gather something of what she had been up to. The room was quite large, with dark curtains on all four sides, which kept the sunlight at bay. As soon as she entered the room, she began to teach a boy half her age, on whose upper lip a wisp of moustache had appeared-or-not-appeared, about sex positions. Anindya watched helplessly as, in front of him, the girl, that girl of his with whom every once in a while he engaged in banter in the darkness of the lake, of whose body almost every fold, curve, and bulge was known to him, conveyed ways and means to a boy half her age. He sat sweating in that room with its dark, drawn curtains. Every now and then his stomach rumbled. He saw how expertly the girl taught the lad about secret crevices and folds. She looked at him and chuckled. Sex too is an art that has to be learned, my boy. And the oriental style is one of the most acclaimed things in the world, which the whole Western world praises so effusively . . . In some parts of Tamil Nadu, even now, when one borrows money, there is a custom of keeping one's wife with the moneylender as surety. Until the money is returned, the wife stays in the money-lender's harem. If she has children then, the responsibility of looking after them devolves on the recipient of the loan, but the wife has to remain at the moneylender's service constantly. Anindya couldn't figure out what to say as he saw these scandalous happenings before his eyes. He decided that, come what may, he would bite the girl right here—he wasn't really into art-fart where these things were concerned. Anindya thought about it and decided. He stood up, just as the girl looked into his eyes and suspected something. At once she stood erect, then she swiftly extended her arm and lifted him up bodily. She, the girl, bared the blouse that covered her breasts and inserted him, the one who had borne the name Anindya till just a little while ago, altogether inside her blouse, and as she did so, she said: My purse stays here, my youthfulness is here, I'm keeping you as well. How overpowered he was! Anindya looked—how big he was, here was his adult body and yet how effortlessly he had slipped into the girl's blouse. He was stuck in the cleavage between her two breasts, it was simply unbelievable. He would never have believed it had it not happened to him. A chit of a girl had supposedly chucked all of a boy like him into her blouse, as if he were a purse, and she supposedly kept her purse like that, kept her youthfulness, and now kept him too. Being so casually close to her purse and youthfulness, he was assailed by a milky smell and was overcome with nausea. He couldn't help himself and thus, for a second time, he vomited violently inside her blouse. As he vomited near the artfully preserved youthfulness, Anindya realized that all this while some kind of bad poison had been working in his system, which was now being ejected, making him feel light in body, bringing back the correct point of view. Whatever he had been doing, whatever he had been seeing—was all wrong, completely wrong. Anindya wiped his lips, he looked through the lens of his spectacles. His habitual condition returned. He regained his normal perspective. He saw that the girl had not been picking and eating lice. She had been eating a bar of Cadbury's milk chocolate. He, Anindya, decent boy that he was, could never have vomited here and there like that, at least not when he was sober. Perhaps a flying crow or something like that had dirtied the girl's posterior. The word "shat" simply won't do here. That pains our refined sensibilities. In fact, people of fine tastes and refined mind never even shit. And the matter of teaching sex had been perceived, at the very least, in an incorrect way as a result of an incorrect perspective. Because girls could only do so much for youngsters—be affectionate. Whereas the whole subject of sex was taboo, which, whether it was legal or illegal, had to be done in secret. And if something had to be brought out into the public arena in broad daylight, that could only be what one wore, no more than that. Never. Anindya felt at peace. His vision was all right. Society-world, justice-morality hadn't yet gone to the dogs. In the interregnum, it was just that a bad man's soul had entered him and made him see things falsely.

When Anindya vomited the second time, the bad man's soul slipped out of his stomach. Trickling along, it made its way to the slaughterhouse. There it entered the stomach of a cow. The cow returned to the bank of the Gobarjhuri lake and began grazing under the peepal tree. Then the soul flew up and slipped into the crow's beak. The crow carried it in its beak and dropped it beside the drain. The crafty girl, not comprehending what the thing in the paper bag was, deposited it in fright under a pillow. And thus the bad man once again regained his lost soul from under his very pillow.

There are, at the very least, three maxims that can be

derived from this story, and if one looks closely, even five. Because people don't like anything that involves too much thinking, only the basic ones are given here:

1. What is emphatically sought to be conveyed in this story is that we live in a society that is completely and in every measure perverted. This perversion is so pervasive that even our dreams about revolution (which boys of a specific age are used to seeing and later, when they have gotten a good job and so on, go around declaring, I'm not a part of it and never was) are overwhelmed by the alcohol of perversion. It is our society, this capitalist social system, that represses the normal development of youth and provides maximal license to deformation.

2. Without a comprehensive vision, it is not possible to see the full form of this perversion. Even if it is visible in bits and pieces all the time, the whole is not that easy to see. As a result we cry ourselves hoarse saying everything's lost, having seen only one part. If we saw the whole we would start to think, we wouldn't run around and jump up and down lamenting that all is lost. Man is good, man is not bad under any system—if one tries to think in such stereotyped terms, the delight of self-contentment is felt all right, but one is untouched by the real thing.

3. The third point is about itching or eczema in the testicles. It is dangerous to scratch and scratch and make the spot sore, because this is a bodily disease of psychic origin, and not just an irritation of the skin.

Okusthol Dodrumoy, 1976

In a Deserted Spot
Measuring a Foot and a Half

Alexander, conqueror of the world, arrived at
heaven's doorway . . . the guardian of heaven
gifted him a human skull . . . Curious, Alexander
had the female skull weighed against all the wealth
in his store . . . the skull was heavier than all
the wealth in the royal treasury he acquired over
a lifetime . . . After much thought and reflection,
the female skull's nose, ears, eyes, and mouth were
plugged with earth, the five sensory doors were
shut . . . It was then weighed once more . . . They
found that the weight of this skull, once deprived
of its senses, was entirely diminished, lighter than
even a thread of a cobweb.

He lay, a small bloodstain on a white wall, four feet pointing toward the sky in helpless abandonment, tail limp,
yellow innards spilling out from the stomach, blood dried
up and turned brown, tongue lolling out from one side.
The town's road skirted the silent human dwellings and
raced ahead, formaldehyde-like pungency in the water,

as from a dissected corpse. One could see the bright red horse licking the muddy face, white spittle foaming along the edges of its mouth, a girl walked next to a boy. Heaps of garbage and carcasses on the river bank, the shrieks of dogs and vultures fighting over a half-eaten buffalo . . . he swam along the other bank, far away—very far away, the shore was barely visible. A square existence like a tree trunk, under the fiery sun a very ugly woman, her face daubed with color, she who always left her hairy thighs exposed to the earth, the clamor of killings from every direction, the monstrous woman joyous. Surupa's physical presence could clearly be discerned through the ring-the-beer-bottle gamble, she walked in the afternoon's desolation, cloaked by the shrubs and bushes, Surupa and her fertility cult, imagining infant Jesus at Mother Mary's breast. Near the green ornamented arch, green men find the much desired machine gun. Soil beneath soil, air beneath air, life within life. A gust of warm breeze floating from the Bay of Bengal lashed against their faces, it burned. Surupa walked toward the screen of bushes, the red machine-gun in a stranger's hands became an unfailing stalker as it spat fire again and again. This illogical body was all that remained; the old, lengthy runaway remained, water fell drop by drop, snakes slithered all over the body, snakebites. Wild bushes filled the courtyard, the sound of water falling on leaves. Rain descended, drenching the body, which was the arrogant rashness of youth, the killers returned time and again to the killing fields, they sniffed the air for blood. Like a meat cleaver, which was the murderer, it came down again and again on Surupa's throat, shoulders, back, face, between the thighs; her body clung to the luxuriant weeds. Before she could scream she was pulled, seized, and laid on the ground, invisible pores in every nerve tingled. Rammed down by rods, small pursuits full of high hopes and emotions, small sufferings, small eddies of joy, agitated man—all were murdered. Despite the events, Surupa's unconventional existence was always present, with rolled-up, youthful, pure wishes— you look wilted, I hope you are all right? They came after a while, men in black masks, we've come to take you, they cuffed her hands, she was made to walk all night long and taken to the bank of an unseen river where it was gods' twilight, furious hell, where the gods were killed and goddesses raped, and the entire universe was enveloped in blind darkness. Surupa's pet name is Rupa, did she still do lacework—did she still enjoy that? The car took off toward the yawning depths, a hand waved, a white kerchief fluttered. Was this a rubber ball flung toward splendor, less death, into nothingness? The table lay soiled after dinner, a male body like a crumpled gray sheet. The death-seed assumed labor pains, between heaven and hell, a wooden chair was placed in a deserted spot measuring a foot and a half. How long before she touched the sky? A winged horse and a one-eyed demon sprang out from the darkness, tore away her personal purity with ease. Tore away the gold, zari-work border from her grandmother's wedding sari, a sheaf of old letters, silver coins bearing the red sindoor marks of divine offering. Tore away the paste-led kaash flowers, the flowing river. Tore away that feeling of tender, adolescent love—sari anchal curled around fingers . . . lips bitten by teeth . . . standing, head bowed, in front of the door . . . Now one could see, next to Tristan's dead body, Isolde, curled up, committing suicide, the climax of love; through the center an arrogant ant walks, busy at work. A light burned at the paan-cigarette shop on the neighborhood curb, a lungi-clad man yawned as he chewed paan. A young adivasi woman with bright-red flowers tucked into her hair sat in the bus, her young man beside her, both returning from the haat, she swayed her body with him and giggled every now and then, the shrieks of basketfuls of chickens on the roof of the bus, far away clouds atop the Massanjore hills. Now there were boys and girls in brightly colored clothes, love, intimacy, luxurious pebbled paths, marble statues of fairy-like women, the golden dreams of Gariahat crossing. Now Surupa lay completely naked in the watercolor, dense forest behind her, scattered trees, the darkness of vines, tiny drops of purple-red sunset light streaking through from above the forest, the dark silhouettes of leaves and creepers in the forest green, and slipped into the middle of it all, spanning the area of vapid light, Surupa nude, twenty-year-old Surupa. Nothing much remained now, everything was decided, everything, like an impenetrable lake. Now in the course of the unending journey along an unknown river bank toward the source, experience, the crow seated on the sill, depressed, the packet of ciga-rettes, a few books with torn pages, the suddenly opened door, everything, everything that was one's own remained behind, flies buzzed around incessantly, almost deserted, deserted, on and on toward the source. Now he, he alone, like the last runner in a race, who knows for certain that he will not win but still runs with his languid, helpless muscles, as a force of habit. And then, like this, one dream kept knotting itself with another, its subject always the same, Surupa's continuous walk toward the darkness and a red machine gun, the one which at the end of the dream he would pull out of some corner of his body and keep shooting at Surupa's entwined waist, and he would wake up to the sound of that gunfire all by himself, without shame. It would seem that these were only dreams and in another dream he'd see the incident in exactly the same form, returned in all its minute details, and in yet another dream he would eventually have to murder Surupa. On a melancholy evening in the month of July, he would be raped in front of an unknown, black-masked woman with the same red machine gun. And thereby the killers would be transformed into dreams, the way they had been many times before.

Foot Dedek Ek Porityokto Jaygay, 1978

Heramba Naskar, Moushumi Naskar, and Jatadhari Naskar

Heramba Naskar lived in a village called Jabla, in the jurisdiction of the Kakdwip police station. He lost his father when he was very young. Of the sister and five brothers, the sister was the eldest. They had some land in the village. With the earnings from the harvest, the family survived, with a bit of hardship. Since his father died when he was little, Heramba had not had much education. His sister Sandhya was married. Heramba wanted to earn independently and stand on his own feet, so he took some money from his mother and went to a village called Bibirhat, near the Bishnupur police station. There he began a business of trading in vegetables. Within three years, he had saved a lot of money. He bought cheap land in a slightly remote location and built a house. His mother was in the village home with his younger brothers, looking after the field there. Because Heramba had not received a proper education, he was keen to get his younger brother, Jatadhari, educated. So he called Jatadhari to come live with him, and got him admission at a polytechnic. Jatadhari traveled from Bishnupur to Calcutta to study.

In 1980, Heramba married Moushumi, the daughter of Nikunja Hazra of Behala. It was an arranged marriage. Moushumi was both beautiful and educated. She was a BA student at Thakurpukur College, and the second of six sisters. Her father was a clerk in the municipality. Heramba didn't ask for dowry. He was content with the three bhoris of gold ornaments that she came with. So what if Heramba was only a vegetable seller, at least he would be able to feed and clothe and keep her. And so Nikunja gave his daughter Moushumi in marriage to Heramba.

Heramba went around with his chest puffed up in pride at having married a beautiful and educated girl. The neighbors said he was truly fortunate to have found such a wife, one who brought light into the household. Heramba's mother, Tararani, too was happy with her daughter-in-law.

The joy in Heramba's happy family was complete when Manasi was born after six years of marriage. At first, Tararani had thought that her daughter-in-law might be barren, but her notion was proved wrong. Before they knew it, Manasi was two years old. Heramba's mother was very eager to see the face of a grandson. Even Heramba wanted a son now. But that wouldn't happen merely by wishing for it. Because it was late night, Heramba and Moushumi lay beside each other on the cot. Manasi was next to Moushumi. After returning from a hard day's work in the vegetable market, Heramba usually fell asleep, snoring. That night he woke up suddenly from his sleep.

He turned around and saw that Moushumi wasn't there. Manasi had wet the kantha. In the dim light of the room, and because he was half asleep, Heramba could not see clearly. After he got married, Heramba had fitted the blue, zero watt lamp with great enthusiasm. At night, the room took on a dreamy ambience. After he had sat up for a while, his eyes gotten used to the dim light and he could gradually see everything in the room. Moushumi wasn't heating water for Manasi. Had she gone to the bathroom? After the wedding, she had got one made per her own design. She couldn't bathe in the pond. He lay quietly for a while, waiting for Moushumi to return. Almost fifteen minutes went past but there was no sign of her. Heramba turned to one side and then the other a few times. Suddenly he thought he heard two people whispering in the adjacent room. His younger brother Jatadhari slept alone there. Why could he hear the sound of two people whispering? Silently, Heramba sat up and then tiptoed to the door. He pressed his ear to the door and tried to listen to the conversation. What's this! It was Moushumi's voice! Jatadhari and Moushumi were whispering to each other with great intimacy.

The next day, Heramba called Jatadhari and told him: Jatadhari, I believe Ma is not keeping too well. She's getting on in years too. There needs to be someone with Ma in the village home, to help her look after the land and our younger brothers. It would be best if you went. I'll make all the arrangements and send you whatever money you require.

Jatadhari did not reply. Seeing him standing there in silence, Heramba asked him: What happened—why don't you reply? You'll go back to the village, won't you?

No, Dada, I won't go back to the village. I don't like it there. And I won't be able to study there. I want to stay with you.

That can't be. Even if you don't like it, you have to return to the village. Didn't I tell you someone needs to look after Ma?

Moushumi entered the room. Heramba glanced at Moushumi from the corner of his eye and began pouring green color into a vat of gourds. Jatadhari walked out and went off somewhere.

15 March, 1988. In the dead of night. Heramba lay on a mat he had spread out in the verandah. Moushumi was sleeping inside the room. It was pitch-dark everywhere. Suddenly, like a madman, Jatadhari appeared and, with a cleaver, began to rain blows on the sleeping Heramba, on his neck, chest, and stomach. Heramba awoke and started screaming at the very first blow. Hearing his screams, Moushumi rushed out of the room. She tried to save Heramba. She held Jatadhari's arm firmly. But Jatadhari freed his arm and began striking at Moushumi's body with the cleaver. Moushumi screamed until she fell unconscious in the courtyard.

Hearing the screaming and shouting, the neighbors came running. They were the ones who caught Jatadhari. They took the severely injured Heramba and Moushumi to the health subcenter in Bishnupur. Some of the locals ran to the police station and informed them. The officer in charge of the police station, Sukumar Thakur, recorded the complaint and arrived at the site of the incident with accompanying policemen, to conduct an on-the-spot investigation. After preliminary investigations, Thakur arrested Jatadhari and brought him to the police station.

At the health subcenter, the doctor examined Heramba and declared him dead. Moushumi, who was in critical condition, was sent to Vidyasagar Hospital for treatment.

As soon as news of Heramba's death reached the police station, the sub-inspector rushed to the health sub-center. After completing the necessary investigations, he sent Heramba Naskar's dead body for an autopsy. After a few days, the report reached the police. The report confirmed that Heramba Naskar had died after being assaulted with a sharp weapon. Severe bleeding from multiple wounds was the cause of death.

Jatadhari Naskar was charged with murdering his own brother, Heramba Naskar, with a cleaver, under Section 302 of the Indian Penal Code. The responsibility for undertaking the detailed investigation for this murder case was entrusted to Sub-Inspector K. K. Goswami of Bishnupur police station.

During questioning, the accused, Jatadhari Naskar, made the following confession to the police: Sir, I used to respect Dada immensely because of the incomparable sacrifices Dada made on behalf of his younger brothers after Baba's death. Dada raised me almost with a father's love. But the day beautiful Moushumi-boudi broke the walls of self-respect and shame and jumped into my arms, I forgot all about the relationship of respect and became mired in my love for Boudi. Every other night, Boudi would silently slip away from Dada's side and come to my room. Soon I began to think of Moushumi not as my sister-in-law but as my wife. I would burn to death in flames of jealousy when I saw her lying next to Dada. I felt as though I had a legal right over Moushumi. I tossed and turned restlessly on the nights she did not come to me. That's how Manasi was born. Even though legally my elder brother is Manasi's father, I know she is my child. A few months before Manasi's birth, Boudi stopped coming to my room. After that she did come, but only now and then, not regularly. This made me angry. Actually, although I loved Boudi with my heart and soul, Boudi did not love me. She had used me, like a trump card, to wipe out the ignominy of being labelled barren. The day Dada told me to go back to the village, I became even more furious within. Dada quarreled with Boudi and began sleeping in the verandah. I realized he had found out about my secret relationship with Boudi. And that provided me with the reason. I bought a cleaver from the market and kept it hidden in my room. At night, I finished off Dada with the cleaver. But I had no plan to attack Boudi. Why would I do that? I did whatever I did only to get her. But when Boudi started screaming and tried to stop me, I simply lost my head in a fit of rage.

The confession was made into a tape recorder. There were pauses in-between and scattered sighs and the sound of breathing. A summary was transcribed in the form of a statement. The incidents after this are brief. The sub-inspector prepared the case papers and submitted a charge sheet against Jatadhari to the court. Jatadhari's mother fixed a lawyer. On the advice of the lawyer, Jatadhari completely denied the confessional statement he had made at the police station. Standing in court, he denied all the charges levelled against him and claimed that he was inno-cent. The police had framed a false case against him. He said it was probably some enemy of Heramba, bent on revenge, who had entered the house and killed him. On hearing Boudi's screams, he had rushed there and tried to save his brother. But the attacker ran away as soon as he saw him, and disappeared into the darkness. As he was escaping, he threw away the blood-smeared cleaver. His own fingerprints might have got onto the cleaver during the scuffle, but he was actually innocent.

On the advice of the lawyer, the forensic and fingerprint reports were arranged in his favor with the help of some money. The lawyer took care of everything. Moushumi too issued a statement from the hospital: Jatadhari did not murder his brother. Some people in the vegetable market held a grudge against Heramba, one of them had committed the murder. She did not want the domestic scandal to spread. Besides, by being killed, Heramba had saved her in a way. Jatadhari's mother thought, I've lost one son, what's the point of sending the other one to the gallows? She too testified that her younger son could never murder his elder brother. Someone from outside had committed the murder out of jealousy. Consequently, the case of murder against Jatadhari could not stand.

On 10 September 1988, for lack of evidence, the sessions judge in Alipore ordered the release, without any charges, of Jatadhari Naskar, the accused in the case of murdering his own brother and attempting to murder his sister-in-law. Moushumi too returned home in about a week's time, after receiving proper treatment from the doctors.

Heramba Naskar Moushumi Naskar Jatadhari Naskar, 1989

Radioactive Waste

Q: Who offered the bride? And who was it that
accepted her?

A: Kama, the God of Love, offered her, and Kama
accepted her. Kama is the provider, and Kama
the receiver. Oh Kama, this commodity [girl] is
yours alone.

—*Vajasneyi Samhita*, 7/48 (Hymn to Kama)

Thirty-year-old Sushma, all of sixty-three kilos, was
showing off her body in an extremely intimate way to
Ajoy, while his father's long-bearded picture hung in
Ajoy's room. It was afternoon, the sun's full blast outside,
unwavering, and from the flat next door, music from the
transistor radio floated in: *Oh mind, what's with you, oh
love* . . . There was no discernable mark on the bright-red,
silk petticoat, and if one wanted to go to the bathroom
one had to cross about two and a half arm-lengths of
light and that place was apparently unpleasant for them.

Pity, for it had taken so long to prepare—Ajoy's house had to be empty (that is to say, his brother and sister-in-law's Sunday-afternoon cinema and the servant boy sent off somewhere for some cock-and-bull reason); Sushma had to take the day off; Ajoy ought not have any work in the afternoon—and they had been longing for this secret encounter for days and nights on end, wondering when it would materialize. But in fact the meeting didn't take place. Sushma had modeled up heavily and put on a lot of perfume and Ajoy was finding it difficult to breathe—because Sushma was thirty years old; because there was really nothing else remaining; because "*I came to your garden to pluck flowers*." The urge to sing out a stanza from the national song had to be suppressed. Perhaps the candle was alight, a soft glow at the head of its long flame, Sushma made appreciative motions with her hand, although she lay flat like a gluttonous beast, paler than the candle; if one rubbed a finger rapidly on her flesh, the smell of gunpowder emanated from it. Like a heavily pregnant woman, Sushma, all of sixty-three kilos, was having trouble breathing, there was a faint moustache beneath her nose, her tummy, entrusted by custom, a waxing moon bereft of a current stream to glide along. Which was why Ajoy had frowned at the nectar and walked toward the bathroom, tying his pajamas. Instead, he turned around and lit a cigarette. And there was Sushma and her candle. Crossing the despised little loop of light, he heard the sound of country bombs exploding outside—the old problem had cropped up again in the neighborhood.

There is a fantastic story in Ethiopian folklore about the ascent of man from demon. On the banks of the river

Meng lived an ogre called Chiang, his lips, like a hunter bird's, were long and beak-like, his body was covered in porcupine-like spikes, there were two immense wings on his back, although the lower part of his body was like a man's. Chiang was king of all the creatures on the riverside. One day when the waters of the Meng were in swollen turmoil, he saw another huge ogre, his face horse-like, with big scales on his body and four long, thin legs, carrying a mouthful of water in his massive, cavern-like mouth but spilling it everywhere, and on the southern bank of the river, standing on top of the hill, was a ravishingly beautiful girl, her lovely form like moonlight springing out from behind clouds. As soon as he saw the girl, Chiang forgot all about the temporal world and ran to receive that beauty, with his arms outstretched. But when he went closer, the beauty vanished with a soft smile, and then, in despair and rage, with trembling fury, Chiang leapt upon the horse-faced ogre, he tore and bit him to shreds. After he had killed the ogre, he heard a divine voice from the sky: You shall cross the threshold to become man from demon; you shall drive away wild animals from your habitation; you shall abandon stone and make weapons of iron. Until that moment, Chiang did not know he was an ogre, nor what it was like to be man. At the outset he thought about getting married, through this custom he thought he could learn all about being human.

After making themselves respectable, Sushma and Ajoy chatted, they drank tea as if nothing had happened, as if an emergency had not occurred a short while ago. Sushma spoke about her life as a nurse. She spoke about the likelihood of becoming a matron at the hospital, every now and then she laughed and Ajoy dozed off to the sound of her laughter. The calamity of before had passed to a great extent. But once again there was the sound of bomb blasts outside, and a few screams. Ajoy went to the window. A boy slipped into the adjacent lane, a knife gleaming in his hand. The sun blazed down, some suspicious-looking boys stood in front of the house on the other side of the street, the neighborhood was completely still. Ajoy shut the window as if no further disturbance from outside could touch them, and as he was about to get up to light a cigarette, there was another explosion. Their windows shook and rattled at the sound. Without lighting the cigarette, Ajoy looked at his father's picture on the wall, he saw Sushma's face, pale and anxious, which meant that Sushma had to leave because it was time for his brother and sister-in-law to return. But there was no way she could step out now. Stuck in the room, they became even more worried as they heard sporadic screams and blasts. A police van drove past. As if in a bid to secure their very existence, they carried on a few words of conversation. Those heaving moments of an hour ago were scattered like broken glass across the room, and as Ajoy went to clasp its last fragment in his fist, he saw blood trickling out of his hand. Standing in the room, he licked his wound. Brother and sister-in-law would be back any moment now, yet Sushma, that big fat girl, had not left. She felt ashamed to step outside now—to sum up the situation, everything was stuck. Ajoy stood in front of his father's picture, gnashing his teeth. The boy pulled his hair out in exasperation with his two hands. If only he could really tear out the coiffured head—even the life of a cockroach was better than this! Or an earthworm! A house lizard! Fuck, how could someone live like this, with a man-eating tiger lurking inside one's chest? Could he?

Zoologists contend that procreation is the first and foremost characteristic of animals. Animal bodies come to an end with death. But by giving birth to a new life, animals uphold the process of procreation. In this way, a life creates a new life. This development of a new generation from the older one is called reproduction. There are a few organs in the body that are necessary for the purpose of reproduction. Through their union, reproductive function is established. The reproductive behavior of all animals is not the same. Sushma's man Ajoy had spoken of cockroaches and earthworms. Let's consider the earthworm. The earthworm's reproductive organs are very strange. There's no male–female division among them, the earthworms that are male are also female, that is, in a single earthworm's body there are both male and female categories of reproductive organs. But an earthworm's eggs do not get fertilized with its own sperm. During union, an earthworm lowers its head beside another earthworm and raises its rear end toward the other one's rear end, and they conjoin lengthwise. In this way, sperm from the first earthworm's reproductive cavity enters the sperm sac of the second earthworm. Thus, despite possessing both sexes, earthworms fertilize their eggs not with their own sperm but with a second earthworm's sperm, and this is how they procreate.

As Ajoy and Sushma walked, they found a place where there was tree shade. It was midday in the Maidan now, not a soul around, and they felt like ponds that had dried up under the summer sun. In nearby Chowringhee, they noticed a sixteen-story building that had come up. Being in high spirits and because there was no one around, Ajoy refrained from calling her "Sushma-di" and used her name instead. Sushma coquettishly said she'd sit on the grass and sat down near Ajoy's lap, lit Ajoy's cigarette for him, and played awhile with Ajoy's hand and fingers. "We could have gone to the cinema at this time," etc.—sundry talk like that, and so a few cigarette butts lay scattered around them. Time stopped momentarily, and soon the woman called Sushma told the boy called Ajoy about searching for a job. Then she could be independent, they could take a separate flat and be free of brother and sister-in-law. The boy understood what she was trying to get at and it made him feel sick, but there was a whiff of fragrance from a mahua grove and it was difficult to overcome such enticements. In Chowringhee a car braked suddenly with a loud screech and a few people ran in that direction. Ajoy thought, "Another accident on earth at this moment." Further reflection along these lines was probably getting dull because at this moment, somewhere or the other, there were more accidents taking place and there were too many people on earth, just too many. As he reflected in this vein, he narrated the thought to Sushma. We shall stay away from all these hassles: the boy lapped up the proposal from the girl and in the sun-bedecked Maidan, he arranged brick upon brick of four walls of their own around them. They laid the walls, became more and more distanced from Chowringhee, from the accident that had just taken place, and eventually even from the sun. No one can see us now, we can do as we please within these four brick walls, that talk, very immature talk, they talked about that, and whether it rained outside or was sunny, whether there was an accident or things were in general moving along sedately, all this did not matter a whit to them. The two of them, in that brick cage, considered themselves perfectly safe in that blazing Maidan and sought to spend their time to their hearts' delight, and exactly at that moment the bomb that dropped on Phnom Penh wobbled the brick cage erected by them, and for the first time they wondered: Is it really possible to be completely free of any distress, like this, all by oneself, solitary?

In 1969, Katsuichi Honda went from Japan to Vietnam accompanied by a photographer. On his return he penned his experience, and with the accompanying pictures his commentary appeared in the *Japan Quarterly* magazine in 1969, in the April–June issue. He had seen the kind of war that went on in every village. He had seen the way an American soldier removed a pair of earrings from a dead woman guerilla, he had seen how, under the scorching sun of a summer noon, American soldiers used a cigarette lighter to set aflame thatched huts of harmless Vietnamese and then had a merry hula-hooping dance party around the sacrificial bonfire. He had seen an American soldier cut off the ear of a dead Vietnamese fighter and stuff it into a plastic bag, and when he asked someone, What will the soldier do with an ear?, the answer was: Keep it as part of his collection, what else! The man added, He will dry it out first, and then take it home as a valuable souvenir. That's nothing, once I saw the liver being removed from the dead body of a Vietnamese guerilla. An American soldier who returned from active duty in Vietnam exposed another incident. The story first appeared in an American newspaper. At dawn on 16 March 1968, in the north-eastern region of South Vietnam, a group of American soldiers raided the village of Song-My, rounded up all the villagers—men, women, children, and old people—lined them up in a particular place and shot them dead. According to the report, the number of those killed was anywhere between 109 and 567.

As they walked, they suddenly halted and began to think, and then thought about what they could think about. There was a cow lying around in the street, they could think about that, they could think about the mist wrapped around a lamp post somewhere, or they could think about how Sushma, fat old Sushma, would look when she became a matron. The wide asphalt road stretched on both sides, all along the roads were people, lights, and frolic in their usual arrangement. One could pick it up and bite into it and suck or lick and taste it as and when needed. After a while the boy wanted to buy a balloon; the girl, flowers. They did not know what the difference between a balloon and flowers was and how much, and they argued animatedly for a while. In the end they bought neither flowers nor a balloon. Evening descended around them, a procession of a hundred-odd people, their arms powerful, their fists clenched tight as they walked under the lights of Chowringhee. He began to think that he too could be in that procession, as one of them, and he felt the stubble of a few days on his face, this stubble, this rough stubble, how Sushma loved to run her cheek over it. Sushma came out of a daze to see a man a few feet away from them staring at her; as soon as she became aware he passed her by, grazing her right breast. Even though she wanted to react, Sushma couldn't say anything, times were bad now, the chap could be a petty goonda, how long did it take to whip out a knife? A string of bel flowers had been bought, it was thrown away on the road. Blood from Vietnam splashed down, it touched the boy and the girl, they went to wipe it away with a kerchief but couldn't because bloodstains are not easy to remove, they accrue, like a debt, over time. A sad-looking beggar girl in a dirty frock, her hair in knots, eagerly picked up the garland and inhaled its fragrance. Sometimes beggars love flowers. Why can't we admit it clearly, the boy began to wonder, but then he saw a sign in the barren field: Do not pluck flowers and destroy the beauty of the garden. The girl, whose name for the time being is Sushma, began to think absentmindedly about a line from a book read long ago, about shame being a woman's ornament, and then realized she was climbing stairs and heading somewhere. Worrying about going alone and so on, she made an act of clasping his neck with her hands and saw that Ajoy's head, down to his neck, had come away in her hand. Ajoy said in affected rage, You ogress, you want to chew my head off, and as he said that he saw the kohl lining the girl's eyes, and various other things under the kohl, and bursting with desire to tell her all this, he began to plant kisses on her cheeks. At that moment, some spiders trapped prey in the waning moonlight and old man moon floated along on the flood waters.

Animals, humans, and gods can all be brought under control through mantra. The root of the word mantra is *mana,* or mind. This root denotes thought. Another connotation of mana is protection of the seeker from the hindrances and obstacles that may be encountered on the path to realizing this secret power. Using the power of the great tantric mantra, the ancient dwellers of Kamakhya in Kamrup, Assam, performed extraordinary magical and divine miracles. When a man could not be brought under their control merely through their affected behavior, they took control of him through their powers of mantra. If a man had to be brought under control, a specific mantra was chanted and a flower was endowed with the mantra's power, and if this was cast on the man without his knowledge, it brought success. Om Kali, Mahakali, sacred offerings of alcohol and meat, invoking Brahma the Creator, and with unwavering faith in the guru's powers—as the mantra was recited and the flower was cast, the boy standing in the verandah was transformed into a billy goat.

The billy goat was tethered in the verandah, it chewed grass and bleated, *maenh-maenh.* Sushma caressed it every day, she stroked its neck at night: oh dear goat, stay with me all my life. As girls her age walked down the street spitting paan juice, they saw the billy goat and said, What a wonderful goat Sushma-di has. Sushma would flash a smile, but sometimes she displayed great gravity. One day, as the goat was tethered in the verandah, it saw a large procession of people advancing, chanting slogans. There had been endless processions all morning, and slogans upon slogans, as if there were a festival in the city. The goat's mind was on edge. If he was released he too could march along with them, he'd shout out the slogans: *This battle is for survival, this battle must be won!* But who would release him? Sushma had become a matron, she watched over him with a serious face; people were becoming more militant by the day, movements advanced rapidly, the fat matron saw all this yet did not notice anything. The furore everywhere increased by the day, the billy goat became restless, surely the great uprising had commenced, he must go. Sushma watched, she said: Oh, cut out the act; she said: Isn't there a term, goat-brained—*Billy goat goes to see the colorful dinner party, and Ram, Shyam, Jodu, Madhu catch and eat him, nasty!* He didn't even know what an uprising was. No matter how complicated the social system, how organized state power and how perfect the military weapons, it was even more unpardonable to mouth slogans like this without proper thought. After delivering her speech, Sushma went away, her hips swaying, but before she left she kissed him. What would the billy goat do now? Tethered for a long time, he began to chew grass, he watched the people on the street, but not once did it occur to him to snap the rope and escape. And as he stood thus, he saw a group of people looking very agitated, and as they marched, chanting slogans, they inadvertently dropped a red flag. He picked up the flag with his mouth and began to chew. But as he tried to chew, his mouth filled with blood and the blood trickled down and flowed for two miles. The billy goat stopped chewing and wondered, amazed, where so much blood had come from. Where?

Sir H. H. Johnson wrote in his book, *British Central Africa*, that the people of Central Africa rarely made obscene gestures consciously or indulged in licentiousness.

He had spent seven years in this land of naked people and not once had he encountered a man or woman making an obscene bodily gesture. Their folk dances would most certainly be viewed as indecent in modern civilized society, but if one considered their significance, they could almost be placed at the level of religious ceremonies. The single indigenous folk dance of Central Africa was initially an expression of sexual activity, but thereafter it was changed and transformed into a rite that could not be understood unless the local folk explained it. But it can be said with surety that compared to the Europeans, the race of people in Central Africa was far more modest and shy, and far more liberated from natural sin. Except for the children of kings, no prepubescent boy or girl used clothing of any kind. The Wankonda males wore a kind of short brass skirt tied at the belly—that was their only garment. The women of this race were almost entirely naked and wore only a small piece of beadwork like a loincloth. The Angoni males wore a penis sheath made of wood or dried fruit skins. A traveler who spent a long time in the Ejimba region of Central Africa said of his experience that although the people of this region appeared to the civilized world to be naked and indecent in their behavior, in matters of sex they possessed propriety and conformed to clear codes of conduct. The traveler describes the investiture ceremony for boys and girls organized at the onset of their youth. There was song and dance and festivity and frolic for several days, through which all the deep secrets of marriage were conferred upon the girl. The whole thing took place according to specific rituals and in the public ceremonies nothing whatsoever was hidden, nor was anything considered shameful. The writer believes that this is why the womenfolk of this race are extremely wise. What needs to be known is known to them from the beginning and they find no reason to conceal natural laws and experiences. In this context, one may refer to a traveler in Congo. He asked a village chief about female nudity and got an answer that is possibly the last word on this matter: it is the tendency to hide and conceal that feeds curiosity.

Madame de Barney, forty-five years old, mother of nine, bent to feed some grass to the billy goat, and as she stared fixedly at him, she asked—

What's your name?

Balzac.

How old are you, sonny?

Oh, about twenty-three or twenty-four.

What do you see?

The forty-year-old woman was so forthcoming but the young woman of twenty gave nothing.

The billy goat thought about a lot of strange things, and as he was lost in thought, Sushma, well-advanced in years, gave him some more grass. In a flash she became a little girl who raced up a flight of stairs and heard: Girls really become girls for the first time when they are about thirty-five. After that she reached the top. But the boy asked, Have we actually reached the top? He still had doubts. If we've reached why do we keep circling around the same lamp post all the time? Whenever he looked, no matter which direction he looked, there was the same mist before them, the same darkness, around the same lamp post. Beneath them, a great distance below, if one looked one could see the river, the sound of a boat lapped by water, the crematorium, chanting of the Lord's name, a bier, bereaved people weeping, and the sound of a motor launch somewhere nearby—they didn't know exactly where the motor launches came from or where they were going. Or he saw the overbridge at the station, and even on the stairs there were a number of tired, sleeping faces. The desolate, floodlit rail tracks at one in the morning. Tired, downcast, they lifted their heads to see the same mist, the same lamp post, and the same darkness. We kept circling the same lamp post all the time. All day, all night. They were unable to get away from the lamp post, couldn't get near it either. As they circled the lamp post, they became tired and downcast. It's been so long since we went somewhere, we don't think differently—they talked, the lamp post, the mist, and the darkness had become akin to death for them. Had they really raced up the stairs one day to go somewhere? They couldn't say for sure. If they looked down, could they see the river, the crematorium, the motor launches on the river, or the heap of tired faces on the steps of the overbridge and the brightly lit rail tracks below? Perhaps they could see, perhaps they couldn't, they couldn't say for sure. Why are we unable to tell everyone what's real? We feel ashamed, and yet, every day, so many people come out on the streets in protest. They talked some more; as they climbed up the stairs they saw how worn out it was, it made them sleepy. The stairs could have crumbled at any moment—that's what they thought. We did not do anything unjust or commit any act of infidelity, so why would we thump our chests about this lamp post, this mist, and this darkness? They, Ajoy and Sushma, thought about all this, they kept thinking, and as they thought, they heard a procession advancing somewhere nearby, the fervor of protest floated by. They were unperturbed, their ears attuned, they listened to the sounds, they just kept listening.

This body of ours, the living body, is a collection of many cells, and the cells are of various types. Every cell is a living entity. The basic functions of a living thing—consumption, respiration, excretion, and reproduction—are coordinated beautifully by the cells. Consumption by a living creature means consumption by its cells. A full-grown man's body has about ten thousand trillion cells. Each individual cell works continuously and in cooperation with the others, thereby fulfilling all their requirements.

Each cell is broadly made up of plasmalemma or cell membrane, protoplasm, and a nucleus. There is a kind of transparent semi-liquid substance within the cell, called protoplasm. The living transparent permeable sheath encircling the protoplasm is the plasmalemma, and the relatively viscous roundish element within the cell is the cell's nucleus, which directs all the activity within the cell. In fact, the nucleus's place is at the very center of the cell, its role like that of the brain in a creature's body. The appearance of the nucleus varies across cells, they are sometimes round, sometimes long and egg-shaped, and sometimes thin and cylindrical. If the nucleus was taken away from the protoplasm, what remains is the cytoplasm and the nucleus cannot survive without the cytoplasm, and without the nucleus the cytoplasm too would die. The transparent viscous liquid substance that exists inside the nucleus is the nucleoplasm. Inside the nucleoplasm there are many thin, thread-like elements, like capillaries, which are the chromatin reticulum. At the time of cell division, these chromatin threads are divided into thread-like parts that are called chromosomes. And it is this chromosome and its central "gene" that carries hereditary properties.

When the male spermatozoon and the female ovum come together, fertilization takes place and a new cell is born. This is how life is accomplished, this is the origin of life. There is a specific number of chromosomes in the male sperm and a specific number in the ovum; consequently, the new cell created through the union of sperm and ovum has an equal number of chromosomes from both parents, because of which every living thing can develop its own unique characteristics.

Before falling asleep, Ajoy sought complete clarity on a few things.

First, he did not love Sushma-di, although he had laid a baby in her belly.

Second, in the process of revealing her magic, Sushma-di, Sushma, had laid her body on his bed.

Third, he had stared long and hard at the luminous darkness.

Fourth, the body, toward which there was all this great love, was only a collection of ten thousand trillion cells.

Fifth, whenever any procession went by near them, Sushma-di tried to sing lullabies to him.

Sixth, he wasn't at all curious about the new cell being created with his cell and Sushma's cell.

Seventh, the idea of leaving Sushma appeared unethical to him, and yet it was also impossible for him to swallow his pride and tell his brother and sister-in-law about Sushma.

As he reflected on all this, Ajoy entered his room, and in no time at all he fell asleep.

How a human being made up of a collection of millions of cells develops from just one cell, which is called an egg cell, preserving hereditary features in the process, and then goes about his life activities, remains a major question for scientists even today. According to microbiologists, at the root of this event lie the DNA, RNA, and protein. DNA, or dioxyribonucleic acid, is that vital part of the living cell that helps determine the structure of the cell, hereditary traits and so on. With each DNA there are different types of nucleotides. It is said that nucleotides are the building blocks of the DNA. In the language of microbiologists, a DNA is like a word made up of four unique genetic alphabets or letters relating to reproduction, each one like a piece of glass of a different hue. Just as a few letters can make up several words with several meanings, similarly DNAs combine in different numerical sequences to form genes. The gene is the key component of the chromosome in the cell of a living creature. Different animals have different chromosomes, and it is these that determine which living being will be human, which one demon or even earthworm. The second function of the DNA is like that of a casting mold; and just as many things of an identical nature can be produced by using a mold, in exactly the same way, from one kind of DNA mold, through an admixture of different chemical elements, the same kind of cell, or component of life, is formed.

If you carry on walking like this, in a few days you will reach the high mountain peak where you can hear the flapping wings of the golden eagle. But it is not advisable to go there for the mother eagle can take away your arm; when she flies to the mountain top in search of food, the two tiny delicate chicks are left all alone. As difficult as it is to search for gull eggs, clambering over huge, razor-sharp rocks scattered in somersaults over the seashore cliff, this is far more challenging. The piercing sun burns down on your head, bruises form all over the body from grazing against the rocks, bleeding, a burning sensation, and you must place every step carefully, never forgetting to keep your balance, because even a momentary lapse of concentration could be fatal. With all this effort, some accomplish it and some don't. Because the golden eagle's chicks live very close to what terrifies many men.

What can be called a living thing?

When a living cell creates another cell of its own kind by itself, it is called a living thing.

What is the difference between animals and humans?

Animals use only the external world and bring about a transformation in that world merely through their presence, but man, while changing the world, compels it to satisfy his own objectives and rules over it.

How did the ape turn into man?

At first through labor, and later, together with labor, speech—the pronunciation of a sentence—the stimuli of these two factors were most significant in influencing the progressive metamorphosis of the monkey brain into the human brain.

Three sick children held hands and advanced toward the sea.

Written on the advertisement: "You don't know what you are missing." At that moment the boy, Ajoy, could not quite figure out what he was missing. He could hear country bombs outside, fighting had broken out again in the neighborhood. He yawned, and just as he wondered whether he should get up and go, the door swung wide open and someone entered the room.

You can get anything if you just stretch out your hand—a gulab-jamun or fat Sushma or a gene created in a test-tube. A commotion could be heard in the street outside. Suddenly, the arrival of a police van with screeching brakes put a stop to everything. No, you cannot get everything merely by stretching out your hand, everything does not stop simply by pressing the brake. A bomb exploded again, the commotion grew. Ajoy wondered why his name was not Ram or Shyam or Jodu or Madhu, or for that matter, Karna-bell or Nucleus—or at least one of the names of those who were in the street now. From today I shall adopt a name like that—Ram, Shyam, Jodu, or Madhu, or Karna-bell or Nucleus—Ajoy thought. Someone entered the room and looked for Ajoy, and everything in the room was in an orderly fashion, the bed to lie on with pillows in their correct place, and interestingly, the corpse of the horse-faced ogre was there too, hung from the rafter, but he, Ajoy, wasn't there. Only three sick children, holding hands, advancing toward the sea.

It is possible to create a gene artificially, and all the genes necessary to produce the human body can be produced in just a test-tube. Experts know all about the cells needed to make a human, and in the future, through such means, humans can be created at will. At the core of human cells are forty-six chromosomes. These are obtained from the twenty-three in the father's body and the twenty-three in the mother's body. And together with these forty-six chromosomes there are at least one hundred fifty thousand genes of various kinds. These genes determine the exact time within which, and how, a tiny human cell is transformed into a complete human being. Almost a hundred thousand proteins, including principal ones like haemoglobin, insulin, and so on, constitute our bodies and each protein makes twenty types of genes. Therefore, one could say that our body is made up of 100,000 x 20 = 2 million genes.

Letting down her hair and spreading it across her back, the girl, Sushma, moved away from the mirror, she took off her blouse, there was a light burning on the second floor of the house in front, a body, its shadow. Sushma stepped away from the window, she did not recall it, although this happened every night. The gentleman peeped into the room through the window. At first she did not realize it, now she could, she had found proof too. Men stare so crazily, seven years ago Amal–Kamal–Bimal–Sukhamoy used to stare. What did they see? One hundred thousand multiplied by twenty, that is, two million genes? Or did they see more than that? At the bottom of the door, where the winter's desolate mist showered down beneath the light of the lamp post, there they were, Amal–Kamal–Bimal–Sukhamoy, waiting for seven years. Now Sushma removed all her undergarments and loosened herself up, she kept looking at the clock.

What is the significance of all these discoveries by man?

Who takes the responsibility of determining the main goal or objective behind producing a human artificially? Everything in the human world depends upon man's self-interest and need, hence man's exact goal or objective is often unclear. Besides, if there is some extraneous influence on man, what could be the means to keep that at bay? The DNA is made up of four nucleotides and in every nucleotide there are some fundamental elements, composed of a combination of electrons, protons, and neutrons. Many believe that radiation from the sun and stars affects the atoms of elements. Scientists like Dr. Bedley say that radiation can lead to changes within the DNA. Soviet scientists had shown that there is a relation between magnetic energy and the human mental condition. The explosion that takes place in the sun every eleven years because of excessive storms affects the earth's magnetic field, albeit temporarily. There can be some influence of planets and stars on the fundamental composition of living beings, because a change in the magnetic field can lead to a change in the atomic structure of the fundamental elements. And at some stage, this may change the electrical properties of the DNA. At this juncture, nothing can be said with exactitude about the influence of the external world on biological evolution. However, preventing mutation by regulating the domain of research institutes is definitely not the last word on the subject. Perhaps man will succeed in creating life artificially, but in the natural way.

What do we conclude about the significance of these discoveries?

There was Rabindrasangeet playing in the house next door. Tinu—Ajoy was called Tinu as a child—picked up a pencil and drew a square, and at its center he made a red dot. The clock struck nine. The pet cat lay in the sun, its body stretched out. There was a spider's web on the wall, sparkling white. A fly buzzed around.

What happens when flapping wings sound
Pollen rains down
What will the fly do
It'll be caught in the spider's web
Where's the spider
In the middle of Sushma's belly

Tinu now wanted a color pencil—red pencil blue pencil green pencil. Tinu drew a picture of an ogre, filling the entire page. But he said he'd drawn a picture of a man. As he brought down the small hand of the clock showing nine, it turned six. The pet cat showed off a trapeze act on the spider's web. As water flowed gushingly and loudly in the bathroom, every kind of laughter and weeping was washed and wiped away. Sushma, open your mouth. I shall look for a spider inside your mouth. Using a blue pencil, Tinu drew walls on the four sides, he drew a gate. He drew a watchman at the gate. He wondered if there should be a gun in his hand. As he tried to draw a huge moustache on the watchman, he ended up drawing a long, straight-line procession of men. He drew red flags in their hands. Sushma, I'm looking for a job. If I had a job the shame would be far less. I could tell everyone, my chest swollen with pride. Tinu drew a happy nook in the room, he drew a parrot in a cage. He made a gramophone. The gramophone adorned the happy nook. Across the river Padma, in Bakshiganj, the weekly market assembled. It was Friday. And today? The villagers bought and sold. And in the city? Tinu tried to draw a bullock cart. He had forgotten what a bullock cart looked like. Then he drew the latest Fiat model.

On the one hand we create artificial humans and on the other hand the oxygen in our atmosphere is progressively getting exhausted. We are advancing rapidly toward a sudden disastrous event. It is from the countless planktons in the oceans that, through photosynthesis, more than 70 percent of the oxygen in the atmosphere is produced. Some fifty thousand poisonous substances and pesticides, radio isotopes, enzymes, etc., that can severely harm life, all invented in the modern era, are now thrown as waste into the sea. Owing to the movement of ships and so on, every year one and a half million tons of oil spills into the seawater. The oil that spills from motor cars and industrial plants on land is almost double that, and almost all of it goes into rivers that eventually reach the sea. Earlier, it was not necessary for the earth to degrade many of these toxic substances. It has been observed in tests that even tiny doses of these substances greatly destroy the sea plankton, thus endangering our source of oxygen.

Moreover, every year, through the increasing use of fuel, we are irresponsibly exhausting the oxygen in the atmosphere. Before the onset of the industrial revolution, the quantity of carbon dioxide in the atmosphere was 280 parts per million, at present there are 321 parts, meaning each year the quantity goes up by seventy parts per million. In addition, by destroying trees and natural vegetation, which enable photosynthesis, over thousands of acres of land, we hinder the production of oxygen yet again. It's not just our air and water that is polluted but oxygen itself that is rapidly disappearing from the earth. Till the very end of his life, Professor Lloyd undertook research on the sources of oxygen. He cautions us with this conclusion: one day, very suddenly, there will be a deficiency in the amount of oxygen in the atmosphere. And the earth's population is advancing rapidly toward that terrible day.

Its teeth were terribly sharp, it chewed and ate humans.

No one lived in the city's old quarters, broken houses, heaps of bricks, a jungle of weeds, derelict factories, people didn't go there, they shuddered even if they went there during the day. It lived there and it ate human flesh.

Once complete darkness envelops the place, it emerges, it searches for raw humans.

Not heeding any obstacles, the hay-laden bullock cart went along the road, it collapsed. A man who spoke of such chicanery—within twenty-four hours his mouth filled with blood and he died.

The sacred offerings in the broken pot lay on one side, goat's blood—standing in the darkness, looking, the sharp teeth were sighted, it ate human flesh.

Searching among heaps of bricks, torchlight in hand, braving the wind that whistled away like a flute being played, the torch slipped and dropped from the hand. Nothing could be discerned in the darkness.

A dog wailed somewhere. Tearing through the darkness, the waxing eleven-day moon rose above the saal trees. Moonlight flooded the grated windows of the factory.

Roads from all directions culminated here.

Moonlight flooded the old grated windows of the factory.

Perspiring profusely, the terrifying sharp teeth were sighted, it ate humans.

Mohenjodaro endangered! Save the "monument of the dead" from the fury of the Indus's floods and salinity! Reading, he approached, and as he approached he saw that someone had thrown Sushma's headless corpse under the dim light at the crossroads. He felt sick when he saw that and in order to overcome it, without looking in any direction, he just kept running fast. After a while, he stopped in front of a cigarette shop, fatigued, and saw some people there. Heaving a sigh of relief as he gave the man sitting in the elevated booth some coins for a cigarette, he remembered that this very afternoon he had seen a man who looked like worn-out, hanging leather, sucking at the leg of a dead dog with relish. Instead of buying a cigarette, he lifted and showed the heel of his shoe to the shopkeeper and asked him: Could you please see whether there's any blood on my heel? The man sitting in the shop was somewhat startled at this, and stared at his disheveled hair. He raised the heel of the shoe higher, and moving closer to the shopkeeper, said: Can you see anything? Any bloodstains? The shopkeeper wasn't startled this time, his attention was directed at the paan he was preparing, and as he applied lime to the paan leaves, he said: Yes, I see it, not on your heel but on your elbow, on your shirt. He was very surprised and said, But it's not supposed to be there. With an air of indifference, the shopkeeper continued to fold his paan leaves and said, I don't know anything about that. Here, take some lime and apply it on the stain.

As he applied the lime, he remembered that Mohenjodaro was endangered. It had to be protected from the fury
of the Indus's floods and salinity.

Man

A kind of radioactive waste

Between demon and man

The ogre kills for need, man without need

Mohenjodaro

City of the dead

Ajoy loved Sushma

And Sushma Ajoy

YOU PEOPLE SAY DAY AND NIGHT

Ajoy hated Sushma

And Sushma Ajoy

What happens when flapping wings sound

Pollen rains down

What will the fly do

It'll be caught in the spider's web

Where's the spider

In the middle of Sushma's belly

But much as he tried to chew it his mouth only

Filled with blood   and

That fresh blood

Trickled and flowed for two miles

The billy goat stopped chewing and in amazement

Began to wonder

The sound of the golden eagle flapping its wings

Could be heard on and on

Because of the genes, two million genes

Today, not a single child is born without at least one unit
of a transuranium element in its body. This poison enters

our body through food. When transuranium (92) enters a pregnant woman's body, a good part of it accumulates in the fetus. What is most worrying is that within ten minutes of entering the body, its terrible radioactivity reaches the bones, where it nestles permanently. Radioactive transuranium elements reside in the body for at least twenty-eight years and there is no way of removing this substance from the bones. A child born with a transuranium element has to live out its whole life as this radioactivity's waste. Not only that, iodine (131) nestles in the thyroid gland and cesium (137) in the nervous system and in muscle tissue, and under specific conditions, these give rise to frightful diseases. Far more harm than that caused by nuclear weapons and tests is caused by the use of nuclear energy in so-called peaceful purposes. The impact of radioactivity on gene mutation is, alas Ajoy and Sushma, unhindered today.

RADIOACTIVITY CONTINOUSLY ACCUMULATES IN THE HUMAN BODY

THE TRANSMISSION PATH OF RADIO NUCLIDES

Strontium (89, 90)	Cesium (137)	Iodine (131)	Barium (140)
From atmosphere	From atmosphere	From atmosphere	From atmosphere
To soil, vegetation	To vegetation	To vegetations, humans	To vegetation
To fatty tissues of animals & humans	To fatty tissues of animals & humans	To fatty tissues of animals	To fatty tissues of animals
To milk & meat	To milk & meat	To milk & meat	To milk & meat
To humans	To humans	To humans	To humans

Pictures drawn by ancient man in Lascaux's caves: between a rhinoceros and a bison lies a dead man, a stick-like body. The bison's body speared, its innards spewing out, its head lowered, ready to strike with its horns. In the middle a dead body, drawn with a few paltry strokes, a rectangular body, arms and legs like sticks, the face bird-like. Killed in battle, that half-man lies between the rhinoceros and the bison, his face flat on the earth.

Tejoskriyo Aborjona, 1970

The Cow Is a Kind of Quadrangular Creature

The cow is a kind of quadrangular creature that conceals the cosmic beam in its eyelids. There are bits and pieces of all sorts of treasures in cows' heads, with which they ruminate over everything in the world as they chew cud. Baba had once brought a cow from Honduras which actually exactly reproduced the work of its forebears and destroyed the colorful slough of plywood, fabricated over thirty years, which people at every turn call democracy. And ever since, we steadily became well-versed in cow-related affairs. Baba explained to us that no matter how confident we might be regarding cows' legs, we weren't correct, because cows could have two or three or four or even five legs—there was nothing certain about it. Cows could definitely declare a state of emergency or, if they so desired, they possessed the capability to bring about a military coup at a whim. They loved to chew furtively on newspapers or the rolled-up pages of the Constitution.

Dry roots and tubers from beneath the soil, syntax: the alphabet system, their own tails, thorny plants, unused cartridges—all this, everything was their fodder, and they derived great pleasure from eating them. But it wouldn't do to think that cows did not possess a sense of beauty or that they were not aware of their own class interest. They dearly loved to sing "*The forests are alive with spring*." When the nation needed pharmaceutical factories, it was cows who reminded the ministers to increase the production of cosmetics instead, and it was cows who advised them to manufacture armaments, keeping people starved. If one were to look at a cow's tail, there would seem to be nothing useful about it, but many believe it comes in handy for nuclear disarmament. Even if cows usually seemed quite innocent, they could become terribly bloodthirsty. If they got the appropriate opportunity and means, they even killed someone as untroublesome as Archimedes. Cows cannot tolerate the views of others. Some people speak in whispers about a special type of cow. These cows apparently use the horns on their head as antennae, and nurture hostility toward every other line of thinking. They say: "Only what I say is correct, and that's what you must do." Asking questions is always banned in the cows' world. There's a worldwide revolution taking place among cows. A perpetual uprising. Their clothes and garb, thinking, everything is changing rapidly. Those who can't stay in step with this get rejected. They become obsolete. There aren't just innards and intestines in the cow's belly, there is every kind of wicked design in there, every evil intent to keep humans human. Cows couldn't attain ultimate bliss unless they feuded among themselves. There are many molesters among cows. Most cows know a Sten gun and can tell a country bomb from a pomelo. The cerebral excellence of cows depends upon a certain cosmic beam. Cows worship in Kalighat, but given the opportunity, they also commit adultery. Dropping bombs on children's schools makes them happy. They love to use diaphragms. The twelfth cow that Baba had reared in his lifetime loved to listen to Beethoven and from time to time it took to sexual assault. It once showed the precise site from where civilization and everything else had begun. But what it did eventually was unimaginable. One night, finding an opportunity, it raped Baba and saw to it that Ma was compelled to go into that room. Although ordinary to look at, cows are exceptional beings. Water is water to them and pistols are merely pistols, but they don't see female bodies simply as female bodies. One hears that in some places the cows' urge for self-inquiry is so profound that they end up writing *Mein Kampf*, or getting into the *Guernica* as mites, they devour it, robbing it of the luster of the hues and curves of the lines. Everyone knows about vampires sitting on cows and sucking their blood at night, but what people don't know is that sometimes cows suck away the vampire's blood, leaving it a paperwhite spine. It is fatuous to say that there are differences of opinion among scholars regarding cows; in fact no two scholars can ever be unanimous about cows. Some cows suffer indigestion from eating too much while some get by with eating very little all their lives and scuffling among themselves. There are divisions among cows along lines of nation–time–role. A cow of 1977 will never chew on dry straw like a cow of 1947. You can't immediately tell the color of the pupils of a cow's eyes but it can rest its entire weight on two legs and stretch its neck and look at the moonlight through the window. Cows love to see nude cows very much—they call it art. In some species of cow, wearing undergarments is also in vogue. Up-to-date cows think about sexuality, they also think about revolution, while for others, arranging cacti decoratively in the verandah is a daily ritual. The shadow of the Tata Center building falls quite often on the cows as they feed on grass in the Maidan. Cows are extremely wary of one thing. If any of them read books or thought contrarily, they were declared dangerous. And if they are extremely wayward they are made to stand in front of a firing squad. In this respect, the cows' civilization is incomparable. However, it is true that cows themselves shall one day decide on the means of liberation of cows.

Goru Ek Dhoroner Chotushkon Prani, 1977

How a Horse Becomes a Donkey:
Horse > Horkey > Honkey > Donkey

No rice in the belly
And the husband's horny

When the massive Mohenjodaro bull advanced, it looked terribly extremist, and Hemnalini coquettishly twirled the bangles on her wrist—sometimes she sang *"Don't love in a tumult . . ."* and sometimes it was *"Love's as sticky as jackfruit gum . . ."* Seeing the bull, the one from Mohenjodaro, still advancing, she snarled, "Why so horny, smartass cow—always standing erect?" and then asked, "Is my body a clove's flower? That whoever finds it, whenever, can nibble away?" The prehistoric bull doesn't stop even at that, and then Hemnalini sees lotuses everywhere, she gazes at them—

A mad elephant's in the lotus bower   a serpent's
in the lotus bower
a pair of swans in the lotus bower

Right then, the son of One-cowrie Mondal of Madaritala considers hawking bread in the train compartment to be far more profitable than going to school.

Right then, in India's employment exchanges

Counting only the registered unemployed, the figure stood at tens of millions

Right then, there's pervasive boy–metaphor–rage–ador-ned–tiger-torment

Some people's calves had been carried away by a tiger

Full of rage, they made a tiger trap—

Before doing it, the prehistoric bull transformed itself into an omnipotent western bull with a bison-like head, a chain strung from the brass ring through its nose, massive shoulders–speedy–young son-in-law–lolling in adula-tion—what we fetch from the faraway west, spending our valuable foreign exchange in order to make a new gen-eration of babies in the wombs of Indian cows with their udders hanging from bulging stomachs; they who snatch our mothers and sisters and do it to them in public, while we the shriveled wait for a future that is bullish in every way. Whenever anything foreign is sighted, Hemnalini sways her buttocks in a frenzy. For one it was a yankee bull, and on top of that, seeing the one-and-a-half-foot-long huge red radish, she can no longer control her lust. Intoxicated with desire, she lies on her back and spreads her two legs

In this fashion, Hemnalini was busy making bullish Indian babies in her womb,

With the western bull's seed

The mangy mongrel on the street walks by, lifting its leg and pissing all the way

An exquisite melody of eternal love plays

In Rabindrasangeet calligraphed in golden letters over deep blue:

Love says I've stayed awake for you age upon age

Yes, yes, yes, yes, yes, yes, yes, yes

Elderly revolutionaries, afflicted by constipation,

Enunciate the objective condition of the nation, spewing Marx–Lenin

They eat cottage cheese morning and night, there's protein in cottage cheese

In honor of their success at being able to admit their sons into English-medium schools

The clerical parents too feel as proud as though they've stepped on the moon

. . . Do you know, Jayanti, our Nantoo speaks only in English

He has almost forgotten Bengali

Speaks only in English even at home, oh, I can't bear it any more—

Calls his father Big Bum

Says, Nasty Papa, you're a peasant with your lungi and bare body . . .

In some parts, pervasive boy–metaphor–rage–adorned–tiger-torment

Some people's calves had been carried away by a tiger

Full of rage, they made a tiger trap

The last few pages of the calendar of the year '76, with the image of Goddess Durga, She who drives away all danger

Blows animatedly in the wind   sometimes it flutters *phur-phur*

The walls of Alipore Jail rise higher

The age of Emergency ripens

Morning's sweet date juice
Becomes intoxicating toddy by evening
We, true revolutionary intellectuals,
Overnight
Cork our mouths, each one of us hides in our respective burrows
We'll think of revolution and all that after saving our lives now
Depending on opportunities and sources, some of us get into banks and into the accountant general's office
Some become professors   schoolmasters   disciples of Sai Baba
Some of us merrily play ball games in the nooks and corners of Victoria Memorial
And some, unable to disregard mother's request,
Select and bring home a beautiful-looking "slave"
We are rapt in our household and family affairs
Going for a few days' outing to a friend's village home
We offer a filter cigarette to Ikram Miya in the village
We find out how bad his situation is
Returning to the city, we boast about our knowledge of the living conditions of sharecroppers
Fondness, affection, and love remain intact in people's hearts.
Hemnalini is busy making bullish Indians in her womb
With the American bull's seed
Every once in a while, she snaps: Why so horny, smart-ass cow?
One-cowrie Mondal's son hawks bread like before
In compartment after compartment of the trains
Only we, youths aged 25–30,   observe and hear everything

গ্রামের একরাম মিঞ্ঞাকে ফিলটার সিগারেট অফার করি
তার অবস্থা কত খারাপ জেনে নিই
শহরে ফিরে ফুটানি মারি বর্গাদারদের ইঁড়ির খবর জেনে যাওয়ার
মানুষের হৃদয়ে হৃদয়ে প্রেম প্রীতি ভালোবাসা ঠিকঠাক বজায় থাকে
মার্কিনি ষণ্ডের ঔরসে
আপন পেটে ষণ্ডামার্কা ভারতবাসী বানাতে ব্যস্ত থাকে হেমনলিনী
মাঝে মাঝে মুখ ঝামটা দেয় : এত রস কিসের লা ট্যামনা গরু
এককড়িমণ্ডলের ছেলে ট্রেনের কামরায় কামরায়
তেমনি পাউরুটি ফিরি করে বেড়ায়
শুধু আমরা, এই ২৫/৩০ বছরের যুবকেরা,   সব কিছু দেখি শুনি
অথচ কোনো কিছু দেখেও দেখি না শুনেও শুনি না
খাই দাই আর বাপের হেগো পোঁদ চুষি
চু ষ তে থা কি ।।

Yet, despite observing we don't see anything, and hearing everything heed nothing.

We eat and sleep and get on with our lives and lick dad's shitty bum

Keep licking.

Ghora Jebhabe Gadha Hoy: Ghora > Ghodha > Ghadha > Gadha, 1976

A Gem of a Man

First God created earth. And then He wondered who would take care of the vast earth. For that it was necessary to create living beings. And so, just as God wished, beings were created. Then came the time to allot lifespans to them. Now He had to determine how long each creature would live on earth. He wanted to seek their opinions on the matter.

The first one to present himself before God was the monkey. He came and asked: "Lord, how long will I live?" God said: "I've given you a life of thirty years. You're happy, aren't you?"

The monkey said: "Must I live for so long? That's just not possible, Lord. It may look like my life is a very happy one, full of joy and laughter, but it isn't. Fatigue accumulates beneath my laughter. All the nuts that people fling at me are bad ones, worm-eaten. Those who throw them think, What better than this would a monkey eat? It'll survive even if it can't eat, rapt as it is in fun and frolic. Think about my situation. And in order to make people laugh, I have to make all kinds of faces. But, beneath all this, fatigue overflows. Every time I make people laugh I feel exhausted. Lord, please reduce a good part of this long life."

Hearing this supplication, the Creator reduced his life by ten years. The monkey was pleased, and left.

Bucket Baba, of Deoria district in Uttar Pradesh, was very famous. He was renowned for a specific reason. If one went to him to ask a question, it had to be written on a piece of paper and thrown into a bucket. After a while, Bucket Baba would insert his hand into the bucket and pick up the piece of paper. The answer to the question would be written on it.

Bucket Baba was not a false baba like Rajneesh or Mahesh Yogi and so on. He had nothing to do with millions of dollars. He probably didn't even have a foreign agent. One heard that Bucket Baba had undertaken penance for sixty-two years. During his penance he had stood on one foot with one arm raised. There was a story in circulation about his powers. Once, Baba and some of his devotees arrived at a forest. It was a vast forest, a lair of tigers and bears. Everyone, including his devotees, warned him about going through it but he did not heed them. In the dark of twilight, he walked into the forest. Halfway through, there was a tiger occupying the path ahead, standing in the darkness, with gleaming eyes. Baba advanced fearlessly. Going up to the tiger, he patted its head. The tiger licked his hand and lay down at his feet like a kitten.

When Baba returned he delivered a sermon: "Love animals. Man betrays but animals do not."

Be aware that on this earth created by God, Bucket Baba was the one with the longest life. Not just uneducated villagers but even accomplished leaders the world over admitted unanimously that His Holiness Bucket Baba's age was definitely a hundred and fifty years. It could even be two hundred.

After the monkey left, the donkey presented himself before God. He was not as clever or as cunning as the monkey. He was late in arriving. Affectionately drawing him close, God asked him: "Tell me, dear donkey, how long do you want to live? I gave the monkey a life of thirty years. Shall I give you the same?"

The donkey wept when he heard this. "Have I to live for so long? Please think about my harsh life. From morning till night I have to go around carrying heavy loads of clothes so that people can dress in a civilized manner and live decently. Every day, all the time, I have to listen to taunts about not being able to carry even more load. Lord, you know that my life has been created to carry other people's burdens. How can one love such a life? I implore you to reduce my life by half."

As he listened to the donkey, God felt compassionate. He stroked his head lovingly. He reduced his life to eighteen years. Happy, the donkey bowed before God and went away to cart more loads. He had wasted a lot of time.

There were many stories in circulation about Bucket Baba's age. One of them was that when the first President of India, Dr. Rajendra Prasad, was a small baby he had been brought before Bucket Baba to be blessed. If one were to calculate, this incident would have taken place almost a hundred years ago. He had said on seeing the child: "The baby shall be President of India." The people of India, eight hundred million Indians, bear witness to whether this came true or not.

Bucket Baba lived on a machan built on a tree, avoiding contact with the sinful earth. The machan was made of bamboo and was fifteen feet high. Most of the time Baba didn't want to descend to the sullied earth. He blessed everyone from his perch on top. Thanks to God's blessings, there was no shortage of sadhu babas in the country. Some of them possessed great powers. Frauds like Rajneesh and Mahesh Yogi had amassed millions of rupees and were in the pink. But Bucket Baba had no money. Yet, compared to them, he was a genuine baba. He did not take money from anyone. He wouldn't even touch something as sinful as money. But if he was offered pure ghee, prepared at home with pure thoughts and wearing pure garments, he accepted it, but not with his own hands. Baba did not receive anything himself, his disciples received it on his behalf. He only blessed the offering. He had no objection to unadulterated pulses and flour, and fresh fruit too. Some Marwari devotees had biryani prepared by satvik brahmins and sent it for Baba. He accepted it gladly. He loved to eat biryani very much. These biryanis were, of course, entirely vegetarian, made using Ganga water, pure cow's ghee, and cooked on a sandalwood fire. He did not object if a devotee offered fine saffron silk. But if the cloth was cotton he returned it. Cotton pricked his soft body too much. He wanted to be turned out in a civilized manner in decent society, so he always wore silk. Recently a devotee had donated him a videocassette player. He watched films sitting on a branch of the tree. He said, "Everything is God's divine play." His enemies said quite a bit of money was spent to get an electric connection for Baba's machan, but in fact this had been given by the devotees. If a devotee gave something out of love, could any guru refuse?

The donkey left. Soon after, out of nowhere, came the dog, panting, and presented himself. He was quite old, his teeth long gone and his vision poor. He was in a bad shape for having come all this way. God asked him to rest for a while and gave him a piece of meat. Because he didn't have teeth, he sucked and gnawed at the meat with great difficulty, but finally ate it up. Once he'd eaten, he felt contented. God asked him: "How long do you wish to live? Monkey didn't want to live for thirty years. Donkey thought a life of thirty years was too tiresome. Shall I give you the thirty-year life? What do you say?"

Paws folded, the dog whined, "Lord, I'll be completely finished with a life of thirty years. Please be kind and don't give me such a long life. While I am young I can run around, I can chase robbers, this is why people like me. As soon as I'm old and my legs are no longer strong and I have no teeth to bite with, they snap at me and curse me and drive me away. One look at me and you will understand, Lord. I haven't eaten a morsel in three days. Please think about my condition, Lord."

God felt compassionate toward him. Accepting his plea, He gave him a life of twelve years. The dog went away happily.

The greatest accomplishment of Bucket Baba was that he was one of the leading voices of the movement to ban cow slaughter. Under his leadership, the cow protection movement spread across India. In his view, God dwelt in every part of the cow. Cow was Mother. The day cow slaughter stopped, India would be transformed into Ram Rajya. Sorrow and suffering, violence and conflict, riots and commotion would all disappear. The fundamental reason for the all-around backwardness of India and Indians was the slaughtering of cows.

Baba was also famous for divining the future. Everything he said was fished out of the bucket. It was said that devotees came from across the world for Baba's darshan. Recently, the Japanese prime minister's paternal cousin's brother-in-law had come to Baba's ashram for darshan. He came to receive blessings on behalf of the Japanese prime minister. His disciples said it was because the prime minister had a lot of work and was so busy day and night that he couldn't come personally, and had sent his paternal cousin's brother-in-law instead. Many political leaders of the country went to Baba and he gave them good counsel. Ordinary people came too, as did businessmen. The renowned film director Raj Kapoor had put into the bucket the question of what kind of film he should make that would do well in the country. The answer that emerged was that he should come up with eternal themes and put in a lot of sex. Only Indians will know what the outcome of that was. *Satyam Shivam Sundaram*, *Ram Teri Ganga Maili*—who in India has not seen these films? Even outside India, in countries like Russia, in the communist countries, these films were well-regarded and highly acclaimed.

Once, Sanjay Gandhi too had put a question into the bucket. The answer that emerged said: "Never be separated from Mother Earth. Make sure your feet are always on the ground. If you fail to do this, you will die." And that's exactly what happened. When his feet rose above the earth, when he tried to fly in the sky, he died. He went away, leaving India in darkness.

Right at the end came man. God said to him: "Neither monkey, donkey, nor dog wants to live very long. How can creation survive then? You have to live for at least thirty years."

Crestfallen, man said: "Only thirty years? No more?"

God asked him: "Why do you want to live longer?"

Man said: "I've just built a house beside a bounteous river. I've learned to light fire. I planted trees and the flowers have bloomed, they will fruit in just a few days. I covered the fields with green stalks. Next winter, the harvest will come home. Can't I enjoy the fruits of my labors? Please increase my lifespan."

God said: "Fine. I reduced monkey's life by ten years. I will give those years to you."

Man said in a disappointed voice: "Only ten years? No more?"

"Fine, I give the twelve years of donkey's life also to you. Are you happy now?"

Man stood silently. He was not happy.

God smiled and said: "All right, you'll get the eighteen years of dog's life as well. But you can't get any more than that."

Man was not content with this either. He raised his head once and looked at God. He wanted to say something. But realizing it was inappropriate, he took His leave with a glum face.

One heard several opinions regarding Baba's age. But no one said it was less than a hundred fifty or two hundred years. If asked, Baba would reply: "I have become Indraneel. I do not age." Baba's disciples explained what exactly "Indraneel" meant. Those who attained self-realization after severe inner and yogic practices were able to transcend life and death. Baba was definitely two hundred years old, perhaps even more. He had seen the Sepoy Mutiny, he had seen the time when Lord Dalhousie was Governor-General of India. When asked whether he had lived in the time of Shivaji, Baba just smiled inscrutably.

Politicians across India ran to Baba to receive his blessings and he distributed his blessings generously. Devotees said: "All those who took Baba's blessings before the elections won. Indira Gandhi lost in '77 because she had forgotten to take Baba's blessings." This was the secret about Indira's loss that no one knew.

Thus did man receive a total of seventy years of life. The first thirty were from the Creator's own compassionate design. The splendid days of infancy, childhood, and early youth rushed past and were gone before he knew it. He did not realize what he was losing. In this period his health glowed, his mind was keen, and he was proficient in his work. Then came the turn of the monkey's ten years. The luster of early youth gradually waned. Outwardly he appeared hale and hearty, but inwardly a sense of fatigue steadily accumulated. Handfuls of dry nuts were flung in his direction but they were worm-eaten, lacking any substance inside. Then came the eighteen years of the donkey. He had to carry the washerman's loads, carrying clothes to and from the washing site all the time. Every day he had to hear rebukes for being unfit to work. The final twelve years of his life were a dog's life. He lay curled up in one corner. He had neither teeth to chew with nor claws to strike with. He ate only if someone took pity on him, or else he went without anything.

The time came for the long-lived Bucket Baba to finally lay down his body. It was because of a mere bite from a snake that had slithered up the trunk of Baba's tree. It bit him in a critical spot: right on his penis. It was rumored that Baba wanted to be taken to the hospital. Some detractors said: "Baba wept inconsolably. 'What are you doing to me? Take me to the hospital immediately, or I'll die.'" But the disciples didn't let that happen. "Let Baba die, if he was taken to the hospital the greatness of his soul would be dented." They tried faith healing, they gave him herbs and roots, but Baba's life was over. And thus did Baba give up his body. Cynics say a lot of things. But who can alter destiny? After all, the circumstances of his death were preordained.

Before being consigned to the fire, his body was daubed thickly with cow dung. He was dressed up in cow attire. Fourteen thousand cows took part in his funeral procession, and there were nine thousand buckets. Nine thousand cow-protection committee members, each one receiving nine rupees a day, marched in front, carrying nine thousand silver buckets on their heads. Behind them was a procession of fourteen thousand cows. Behind this came Bucket Baba's dead body. The government of India volunteered to bear all the expenses of the funeral procession. Photo features of the procession of cows were published in newspapers across India and, for that matter, in foreign newspapers too.

Manush Ratan, 1987

Drumstick Flowers Make a
Fine Chochchori

The drumstick tree in the courtyard has flowered   white
flowers, the color of terrycloth
Sway in the breeze
Drumstick flowers make a fine chochchori   with bori
The seekers keep track
One and a half babies are born in the country every
second. There's nothing to fear, more than half of them
kick the bucket even before they can eat properly. Red-
blue festoons were being put up in every direction. The
International Year of the Child was going to be inaugurated. My brothers, look around you, today there are
dense clouds of disaster on the firmament of Bengal's
destiny. There were tears in Malabika's eyes because a
mosquito had entered her mosquito net. The fields were
laden with the landlord's harvest. It was as if the very
country now belonged to Anadi Dam, the village land-
lord-cum-don. Just as it had been his father's earlier.

The green harvest was ripening to gold. Donning khadi dhuti–punjabi, Anadi Dam—look at his neck, just like the buffalo's in the cattle shed—had entered the political arena in order to serve the people and be one with them. He had joined the successful party, the one that would yield maximal gains, and obsessively engaged himself in party affairs. Actually, politics had been his father's forte. Like him, his father, Three-cowrie Dam, simultaneously managed his lands, oil press, jute warehouse and a trucking business, and was a bulwark of the local Congress establishment. His son, our Anadi Dam, matched his dad in every way. He watered his own pumpkin fields with the fire-fighting hosepipe provided by the government, and did so with pride. The people didn't snatch it away! After completing his chores with field-farm-workers- accounts, wearing his khadi outfit, he headed straight to the local meeting of the red party. At night, when he sat down to eat, he whispered to his Calcutta-based, younger brother-in-law: I hear that in your Calcutta one can get memsahib whores? What's the rate, pal? Come, let's go one day, drink English liquor, and have some fun. The Coffee House stamp-bearing lecturer brother-in-law—for want of flesh, the rear of his trousers hung loose—kept his Marx–Lenin carefully arranged at home, he was ill at ease but he couldn't protest. After he arrived that evening, he had gone around and seen his elder brother-in-law's farm lands and rice mills, and got a sense of his reputation and influence. In front of him lay rui fishheads and a pitcher brimming with creamy milk from their own cow. A goat had been slaughtered in his honor. The intellectuals' faces turned glum sometimes, and at other times took on the look of Bruce Lee. Established writers never think of removing the cataract in their eye—what if one loses the eye in surgery? "Moshai, you could make a buck and get by during the Congress regime, with some help from mantras, and you can do the same during the Communist regime"—those who earned a little bit from politics were enraged when the question of investigation or punishment was raised. At the railway siding, the engine went and pushed the standing coach—is this what's called railway shunting? After three love affairs, it was Malabika's prenuptial turmeric ceremony the next day. The son could be heard quarrelling with his clerical father: Hey, Dad, you fucker, you gave birth to me by doing you-know-what, so what the hell do you mean you can't feed me—do you think you can fuck with me? Two blooming schoolgirls, wearing red frocks and with red ribbons on their heads, pushed open the iron gate of the park and ran to the flowerbed. The expanse of the sky in every direction, how immense this deep blue sky was. He didn't think it necessary to read the *Manifesto*, those who had become heroes by burning trams and buses now controled leftist politics. The babu-faced revolutionaries standing beside had done well for themselves and prided themselves on explaining the politics of wage hikes to the people. In the same district where in a span of ten days as many as six class enemies were annihilated in various outlying regions, the landlords had returned to their erstwhile glory, they had become friends with the electoral revolutionaries. And of course, it was well known that the electoral babus had to spend most of their time in the city, they had to be on intimate terms with leaders and ministers, for a vital need might arise at any time—they didn't have the time to show their radiant-as-moon bodies in the village, except during elections. All around lay muddy pebbled roads with dried sludge, terribly furrowed. After a whole day's work, the middle-aged farmer sat with his back against a wall and sang: "*I'm a sad soul in love's marketplace . . . I've come to love . . . Oh, innocent heart, heart of mine . . .*" Sixty years ago, his grandfather too had sung this song. His son, who was born the same year the tricolor flag was flown aloft the Red Fort and the country became independent, says—listen to what he says in his own words:

> We are earth-diggers, we dig earth . . . we have to pay a commission to the contractors, middleman, and village headman . . . Babu, we can't survive and toil with what's left . . . After working all day, man and woman together get three rupees . . .

Hey, wouldn't it be nice to catch a few ministers and make them sit under a tree in the village and sell paan and cigarettes? The unending flip-flop of rubber slippers on feet. It's been cloudy all evening, it was windy just a while ago, with fleeting eddies of dust spreading across the fields. Malabika whispered: Keep quiet about the affair with Sitesh—if some people hear about it, there'll be all kinds of talk. But even if they did hear about it, what the hell—tell me, who doesn't have a bit of friendship and love before marriage these days? A crow sat in the village bakul tree, the crowd of sparrows grew. Whether it was a whore's pimp or the editor-cum-literary chief of Baghbazar, if one tried to speak out about their disposition, the police would definitely arrive to protect law and order. "First and foremost, middle-class careerism has to be destroyed"—having written this, Subimal wondered where he'd publish this article, and in which paper. It was unfortunate that he hadn't yet become a Mahasweta, weaving leftist tales of rural Bengal that could simultaneously be published in the Sunday supplements and in little magazines. One could have become a revolutionary writer from a very safe position—there would have been money as well as fame. But how much could one tolerate this petty bourgeoisie abusiveness in the name of literature? Not much. Just a few days in the lockup, strung up; and beaten on the soles of his feet (causing merely a minor problem of the spinal cord), all the revolutionary talk reeking of middle-class values will be finished off for good. He too had protested, just for the consolation of standing with a few hundred prisoners, holding the bars and gazing at a slice of the starry sky. Peddlers of tooth powders in the Maidan now organized interesting magic shows, bending thick iron bracelets through the force of their strength, and performing tales from Kathmandu. People crowded around to watch. The heroines of Bengali novels became evermore progressive. The heroines tell their mothers, without inhibition, about all that they did with their boyfriends in the evening at the lakeside. The road to the District Board was metaled. During harvest, if the peasants failed to deliver the harvest of their labor at the landlord's house, police jeeps arrived in a flash, raising clouds of dust—law and order was a very strange thing indeed. Radhu Mandal bit his hand, this road had been built by them under a food-for-work or some such state program. Radhanath's grief was that his matriculate son hadn't found a job and had become a truck driver's assistant, an unsalaried cleaner. He could be found in the garage day and night, he had learned to use intoxicants, although he was only fourteen years old, and he didn't want to return home. But what a fine boy he was, babu, the teachers used to say that if he got just a little guidance he would get a distinction in the exam—he never even raised his head and looked you in the eye . . . How had things come to such a pass, Radhanath sighed. Along with his family members, Radhanath was a beedi-worker. And it wasn't just him and his wife. Although it had been thirty or thirty-two years since independence, even his little children had to stay home and make beedis instead of going to school, not to earn money for their studies but for the family's survival. Backbreaking labor, sitting and working day and night, tobacco dust—in the process of erecting the owner's mountain of wealth, the lungs of eight- to ten-year-old children were damaged. These perpetually beedi-making children of Radhanath would never get the opportunity to hear about the International Year of the Child. There was talk of a chest clinic being opened here very soon. A site was acquired near the station. Donations amounting to about twenty-five hundred rupees were collected. With this money, only the foundation stone was laid. And one day, the labor minister came and ceremonially inaugurated the foundation stone, sipped a cool drink, and left. That's it, game over.

The sun grew hotter, some people dried clothes and some dried fish.

Just two people, face to face, waited a lifetime to recognize each other . . .

Would you like to act in a play, Malabika? The role would really suit you, a sad-faced, sari-clad daughter-in-law from a poor household—I'm serious, it's not a joke.

In the late afternoon sunlight, putting down their rag-picking sacks, two weary-faced boys played "tiger-captive" beside the tram track. One was bare-bodied and wore just underpants, with about a month's grime on him. The other had slipped something resembling a torn punjabi over his body, it reached his ankles. Behind them, the shadow of Grand Hotel grew longer. That did not bother them in the least, they were rapt in playing "tiger-captive."

Ti- . . . ger! . . . Cap- . . . tive! . . .

The potbellied landlord, just a few strands of hair on his head, his eyes like a swine's—who until a few days ago had been afraid to step out of his house—was now fearlessly health conscious. In order to stimulate his appetite, he was going for his daily walk along the riverside, a silver encrusted walking stick in hand. Mrs. Malabika now busied herself with the complex subject of which color of paint to use at home that would go with the furniture and please both the eye and the mind. In the jungles of the Terai, some impossibly tall people now wanted to light a fire with shrubs and twigs collected from the area between the jungle and the settlement, they crouched low and blew into the fire before them, their eyes turning red with the smoke. Hey, the drum's playing—the monkey-man had arrived in the neighborhood corner—boys and girls raced up to him as if their very lives depended on it. The mentality of the people of the country had reached the point where even if it was a collection drive for flood relief, a cricket match with film stars had to be organized, or else people did not want to make donations. A tomcat sat crouched on the wall, its eyes fixed unwaveringly on the householder's room. A swarm of brown grasshoppers hovered over a date palm. Wearing brown silk punjabis and tulsi necklaces, the head-shaved sahib vaishnavs beat drums and cymbals and drew the chariot down Chowringhee. Pretty birds flew around beside the lake in Ballygunge. As the night advanced, the neon lights on Park Street turned fiercer, pop music played to a lusty beat, music to warm the blood. The mother of the boy in the hammer-and-sickle party went to see a girl for her son. The boy worked in a bank, the girl had to be extremely beautiful and belong to the right gotra. The little boy sat in the verandah and ate muri; scattering it on the floor, he called out to the crows and fed them. How would he know that even if there was a record output of food grain, three-fourths of the people in our country went through each day with half-empty stomachs.

Trams and buses were laden with returning soccer fans—victory flags of Mohun Bagan or East Bengal burst forth here and there. Shutting the door to his room, the honorable minister furtively opened a book on palmistry and studied the fate and sun lines on his palm. In the slum, a man beat his wife mercilessly for ruining her character by going to work as a maidservant in a babu's house. *"In this education system, the more one studies the bigger the idiot he becomes"*—the boy who had written this on wall after wall was now a teacher, he was concerned about whether he could get into university by doing a PhD. All the neon lights were suddenly going off. The policeman lurking about blew his whistle loudly. A burning piece of lead pierced the left breast of the comrade from Medinipur. The blind lunatic woman began to scream from the central tower. The rapid pace of the melody of the *"International"* floated out past the bars of Behrampur jail. Krishnan Chetty was hanged silently. Babu revolutionaries—big fellows, the belly most of all—chewed the moshla-muri of socialism and looked on, they pursued and savored Marxism–Leninism. It was winter now, the old kaviraj heated chawanprash in a large griddle. A swarm of brown grasshoppers hovered over the date palm. The girls in the circus, clad in sparkling satin bikinis, were about to begin tiger tricks, having completed cycling on wire, trapeze acts, the death well, etc. The traffic on Lenin Sarani was increasingly snared in ugly jams. Krishnan Chetty's hanging was today—a thin boy, completely dried up, walked down the road grimly, absentmindedly twisting his left thumb with the right thumb.

Serpentine Lane and its darkness dissolved before his eyes. It dissolved, and now it was like the mysterious winding stairs painted by Gaganendranath Tagore, as of now . . . at this moment . . .

Sojney Phuler Bhalo Chochchori Hoy, 1979

Secret Vrindavan

1. THE KING'S SHIP

Standing in front of the station's shiny, freshly painted, silver-colored bridge, Sulu Majhi from Hatpukuriya finished spreading the wet, red sari over the platform—she was wearing only a knee-length petticoat and blouse—and fixed her eyes on the magic machine: the bioscope. She saw the city of Bombay, saw Howrah bridge, saw a secret Vrindavan. How beautiful and colorful everything was. In exchange for ten paise, she looked into the bioscope and took it all in. A dark-skinned, five-year-old girl wearing only a red string-band on her waist chewed on a raw guava and tried to press close to the glass window of the colorful box. Beneath the huge clock, which had been frozen for ages at 11:55, squatted the man, as if timelessly, puffing a beedi, gazing ahead vacantly. Just a while ago, so much argument and counterargument had taken place between them about this pleasure worth ten paise. A baby boy, about a month old, was sleeping beside him on a sheet of plastic-coated paper. A swarm of bluebottle flies hovered around him; some had descended to his lips, as if they were about to enter his mouth. They were going to Calcutta to find work. They waited, the train hadn't arrived as yet. There was a green clump of bougainvillea on the brown walls of the railway quarters. New houses were coming up next to the railway station. Men and women clambered up and down the scaffolding, bearing trays full of cement mortar. The mortar was being prepared in a noisy machine. Strung at the top of a long bamboo pole were a broken basket, a torn shoe, and a straw broom. They had eaten a short while ago, wetting at the hand-pump the roasted rice that they had brought with them, wrapped in a gamchha.

This was the screenplay of a ten-minute color film in which there was no dialogue. Throughout the film a drum would thunder, sometimes to a gentle beat, sometimes to a rapid one. The matter of holding up a sari spread over the platform belonged to another dimension, which could never be brought into writing. That old nine-yard was the only and most precious sari of the girl, which she wore to go to the city. The color was a bit faded, if one looked closely one would see that it was quite frayed, although not yet torn. This had to be captured clearly by the camera. The camera would chase the sari from afar, slowly, so that after a while it would occupy the entire screen. The close-up of a faded, worn-out sari. That was essential for this film. The bioscope, a magical cinema box made of colorful tin, whose gleaming lid the girl would pull open to place her eye and watch a film: this needed to be extremely colorful, an eye-catching color whose red, blue, and green would dazzle. The boy laid out on the sheet of plastic-coated paper and the blue flies would be presented from a different angle. No flashback would be employed, for that was too cheap.

Past and future would appear in the present itself, they would merge. The torn shoe, the broken basket and the straw broom were symbols of a specific belief, of the building masons. If kept this way, atop a bamboo pole, they would not fall down from above while working. They knew about this special rite, it would flash before their eyes, just the sight, a ritual to protect them from falling, under the influence of some evil spirit's powers.

2. THE PINK PLASTIC SLIPPER

A pink plastic slipper lay about ten yards away, the other was still on the foot. On a dawn in September '82, she lay beside a metro-rail construction pit, her breasts exposed, the red blouse ripped apart. Thrown to the ground, face turned a bit, diagonally, between the rusted iron beam and the green grass. Blood had trickled down the left side of the mouth and dried up, blackish, the mouth agape. There was blood on the lips too. A single hairpin, made of aluminum, lay on the green grass, covered in dew. A few broken pieces of colorful glass bangles lay scattered here and there. She had come to this city to dig earth for the metro rail. A straw-colored grasshopper scampered over the torn, red, knee-length petticoat. I saw all this that September dawn when I went for a stroll in the Maidan. Jogging along Red Road in the light mist was a fattish man wearing a white vest, trying to reduce his paunch.

And piercing through the mist, Mao Tse Tung's red sun was about to rise. Oh, how wonderful! *Assailed by a fart the cot breaks, startling the zamindar!*

A short, paunchy man, Lalji, entered the room. He was financing the film. A diamond ring on his finger, larger than a pigeon's egg—a patron of literature and the arts, especially nude art. The exact significance of the pink plastic slipper had to be explained to him.

_____

Guptobrindabon, 1982

Babbi

Who's come to see the patient in bed number nineteen? The patient died at dawn. Do you see the red building on the right? The one with the rusted collapsible gate? That's the morgue, that's where the body has been sent. All of you can go there and see it, but one person at a time. All around was a cold blue haze of rotting corpses. In the darkness of that haze, a fat, paunchy lump of flesh dressed in a finely pressed dhuti-punjabi descended weightily from the vehicle. He came near, put his hand on the shoulder of another and whispered: Got matches? That was code language. After that the two of them disappeared into the darkness. A hunched man, leaning on a staff, crossed the road. At that moment, the earth seemed to turn still. The man crossed the road slowly, knocking his staff on the ground as he supported himself with it. He kept crossing the road. The story now takes a turn toward the night fairies. As the night advances, they pluck out all the feathers from their wings. In the burial ground, hammers hit nails, gallows are being erected. Drawn by the sound, a few hazy, shadowy figures leave the settlement and go toward the factory, now overgrown by jungle, lanterns swinging in their hands.

All these disjointed narratives, coming in succession, produce a reaction in the readers' minds. To extend their influence onto feeling and then go beyond that—to poison. This is what shock treatment is all about. Their mental balance wilts. The insensitive calculus of reason is shaken. Everything animate and inanimate, here and now, is mired in blood.

The old man says, laughingly: I chew and eat flowers raw. Then, halting his laughter, he informs everyone that his entire right arm was in fact not his own. For a long time, he didn't have a right arm. He had found this arm in the garbage vat near his lodging, and later stitched it to his body. But, Sir, where did your right arm go? Oh, I lost it when I was a child. At that time, my father . . . not for anything in particular, you know, but just like that, you know . . . the thing happened . . . And one didn't have a choice regarding what happened. When my father's dead body was being cremated, all of a sudden, swelling up, he broke out in loud laughter. He was compelled to leave the crematorium quickly. Naturally he was in considerable distress, but even then there was no letup to his hysterical laughter. Father was everything . . . all this . . . taught me everything. Yes, he loved his father dearly. The old bloke's teeth were marvelous. He said he chewed and ate flowers raw. He started laughing the moment he spoke. And laughing, he argued: So what if I chew and eat them? Do you have an objection?

In the dead of night, the smashed body of one Monish lay sprawled across the overpass. It occurred around midnight but even at dawn no one knew about it. Many cars passed by, but nowadays who likes to get embroiled in trouble, knowingly at that? A tallish youth, and hugging him from behind, a girl dressed in black bell-bottoms and a red sweater. The road was so wide and smooth that everybody indulged their foot and pressed down on the accelerator. The motorcycle lay smashed on the overpass. Later they found the twisted, smashed, limp body of Monish lying on one side, and on another side lay Rebecca Chatterjee, unconscious, with a head injury. Monish's wife was at home then, looking at the street, anxiously awaiting him. Cruel fate, in a long, bluish-black barrel. Love does not die. Not even if one lives together forever. Absolutely everything—from the enamel bathtub in the bathroom at home to the brass handle on the door, I just love everything. Impenetrable forest in every direction. A river. The Simlijhora resthouse in the middle of the Western Ghat mountains, under the shadow of an immense tree. One could not help getting ensnared by its desolation. There was a gushing waterfall behind the bungalow. Two cane chairs on a neatly cropped, grassy patio in front of the resthouse. Rebecca was sprawled in one of the chairs, and far away was Monish's motorcycle. Dry leaves fluttered in the breeze in the verandah of the bungalow.

If harshness prevails over scintillating prose, the mercilessness of the event becomes ever more prominent. And self-opposition is part of the work process, a two-pronged process to penetrate into the character—it can also be three-pronged at times. This suspicious investigation should be there at all times.

A girl writes: I am twenty-six . . . I am slim . . . about to take the state civil service exam. I consider it an affront to my dignity to add "Miss" or "Mrs" before my name. I wanted to go to Delhi last year to spend a few days with you, out in the open, but I spent all my money in three days.

This is one side of opposition. That is, me thinking in my own way. In this process, the character keeps asking this and that. The writer feels happy. The curiosity of the character who reads not only his own part but carefully goes through the entire piece of writing naturally makes the writer happy, it makes him feel enthusiastic. All the characters sit together for discussion, they want to know the meaning of every word, what they do, why they do it—they discuss everything threadbare with the writer, and become aware. They even express their opinions. They argue. But often the writer must feel helpless. Does everyone know about that shit? It was only once that he saw the paunchy man clad in a finely pressed dhuti–punjabi get off his car in front of Victoria Memorial after 8 P.M. And right then he fathomed the truth—behind the existence of all the male eunuchs of the land, the boys younger than primary school age, and all their typical customers. Rebecca had wanted to know what readers thought of them. In my opinion, the readers' gaze would always be on your black bell-bottoms and bright red sweater . . . actually it's very bad for a writer to race toward a particular character. They should be allowed to do their own thing.

Suddenly, all over the country, after exhaustive searches, the police discover huge quantities of illegal firearms and many arms-producing factories. They recover freshly made country bombs and bomb-making chemicals. In just one day of seizures, almost twenty-five thousand firearms were recovered, including rifles, revolvers, pistols, and pipe guns.

Then the fellow—everyone knew him as the mastaan of the neighborhood—said: Here, take a look, I brought these for home—a mother's shawl, a middle brother's silk punjabi, a youngest brother's wedding shoes—I'll dispose of them in the thieves' market. He said it all right but he did not really feel very comfortable about it. He was in doubt. He was unable to desist but didn't feel any better for doing it. This always happens in the binary construction of a character. They have different objections at different times. The oppositional thing was simply part of the character's working. For sure, the old bloke, the flower-chewing-and-eating old bloke, had admitted that he had a special physical relation with the person he had killed—a romantic relation. After that, both of us transformed ourselves. The romance vanished. There was something else that came in-between the bond between the two of us. As he said this, he laughed loudly. I'm the kind of person who chews and eats raw flowers. All the while, nearby, the girl's face emerges clearly. Meaning, it was she who was on the same motorcycle as Monish on this new overpass. On quite a wide road. At eleven at night. Monish had raced at great speed—he had to get there quickly. His wife Anupama was waiting for him at home. It happened just after that. But there wasn't anything else on Monish's mind, anything different . . . Monish stands up from among the unseen. With matching prose, he keeps falling into the pose of a speaker. I love lies. I'm happy telling untruths. I like everything that is untrue. All that's prohibited makes me blissful. It is he who now takes Rebecca and . . . as he reads, he keeps smoking. The characters are seated on scattered chairs, unmoving. Utilizing the opportunity, there's some candid conversation with Rebecca.

Writer: Are you very fond of going around with boys?

Rebecca: Of course I am . . . I like it . . .

Writer: Have you ever gone somewhere with your boy-friend, I mean, spent the night there . . . ?

Rebecca: Is that terribly wrong? But that depends a lot on the situation . . . sometimes such things happen, you know . . .

Writer: What are your views on democracy?

Rebecca: I don't bother about politics.

Writer: Do you keep yourself aware of all that is happening around you?

Rebecca: I do glance through the newspaper, but I don't like politics. There's so much more in my world, it's those things that interest me.

Writer: Don't you ever think about things you don't like?

Rebecca: That's right, Sir!

Writer: One more thing . . . you know Monish is married, he has two grown children . . . he's happy with his marital life . . . despite knowing all that . . .

Rebecca: Yes, I know. I've thought about it. But what of that?

The mastaan youth stood up in the midst of the conversation, his hand in his trouser pocket, clutching an unseen revolver. He burst out: Why don't you give me a note, Mr. Writer, we'll play the numbers game. He kicked the upturned clay teacup lying beside him.

Everyone sees but no one says anything. The evenings echo, like the tang of lime in country liquor. A new anxiety-free life. Each person casts twenty to twenty-five votes. They style their hair so that it covers their ears. When the local girls' school is about to get over for the day, they hang around the curb with their mates, they whistle. The camera pans slowly. One can see an old beggar lying dead at the end of the road. The day continues. The boys of the neighborhood walk down the lane, carrying the old man's dead body. They chant the Lord's name. Hearing that, a housewife on the second floor automatically knocks her hand on her forehead in pranam. People crane their necks to watch the funeral procession. The red building is a blur in the light and dark of the mist—it is the morgue. Next to the morgue, the slowly trickling river. And beside the river, the cottage of peace. A clay photo frame beside the broken wall. In the corner of the verandah, an old she-goat offers her teats to her jet-black kids, and down below, a full-fledged sparkling river. A large hen accompanied by a troop of chicks runs toward the verandah. The hibiscus shrub in the courtyard is in full bloom. Pumpkins hang from the elevated pumpkin platform. An eleven- or twelve-year-old girl in a striped sari stands up and watches the train go by, far away, at the very end of the fields.

A commotion breaks out. Nothing of who says what can be heard in the infernal din. The problem arises when I make them, the characters, sit around a table in order to try and understand them. But, but . . . the flower-chewing old bloke starts off, but eventually he comes. He takes a chair and sits down. Rebecca too comes and sits on one side, although she is somewhat disinterested. She mutters: So what if Monish is married . . . Monish too arrives, cigarette in hand. Every now and then he puffs absentmindedly. Most of the cigarette burns out in his hand. Then he lights another cigarette. The paunchy, non-Bengali businessman in finely pressed dhuti-punjabi comes too. He can't really figure out what's going on. But that fellow, the mastaan, does not want to come at all. He is happy to simply hang about on the neighborhood curb and extract gambling money from this, that, and the other. With all these people . . . someone's a lady-killer, someone an old geezer, someone's a half-whore . . . but the Marwari's a homo of the highest order. The chap buys our wagon-breaking goods for the price of water, meaning he coerces us to sell—to sit on the same table as him—fuck, no! It just isn't possible to have a discussion with everyone. Whether there was any latent affinity between the persons—what may emerge in the course of discussion does not happen at all in reality. The chap stands at the curb with a long face. Nearby, there is the sound of a country bomb exploding. Windows are being closed. People running for safety. Rebecca stands up. I have to go. I have an appointment. Will you drop me, Monish?

The 7:55 local news wafts in from the window of the house next door. Ascending twenty yards, a huge concourse of flat stone is clearly visible. And just after that, a dark tunnel to descend through. If one descended the stairs, sticking to the edge of the stairwell, at the very end was the secret coffin-house, the most ancient neighborhood of this ancient earth. Urine. Patrolling police vehicles. Country and English liquor. Ganja and bel flowers. The aroma of fried onions and snacks suffuse the place. Suddenly the tunnel comes to an end, and the journey of life begins. City and town, field and farm, all packed with humanity. A troop of big black ants at the base of the thick green crop of grass sets out to change location. If one were to observe them closely, one would see that they have all set out in search of high-lying land. So the rain is going to descend very soon. Set in a thicket of screw pines, the inhabited quarter of the village gets agitated on hearing the cries of the chicken-thieving fox. Somehow, a malevolent fissure begins to accumulate within the blood. Corpses keep burning in the crematorium beside Deerslayer lake. The washerman's mule enters the mango orchard and feeds on the grass, unfazed. There's a crack in the slothfulness. The fissure keeps getting enlarged, its cold blue haze expands.

But it's just this that's most difficult. Getting all of them together for a discussion. Making the social aspect clear to them in the course of discussion. The strength of the effort lies precisely in this, and it can overcome all existing and associated opposition. But that's what never happens. The blue haze keeps expanding. As before, the mastaan youth stands at the neighborhood curb, hands in his trouser pockets. Rebecca keeps going away, she takes Monish along with her. As the bulging paunch stood leaning against the Ambassador car, he said, Sir, I must leave now. Rebecca burst out laughing at the mention of the word "abortion." Why should I get it done? This lack of fear on her part to own up is something the writer makes special note of. As well as her habit of owning up in this fashion.

The mastaan youth had once admitted: Do you know who made us? The country bombs were thrust into our hands. And the money came after the work was done. Hey, go and have some fun, boy! Who the fuck cut us off from normal life? It's the railway yards that now determine Bengal's politics . . . You don't believe me, do you? The old fogey says: My right arm is not a real one, it's just something I found. I chew and eat flowers raw. From normal life . . . yeah, me too . . . Then Rebecca hisses: Believe me, believe me, I am not afraid of the truth. Her hand still holds Monish's thumb. It's impossible to get them all together, to make them sit at one table. Although everyone came, albeit with their "buts," the mastaan didn't come. He stands at the neighborhood curb, unmoving, hands thrust into trouser pockets. He observes who comes and goes. When he spots a new face, he looks carefully to assess whether it might be a fucking cop. Seeing Rebecca strutting along, he says: Why are these half-domestic females here? There's one unoccupied chair at the table, one cup of tea gets cold, it's determined . . . There's the red building—the morgue. A rusted collapsible gate. All the bodies have been sent there. The night advances, the story keeps turning toward the night fairies. The same cold blue haze keeps extending. One can see Achilles and the tortoise. The race between Achilles and the tortoise. The tortoise is a thousand yards ahead of Achilles. The race begins from this position. In the time that Achilles covers a thousand yards, the tortoise covers a hundred yards. How long will it take for Achilles to catch up with the tortoise? By the time Achilles closes the thousand-yard gap, the tortoise is a hundred yards ahead. When Achilles runs a hundred yards, the tortoise has advanced by ten yards. Even when

Achilles runs these ten yards, the tortoise is one yard ahead. And in this way, there is always a gap between Achilles and the tortoise, all the time, forever . . .

Babbi, 1981

Mohandas and Cut-Ball

Hey, look, there's Gandhi!

A staff fashioned from seasoned bamboo in his hand, he gazed vacantly at the road in front, toward the profuse line of krishnachura trees, and the people crowded all around, threw money at him, at his standing image; they threw clinking, easy money. The same shaven head (Did Gandhiji have a shaven head? Oh, I don't know!), draped in a thin, sheet-like something, the dhuti he wore not quite touching his knees. Only if you looked carefully could you discern that his staff was not so well-seasoned and had not been pared, while Gandhi's staff had been of seasoned bamboo, finely pared, and polished with oil. Cut-Ball did not hold such a finely pared bamboo in his hand.

Who's this Cut-Ball? People have forgotten his real name. The people in Karnataka's Shimoga district know him as Drama Cut-Ball. When he was about forty or forty-two, while he'd been bathing in the river to the recitation of the Lord's name, a crocodile had chomped on his testicles. Of course, it couldn't bite away everything. He managed to recover quite a bit from its jaws. Half, or even more, was left intact. Thereafter, his name became Cut-Ball. As he often took part in drama performances, his name soon became Drama Cut-Ball. Of course, before this incident, he'd already had two sons. Otherwise, the lineage would have been a goner.

As he grew older, Cut-Ball searched for some other means of livelihood. He even sold lottery tickets for a while. Exactly two months ago, he went to pray at an important local temple. It was the custom for devotees to shave their heads before praying at this temple. Cut-Ball shaved his head and went to pray, and when he was returning home after doing so, something funny happened. He was walking along with an unpared bamboo staff in his hand. He'd retrieved it from a heap of garbage at the temple. Seeing him, the poor urchins playing in the streets exclaimed, "Hey! Gandhi Maharaj is coming this way," and set off a howl, created a stir, and their parents too, hearing the shouts, streamed out from their houses and stared with amazement and disbelief at Gandhi. Perhaps some among them had actually seen Gandhiji. But their sight had lost its sharpness, they could not distinguish between true and false any more, and in particular, they had not noticed the unpared bamboo staff. Or even if they had, they had not attached any significance to the detail.

Returning home, pondering over how he would feed himself, the incident provided a hint to Drama Cut-Ball regarding a possible source of income. Why, in this country, one could surely make a living playing Gandhi! His head was already shaven, and to make the likeness perfect he decided to get himself a pair of round, nickel-framed spectacles. Keeping a picture of Gandhi in front of him, he dressed in a knee-length dhuti, worn in the exact same way, adroitly wrapping one end of it around himself. It was just like the real Gandhi. But he did not relinquish the knotted bamboo staff. Let that be, after all it was this unpared bamboo that had proved to be providential for me. He went to the main road and stood in a Gandhi pose for about an hour. There was the clinking of coins flung by passersby. Quick money, gray coins. Drama Cut-Ball paid inward homage to the father of the nation, to the determiner of the destiny of India. He thought, Bapuji, don't blame me. I'm Cut-Ball, who has to make himself up like you in order to be able to eat. But I am me, and you are you. I can never become you. Don't want that either. That would be a great sin. Not for a moment do I want to be like you, discarding this unpared bamboo and taking up a fine staff.

After this, Cut-Ball went ahead toward an even more difficult sadhana. He wanted to stand for hours on end, one foot forward in arrested walking motion, imitating the father of the nation. For a few days at a stretch, if need be. Let there be thousands of spectators crowding around him. Let them behold that in affecting a good likeness of Gandhiji, not a muscle of his body twitched, his chest was no longer rising and falling to his breath, he stood like a replica of Gandhi, cast in stone, before the people of free India—most of whom had never laid eyes on Gandhi—even if they had, they had forgotten to distinguish between true and false. Someone actually said: Here's Gandhi No. 2. Your makeup is great, brother!

Recently, he stood as Gandhi for seventy-two hours at a stretch, perfect makeup, perfect attire—

—he stood   at the crossroads.

Where one's eyes go.

Beneath his feet was green grass.

A hint of the red of crushed brick in the gaps.

Just this one sight at the crossroads.

When he was like that, standing absolutely still for long stretches of time, little boys and girls went up to him, pinched him on his stomach, and ran away. Some threw pebbles at him from a distance. As he stood between two red lines of trees, a skinny slum girl came up to him, holding a mug of milk that she'd brought after milking her goat. White foam still frothed on its surface. She said, "Take it, drink it, it's not bad, it's pure, good milk." But Cut-Ball's concentration was not broken by this. When he related this incident, he said: "Actually they want to see if I'm the genuine Gandhi. I have to pass these tests. I don't mind." When he heard that I was a journalist from Calcutta, from Jyoti Basu's land, who had come to interview him, he paid more attention to me. After talking about this and that, he said: "Two unemployed sons, the younger one's eleven, he works as a teashop boy, from this age he's started smoking beedis. The wife is not in good health. I've heard one can find a job if one goes to Calcutta. Is it possible to get some kind of job, Dada? Should I send my elder son there?" As he told me about his various joys and sorrows, he was on the verge of tears. It was of great sadness to him that he had not been able to get himself a pocket watch like the father of the nation had. "I can barely survive with what I earn. I haven't been able to buy a pocket watch yet. Can't be a full-fledged Gandhi without a pocket watch, can I . . . ?"

I asked him, "You're earning money by dressing yourself up like the father of the nation. Isn't that unethical?"

Cut-Ball became agitated. Knocking the unpared bamboo staff on the ground, he exclaimed, "I . . . only me . . . am I alone . . . you . . . all of you . . ."

Let me take this opportunity to say something about myself. I returned to Calcutta the very next day after the interview. Earlier, I used to teach, but for the last few years I've been a film journalist. Art films are my favorite. Even if people use the term "intellectual" in a pejorative sense, I've personally felt elevated to be so labeled. I've put on a sad-sad face but felt quite pleased inside. Recently, I wrote a wonderful article about the wedding of Sarah and Andrew in England, which was a great hit—the sex life of the future princess, who hadn't the girl slept with—accompanied by some hot pictures . . . I haven't seen the article yet. Of course, some friends have complained that this article borders on pornography. But I've explained to them that I am a gentleman, I uphold a wholesome culture, I only bring facts to light and in gentleman's parlance. I've portrayed the sex life of the elite of the contemporary world, and that can never be compared with pornography. Pornography contains perversion, and the language is extremely obscene. Pornography cannot be written in decent language and it can never be published in the largest-selling weekly of the Bengali language—after all, they too have a notion of taste. I've demonstrated that I can be no less proficient in popular writing, that if I wanted to I could have become at least another Ganguly-Tanguly. An intellectual journal is bringing out a special issue on Eisenstein shortly. They've asked me to contribute an article. I'm thinking of beginning the article like this: "Just as one cannot conceive of the existence of *Battle-ship Potemkin* without the Bolshevik revolution . . ." I praise myself inwardly. The opening is fantastic, at once left-wing and intellectual. But the rest can be written later, with more thought. Today I must write a rousing article about Cut-Ball, and it should be written in simple language, from an objective point of view. There can't be any communist sloganeering in it, the owner of the paper doesn't like that, besides, since the article is for ordinary half-educated people, it's safest to write it in simple language, with a tone of objectivity. Oh, the sound of money falling! Cling-clang! Easy money, gray coins. The name Cut-Ball's really fantastic! The subject has to be explained simply . . . a man in free India who makes a living by playing Gandhi . . . adopting the name Cut-Ball—oh, it'll sell like hot cakes!

Mohandas O Aenrkata, 1986

Calcutta Dateline

PREFACE

It is easy to point to the Tata Center tower and identify the class enemy. But it is not so easy to recognize a culture that loves to denigrate the son of a peasant who has become a civil servant as an ingrate for concealing his father's identity, and the next moment has no hesitation in jesting with another about his being a peasant's son and imagining he's actually an IAS officer . . . All of us believe equally in democracy, but the responsibility of running the country can't be handed over to a peasant's son, to a block-headed son of a peasant . . .

BITU

I hate the word "tradition." That my father's correct merely because he was born before me, I don't think there's any logic in accepting that. If one must talk about tradition, well, I'll say that my generation is far more progressive than the earlier one. I openly read *Playboy*, of course I do. I enjoy reading porn, much more than the classics. *Playboy* is like a bottle of champagne. *An adult needs pornography like a child needs fairytales.*

SOMPRAKASH

You're making a mistake in one respect, Bitu. *Sex is not related to pornography but to health, and to enjoying sport.* In fact, our society is afflicted with bedsores. *Something rotten in the state of Denmark . . .* And my own life, my responsibilities—I just act out everything. I'm greedy to live on even after I'm finished, so that I can transform my downfall into another acting experience.

BITU

In these nineteen years, I've realized that the male is indeed a peculiar creature. When a man isn't in a relationship with a girl, just observe his behavior as he pries into her affairs. For all you know, he treats the girl in his life, whether through marriage or some other means, quite badly. But when he's with a girl with whom he doesn't have any such relation, he uses every opportunity to be nice to her—I wonder why the male species has this mentality. Perhaps it isn't wise to wager too much on personal relationships.

In the course of this conversation, the massive staircase becomes visible. The wooden planks on which Bitu descends elegantly, completely naked. She climbs down to the door on the landing. Perhaps it's a solo exhibition—meaning a nude female body being shown for a long time. A mid-shot of nakedness from the breasts to the feet. Only the head is not visible. Just the head. By being present in front of our eyes for a long time, this raw nakedness makes sex seem dull and insipid. It also revolts against the male conception about women's liberation—the view that relegates the whole issue of women's liberation to a fad for conversation . . .

SOMPRAKASH

He once had a dream that he was standing in front of the throne of the Great Adjudicator. But he was not at all afraid. What can you do to me, boy—sitting in peace on the seashore, you carry on playing chess with Bergman; the sea, the lifeless sea, roars behind you, as if it is only an arid backdrop. I have survived forty-four years, after all that the world has done to me, what more can you do? The night advances, I get drunk. Rats emerge in stages from the darkness, hordes of them, green-eyed, they come and nibble at me and eat me alive—every night. And I, a hired killer, out to reach another form of existence. For which I could murder my own daughter. I could even poison my own blood in order to survive. The red-masked man snatches away everything from him, everything he struggled for. He exists wherever I go.

He is there, my rival, a king above everyone else, supreme monarch, a looter, universal and cold as death. It's very real, all this, a terrifying thing, and yet, whatever I am, why should I be ashamed? I don't think we have done anything wrong, anything for which we need to be ashamed or hate one another. Believe me, Bitu, there's nothing in the world that's more meaningful than life, there can't be. That's why, for me, our relation is not frivolous or reproachable, and that's why I don't consider myself wretched or corrupt—no reason at all to think that way. Not even after seeing the array of green eyes staring intently at me.

Our protagonist Somprakash is an affluent, sociable man who has pushed his way ahead through the crowd of ordinary people. He has a fridge, a color television, and a guitar at home and, what is unthinkable, a huge collection of books. A middle-class Bengali, a product of the managerial revolution. The story pursues him and sees his typicality, his connection with the masses or lack of it. The personal tragedy of this apparently well-to-do man, with his office, bar, club, and sexuality, surrounded in turn by oppressed humanity, is in fact the tragedy of every half-conscious man in the third world who is neither able to rise above his prejudices nor accept them. Hence ambivalence manifests itself everywhere. At a glance, this might appear to be a cheap story of perverted tastes, but this is the story of a society in which one destroys human relationships and moves rapidly toward the lowest station, to a culture based on unequal competition, where even mother and daughter are mutual rivals and no more. Normally society accepts this inhuman competition as a precondition for success, it's seen as part of the warp and woof of unseen social forces. At the end of the story, when he wishes to reach the final stage of the relationship but fails, in order to find a rationale in favor of his morally compromised life, he tries to provide his attitudes and conduct with a rational basis. In this way, then, society selects him as an object of collective hatred. "Thinking is the greatest pleasure known to mankind," he cries. Self-centered sorrows and pleasures find multidimensional expression. The death scene is rendered keeping green nature as witness. The screeches of vultures in the crematorium are audible, beside the body of flesh and blood. Water continues to flow in a gentle stream. But for that, all is silent, like the white of bones. As the night advances, his teeth become keener. One cigarette after another burns away, dangling from eager fingers. In the next scene, Somprakash and Bitu are shown in close-up. They move swift-footedly through blueness, across a blue-carpeted bedroom with curtains of smooth silk drawn on windows, and hold each other tight. Behind them, the dim light of the inner quarters floats into focus again and again, illuminating different parts of their faces and bodies, their blue amorous moans on the silver screen. The characters behind the curtain seem impervious to all this. After about fifteen minutes, having set their clothes in order, Bitu nudges Somprakash. Nobody knows who reaped profit from the game. Music plays to a fast beat behind the sheet of glass. He looks at them through a window—

— *Do you think it is creditable to become pregnant at nineteen?*

— *My mother was also nineteen when she conceived.*
— *But she was married.*
— *You mean she had a license to fuck!*

A dog stands over a dead body, tears apart and eats the flesh. It wouldn't have been proper to show this scene too vividly. Why does the moon cast so much light on the dry riverbed on the night after the new moon? Bit by bit, the past arrives and gets enmeshed with the present. Bitu had just finished reading *Slaughterhouse-Five*, furtively. Feeling hot, Bitu took her shirt off and lay down beside Somprakash. Only a beer bottle lay between the two of them. Such a fragile and transparent barrier! After some time, she comes closer. She whispers: "It's hot—what intolerable heat and humidity today . . ." Somprakash stands in front of the door wearing a lungi, his hands covered in blood—"The bulb broke in my hand . . ." "Oh god, so much blood . . ." She is frightened and a little nervous. Drops of blood splash onto the floor. Bitu comes running in a flash. "Come, let me bandage it, don't worry." As she shuts the door, the episode vanishes from the room, leaving behind only the bloodstain on the blue carpet.

The next film begins with a rape scene, which runs for almost twenty minutes, in a film within a film. The entire incident takes place in a desolate room on a winter's night. Later, the girl who was raped is interviewed. And one after another come little girls, young women, and middle-aged matrons who have at one time or another been abused by men. We hear the immaculately dressed little girls, adolescents, and young women utter one by one, "I was first raped by my father . . ." and then the vulture on the dead body tears out and eats flesh. Images, and images after images. It could instead have been that this nineteen-year-old buxom heroine, Bitu, prances and dances around throughout the story, under soft light, with the hero . . . TDH (tall, dark, and handsome). But it isn't so. Now even the deep-green valleys turn gray, even the closest relations lose brightness steadily.

Murder for Salt
Jalgaon, 22 September, 1982

Too much salt in the food—for just this grouse, mother-in-law and brother-in-law beat up a newly married twenty-seven-year-old bride. While cooking, the young woman had put a little too much salt in the vegetable curry. There was a terrible furore as soon as the family sat down to eat. She was taken to the hospital with severe injuries after being assaulted by her mother-in-law and brother-in-law. She died in the hospital.

The face in silver color, the moustache and its environs, till the throat, are blue, only the inside of the wide-open mouth is red. The square of white lines on the four sides steadily becomes larger and goes out of frame. On one side an orange moon hangs from the sky. Children hold hands and dance among trees and shrubs, the trees are deep green. Our impatience mounts. We move forward. The episode begins.

The scene, made up of things collected bit by bit, is one of complete disorder. It takes some time, naturally, to get used to the jolt of this introduction. A bathroom fully done in pink porcelain comes into view. Bitu with her body immersed in lukewarm water—the water is still, Bitu's eyes are closed. A herd of wild buffaloes graze in a meadow of tall, green grass atop a hill. One must admit he has aesthetic discernment. In the disorderly background, string-like, linear, colored snakes have been released with artful brushwork. Men, trees, and rocks wriggle on the lines. One is informed that in one version of the tale of Rama, Sita was Ravana's daughter. Rama lured her away from the forest. Thereafter, Ravana steals her away from Rama, with evil designs. Through discussions like this, the story gets written. The descriptions and dialogues are written out on a page at first. It is read out to Bitu from time to time. If there are to be any changes, there are further discussions and arguments. After that it begins to be written anew. If Bitu is displeased, she changes it herself. The task is so complex and mutual that it can't be explained in words, there's no formula here. Simply writing and cutting, cutting and writing. Sometimes it attains such immense depth that one is unable to comprehend exactly what's happening. It's necessary to observe how Bitu acts in every single scene. One has to watch, alertly, how she brings a character to life. Despite the impediments, the desire to write out the story is born. It is necessary to sit with pen and paper. Do you like it, Sir? A very difficult question indeed. Summer's around the corner. There's so much soot in the lantern that hardly anything is visible, everything is shadowy, there's only gloomy darkness. *We are all born socialist and they have to work very hard to change us*—a wry smile plays on Somprakash's lips. As a college student he frequently quoted this line from Engels. The stairs on the right side, the door on the left side, and in a corner, Bitu's room, the door ajar. She sits with one leg propped over the other, the hem of her skirt has risen considerably above her knees. What's in her hand—Barbara Cartland even now! Somprakash gasps and says, There's a terrible ache on the left side of my chest. Bitu, please hold me and take me to the room. The story begins in this way. After that the attack on the story begins. It is challenged, it is broken into smithereens, its storyness lies in pieces. Questions are asked about the way we read. For instance, in one scene, Somprakash and Bitu, with great élan, watch a blue film, freshly acquired from Denmark, on the video-cassette player. As she gets tired, the girl wipes beads of perspiration from her nose. Such an excess of all this every day that it no longer holds excitement. On the tip of her nose is a bead of sweat. The wildness is subdued, the bead of sweat becomes clearer than the image of the bra being undone. And furthermore, this has no physical meaning any more. The music playing lacks sweetness. Sound is used as the seventh note, consequently every composition loses its meaning. A vast wetland can be seen through the bedroom window of the huge apartment, a forest through the window of the living room. Childhood's butterflies enter through the open window in the east, they fly round the room. Somprakash thinks the colorful butterflies are like the pattern on the border of a Dhakai jamdani sari that floats in from the recesses of his memory. What had the jamdani butterfly begged him for? His eyes are vacant. The butterfly touches the wobbly study-table in the room, it touches the timepiece with its legs and then flies around, working its restless wings. And in the middle of this shot, a three- or four-year-old girl, dark in complexion, wearing only a red string around her waist, dances animatedly, singing a love song—

Crooked your flute, crooked the melody
Hold and play it crooked, dear
Cast your crooked eyes crookedly
And steal this maiden's heart, oh dear

A brilliant socioeconomic explanation could be included in this—what rural life is like, Somprakash's childhood, the destruction of village life, and the rapidly growing immorality of the metropolis. She has no objection to being completely naked. There is a very fashionable drawing-cum-dining room. ABBA and Runa Laila play all day on the stereo, and Bitu dances in bright red jeans. The loud strumming of a harp playing continuously, the sound of stones being broken, the shriek of a vulture, the roar of thunder, the splashing of a waterfall, and Bitu's amorous moan—which is natural, like the rhythm of the breeze or the blue of the sky. Remembrance: on a night in the seventies, a pregnant woman's body was cut into pieces and left in a flat in Jodhpur Park. And the scandal of raping a minor girl. Later, it was found that her age was nineteen, she wasn't a minor after all. All this clotted darkness, the environment of memories mingled with terror, is never a matter of pleasing romanticism. All the ups and downs of his own life—childhood poverty, terror, dreams, memories, pains, and yearnings—all of it, every single thing, gets mixed up as they are written out, they become hazy. In his own married life, is he quite what they call "happy"—or is he something else? He had married for love, Joya and Som both liking each other, all those things of college life. But nothing is too clear or illuminated to be probed or justified. Does Som now inwardly desire death—Joya's death? Nothing is reliable and dependable. I don't fear defeat or suffering, that's why I see Dostoevsky's hero as much braver than James Bond, Somprakash thinks. In my eyes he is a hero because he is on the verge of defeat—a man, a tiny, insignificant, imperfect creature in the vast expanse. In this way, incidents and characters move simultaneously in dream and reality. Place, time, and character are entangled. Robert McNamara pops his head out from a pile of old newspapers. At one time, when he came to India as President of the World Bank, what an outburst of protest there was from the communists. "Go back . . . go back." He returned after a long time, precisely during the regime of communist ministers, to West Bengal itself, to Calcutta. There was no protest at all. No one said, "Murderer of Vietnam—go back." The newspapers report that the murderer now looks at the communist ministers in the Writers' Building and smiles wryly as he listens to their demands and appeals. There is an abrupt sound, the line gets disconnected. *Calcutta Dateline Heavy Damage.* Somprakash thinks that socialism is not just the language of protest, it is also a rich lifestyle—as far as he understands it. When the shameless god comes around dawn, hobbling on his crutch, piercing the veil of carbon monoxide emitting gustily from the chimneys, Bitu is sleeping in her room, lying naked on the bed. Her mother makes tea and calls her. Here, when Somprakash talks face-to-face with the author, the story remains the same, although Somprakash himself thinks that he is playing a radical, left-wing role. The story shows it from a particular angle but doesn't get into direct criticism. The intelligentsia have a certain view of themselves, and are habituated to seeing themselves so. Somprakash too observes his role in society, and the effect of criticism on him. But here the criticism proceeds into deeper territory, drawing the reader also into the equation. In the whole process, the classical form of storytelling is demolished. Again, sometimes, while keeping the process of construction and deconstruction active, the new framework is prepared for emotional reasons. His is a solitary, individual rebellion against total dehumanization. The huge sitting room in Jodhpur Park comes into view, its splendid lampshades and bronze-colored silk curtains on the window lie in shadow, a Japanese kimono, soft slippers on the feet, *Economic Times* on the lap. Bitu has gone to Trinca's with her friends, and Joya is on the sofa, knitting a golf-sweater for Som. There are bottles of whiskey and soda on the center table. Somprakash was pouring from the bottle for Joya, taking some for himself too. There was no peg measure. When Bitu returned, she too would join them and sit next to her father. As the cabaret began, the people there got excited. Bitu sensed hands on her back, buttocks, and thighs, perhaps suggestive finger signals, but she did not pay any heed to all that. Recently a young man who loved her had committed suicide. He had shot himself. Bitu says, that's the only thing he did well. She didn't cry one bit. She went off in the car with her friends to eat ice cream at Kwality's. Joya said to her husband, The girl has been thoroughly trained, *she never misses a pill.* The three of them set out on a voyage aboard three different ships. When the ships sank in a blue storm, they returned, having salvaged the broken stories. A group of three persons: mother, daughter, and father. Whatever else we may be, after all we are bhadralok, cunning through and through. Once, in the scavengers' hamlet, a girl of about seventeen or eighteen—she would be about the same age as Bitu—Somprakash had then passed with a first division and gone to study in Presidency College—she was wearing only a gamchha, and seeing me suddenly, not finding anything else close at hand, she wrapped a torn floor-mat around herself, I remember, as a means to avoid shame. Even after all these days, Somprakash hadn't forgotten the incident, it was so long ago . . . Come, let's go and sit somewhere, let's have something to drink. Beware, whatever you do, don't let your own daughter wear a punjabi and parallel trousers. A smile plays on the corner of the lips. Calcutta has a new culture, of wearing embroidered punjabis and expensive handloom saris. Attending solo recitals of Rabindrasangeet in Rabindra Sadan. *Splendidly flows the unceasing, eternal stream of joy.* On returning home, the better half dons a nightie, and the girl a kaftan. The bar cabinet between the two windows. Pull the long wooden handle, and there are rows of expensive scotch whiskey, cognac, and bottles of wine. A dark-skinned adivasi, his wavy hair flowing down to his shoulders, plays a dhamsa like a crazed man—who knows how long he has been playing? The dhamsa was about six or seven feet long, as tall as a person and a half, made of ancient buffalo hide. It had been carried on people's weary shoulders. Dark-skinned, muscular, and bare-bodied, he kept assaulting the dhamsa in drunken intoxication with two saal sticks, and with the assault awakens Sing Bonga, the clan god . . .

Kudchi flowers, kudchi flowers
Bloom in bunches everywhere
A tiger ate the landlord in the forest

The rays of the setting sun penetrate through the tree canopy and spread in every direction. The girls supporting

Women's Lib, the ones who burn their bras, attend the enchanting program. They wear thin, see-through tops and jeans, despite it being a winter's evening. The jeans start below the navel, and the two ends of the shirt are knotted together four inches above the navel.

— Could you eat the flesh of a corpse?
— No!
— Drink your own urine?
— Not at all, Babaji, I know nothing at all of all that.
— But I can. I've learned hathayoga. For twelve years I practiced the occult in the crematorium, sitting on the five-skulled seat. I can turn brass into gold.

Then one day, the Guru came home. Like an offering to the gods, lychee are served on a stone plate and Kissan squash in a stone cup, with ice. The Guru, clad in saffron-brown silks, an India Kings lit in his right hand, his drooping eyes gazing fervently at the shishya's buxom maidservant. An eighty-year-old woman had once remarked: Lord Shiva is always aroused so don't disturb him too much, dear . . .—Bearer, bring the bill please. Someone said—It's the self-made men, I mean, those who've risen from humble beginnings, who despise the poor. A long time ago, quoting an American sociologist, Nehru had written: Politics is the beautiful art of obtaining votes from the poor and money from the rich by giving assurances to both rich and poor about saving one from the other. And he was a great artist in this respect. In a country of six hundred million people, 70 percent of the world's illiterates were Indians. And in 1969–70, class struggle and class conflict were dominating the minds of even nineteen– to-twenty-year-old boys. Well-paid journalists in big newspapers gave it the name "politics of annihilation" . . . He does not know whether power flowed through the barrel of a gun, but he did know that the number of illiterates in the state of West Bengal alone was greater than the number of illiterates in the whole of Europe. The lady's voice was as soft as silk. Giant posters requesting tax-free saving in the National Savings Fund, right next to posters advertising Nirodh. This huge world was God's farmhouse. All the people would be judged by his inviolable law here, for as long as the true could be distinguished from the false. In human society now, the chaff was more than the wheat . . . Yes, one by one, all of them were killed, and before being killed their eyes were gouged out, nails were driven into their skulls with a hammer, their argumentative tongues were pulled out, and the breasts of young women were sliced with a sharp cleaver. At that terrifying scene, loud screams fill the cinema theater. In the wintry night, the flowing river and the mysterious forest nearby, deep in intimacy, side by side.

Bitu had passed out.

Other than a few drunkards, no one was awake in the hotel.

Atolyus stole Sisyphus's sheep. Sisyphus eloped with Atolyus's daughter Anticleia. Salmoneus occupied the throne of Sisyphus. Sisyphus raped the daughter of Salmoneus. Tyro murdered the son of Sisyphus. Salmoneus was accused of the murder and expelled from the country. Tryro married Uncle Graham. Sisyphus got back the throne.

In the middle of a herd of buffaloes, bullet-riddled Balthazar, Bresson's donkey. It is dying by the minute. Before that it had participated in the religious procession.

— *Where are you*
— *Somewhere in the dark*

And then the titter of laughter.

All the while, something happens inside, in this way. He changes, he experiences. He experiences the change himself. After losing God, a huge void was created in his life, and now he fills that void with experience. Nothing was contemptible to him any more, human greatness as well as human bones and filth, were both the same and equally natural. What has Bitu given me? I have to ask myself this question, and I have to answer it too. I got life's secret from her. If I have to fight against life, I'll fight, and this very life will then select one of us. And Bitu, you probably won't believe me, but my sliding and falling in this way is not shameful, there's nothing to be pained about. This is how I lie in wait to ambush life. That's how I survive. The survival is not of the everyday variety, like it is for others to whom life only shows its fangs, to whom life appears mundane, bloody, and hollow. An acute strangeness develops in every individual. And it grows. As he wakes up, a terrible hangover. He can't see properly, a headache, a nauseous feeling. Through the mist, the tall trees on the sides of the road take on a ghostly appearance. Pictures hang on the walls, oil paintings, such refined taste. He pulls them down and throws them away. The sound of breaking glass shatters the silence. Mother and daughter titter in laughter. I'm not jealous, am I? It's not clear whether it's the mother's voice or the daughter's. Somprakash, tall and lanky, had taken her out. At first she was quite curious: Oh, no more, Som, please. How the two of them had cavorted! The tips of the blades of grass pricked the bare back like needles. I forced her to drink quite a bit of brandy. My mind wandered to the desolate hotel on the sea coast. She stands on the balcony, gazing at the endless stretch of sea, still and calm. After that a cigarette, gentle puffs. Bitu loved striptease. She had even performed a few times, at private parties, at the request of friends. Somprakash knows. On the last occasion he had seen it himself. A yellow woman, naked, on horseback. Behind her, on the vast backdrop, a sunset. The picture becomes clearer and more vivid. If one strains one's ears, one can almost hear the neigh of a horse. Right underneath, beneath the supreme teacher Mao's picture, the mother pulls out lice from her daughter's hair. The party wanted the masses to learn to respect the leaders. On the right side, the local arts center. The subject of the exhibition, Socialist Realism, devoid of any hint of nudity, of course. On the left side, a classroom in Sweden, project- ing a "blue film," the teacher conducts a sexology class. Joya nudges and says: Hey, what do you think . . . Isn't Bitu there? The door is open . . . So what? Bitu's grown up now. Joya keeps thinking that Bitu will become even more beautiful. She suddenly remembers her own age. What does she give to Som? "Shh, quiet. Can you hear that?" "Really, amazing." They spent a few days in the hotel, lying under the blanket in the soft bed. There was hardly anyone else awake in the hotel, other than a few drunk- ards. Something fell from Joya's hands in the kitchen, something made of glass. The sound of shattering. When the sound entered the room, Somprakash was suggesting to Bitu that they watch a blue film. But she doesn't feel like doing anything at all, it's terribly monotonous. When the whole system is false and devoid of morality, it's idiotic to stick to some bloody old sentiment . . . Wonderful aroma from your cooking, Somprakash forces himself to make a compliment. The scope for acting is quite limited here. The dialogue begins like this—

> My friend Tiya had an abortion, but I don't want to do that. After all, there are contraceptives. And even if I don't have it, so what? I don't make a fuss about sex. I like him, so, he's my father. But I like him. And I like Subroto too. But then everything depends . . . I don't mind sleeping with anyone. Actually, I don't love them at all, I just want to own them. Are you talking about the London *Observer*? I've read that article, very interesting—

LOVE "DOCTOR" HITS THE JACKPOT
[From Peter McGill in Tokyo]

Sex and education have long held pride of place in the Japanese list of obsessions, but until the arrival of the Junior Health Club in Tokyo, no one had tapped the enormous potential of joining them together to make money. An enterprising businessman called Yasuo Ishii recently hit the jackpot by offering evening classes in sex "counseling" as well as a chance to improve sexual technique, and to work out frustrations through stimulating sex with hired "models" . . .

Here, a class of affluent readers would definitely support me. They would support this so-called unhealthy relation. But they will surely take from me too, in another way. "They're human too, they too are rational"—they'd also like that to be said. Actually, they compliment me in the hope that they, this class, can employ my support as capital to legitimize their own doings.

— Am I going too far in trying to help you?

Whenever I recollect past conduct that's fearful, I try to get busy with some kind of work. The condition becomes dangerous—it would be wrong to call it fear. I don't feel like doing anything. I become like stone. If I had a blade nearby, I'd commit suicide. But in order to do that I'd have to go to the bathroom and search for the blade and get it. Eventually I don't do even that. Bitu, give me company, let's get a couple of beers and sit in the lounge. A bruise steadily becomes clear on the girl's breast, from which pus oozes out and trickles down, an angry red sore—is that a symbol? Here, in these parts, instead of seeing something or showing something, understanding it is most vital. Trying to show something to her, waiting until the very end to see where it goes—all this is very complex. But one advances and then leaves it, leaves it to others to understand. It all depends upon the person who understands this endeavor. Not all of it may be true either. Apparently it may seem that no one has any relation with anyone else. That may be, but it will all still continue; these characters, in the way they have crystallized, the incidents that they bring about in the normal course. And another point, what the writer wants to bring about. And yet another point, what the reader thinks. A fourth element could be added to this, the way the whole thing is presented, that is, the relation between sexual repression and social repression. And another element, perhaps an emotional reason—why perhaps, definitely so, and at this very moment. Someone enters the bedroom. She straightens her clothes vigorously. I heard you, Joya said. Setting his clothes right, he saw Joya standing at the door. He clutched his two shoulders with his hands. Resolute, he advanced toward Bitu brazenly. Putting on the shirt in her hand, Bitu moved to the other side of the bed. Then she stood near the window, a cigarette lit in her mouth. The mother standing at the door, the father standing with his back to her, with a hastily worn dressing gown, Bitu wore only a partially buttoned shirt. Suddenly, in front of her very eyes, Joya saw Somprakash grab and rip open Bitu's shirt. Bitu tried to hold onto the ripped shirt somehow or the other. The jeans and everything else lay beside the bed. Father and mother were in the middle of the room now. Both were looking at one another. Joya saw the father advancing toward the daughter. She pushed him hard. From the corner of her eye, Bitu saw her father fallen on the floor, mother bending down over his head, what is it that one sees—violence or vengeance? She puffs out smoke absentmindedly, as if unaware of where she is. The cigarette dangles out of the corner of her lips, blood from a cut on the lip, blood on the tip of the cigarette too. Don't touch her, Joya repeats. Somprakash comes face-to-face with the girl, the cigarette dangles, face turned slightly in the other direction. He extends his left hand to the girl's shoulder, his other hand was moving toward the front of her shirt, its shadow falls on the wall. Bitu is willing, he says. Joya drops down. Right there. On the doorstep. The shadow of that too, there. There was no scope for oversimplification, one incident on top of another incident, one ingredient on top of another ingredient, all becoming so saturated that no tendency is separately identifiable any longer, in an immaculate way. The whole scene needn't have been seen in slow motion so far, but this shrill poison-blue incident is employed to scorch and nail our conscience. Although this particular incident is about debasement in a specific section of society, once it's shown as a still image it enables one to discover its links with the general crisis in society. Again, the ethicality of the act can be evaluated. Here is someone who tries to bring about a balance between two opposing forces. A stone of appropriate size always reaches the fist of the one who dares to defy, as soon as the muscles of his arm are stretched. The whole room is in a disheveled state, the mattress and pillows on the floor. In one corner of the bed, Bitu's bra. While ascending the stairs, a large reproduction of Boticelli's Venus on the landing. It comes to mind. As he ran for his life, he felt as though his bones had turned to water. Not finding booze, he drank two gulps of oil by mistake. Hair oil, Joya's, Bitu wasn't born then. And then he was vomiting. Don't think I missed the stories about you on the walls of the college bathroom. As he vomited, he blurted out, I saw the writing: Som + Joya—the two come here, at night. You think you're very beautiful, don't you? I also remember, it was written on the wall of the college urinal—how many times Somprakash had noticed it: "I want to see Joya's —." In place of the dash, a vulgar word denoting the private parts. As he fondled Bitu, that line floated into his head. The two of them were active in the Students' Federation then, and then love, and love marriage. So who did Bitu get the disease from? He strokes

Bitu's body. Flirtatious whore. And wasn't it imaginary—but even higher mathematics was imaginary. The bad times made me realize even more that life was rich in every way, with infinite variety, and it was beautiful, the value systems that we keep thinking about have no significance when it comes to life's necessities. The trees themselves burst into new leaves. He saw dark clouds on one side of the sky rapidly spreading across the other side. For the last few days, there had been kalboishakhi-like gales and thundershowers at this hour. Through the window with open curtains one could see the well-dressed men and women who had been invited there, plates in many of their hands. Suddenly, like a gust of wind, a burst of laughter, bright lights, the fragrance of the bunch of rajnigandha on the table. The gentleman looked completely different in a dhuti and silk punjabi. A thick garland of bel on his neck, a dot of sandal paste on his forehead, he looked just like a bridegroom should. In the course of physical exercise, there had developed in Somprakash a kind of narcissistic restlessness for full satisfaction from the "taste" of his own body. Within this obsession with his body lay an intemperate wildness, which in another sequence is manifest in Bitu's and Somprakash's intimacy. If one observed closely, one would find that it was a kind of wild game they played with one another, resembling animal sex. In the delight of the game, Somprakash gets a taste of the satisfaction of unbridled freedom of his body, and the bodily right over another body. There's no element of love or surrender or suchlike attached in any way. In the shot with which this scene reaches a climax, Bitu is lying on top of Som's supine body, he lies in carefree pleasure, sheltered by the softness and warmth of her body; Somprakash's supine body, his sexuality submerged in narcissistic ecstasy. In Somprakash's own language at that time: this is really a battle against one's own body, in which the body becomes very eloquent, as if every nerve is a string of a melodious harp. After that, the scene of the final farewell is a grand one, when Bitu, without saying anything, tip-toes away slowly from the room, and he, lying in bed pretending to be asleep, is silent, knowing that neither of them will ever meet again. Perhaps they would meet once, fifty, sixty, or a hundred years later, for just half an hour. Bitu's body would then be ugly and deformed, one leg shorter than the other after a failed operation, her body grown bent. Just here, in the middle of this, after the sex scenes are shown, a negative is placed on the opposite side, and the two things become clear: what you see and how you see your seeing—upon which the whole matter depends. Meaning, this exciting sexual movement—one in front and one behind—the seeing itself, to a great extent, and how it is shown, together determine the process of your classification, which way you are going and how far you are able to come away from your class-determined situation. You are looking at a nineteen-year-old girl who, at specific times, is nothing but a pleasure object to her father, and at other times, she is different, normal, and sensitive, and in that sense complex too. Again, there's the side of the father who breaks social codes, at least that's his boast, and from that point of view he's radical, and he too keeps a sharp watch on how he is being presented, what his flaws are and why, the symbols and such like are observed minutely, and the endeavor to extract meaning is undertaken. The word "endeavor" is necessary here because his mental makeup has compelled him to see the exploitation that has gone on in level after level of society as being on par with sexual exploitation. And so he too did just that, and did it expertly. Through all this, Bitu is brought down the massive staircase, taken deep into the spotlight of civilization, which chases her and brings her down. It was as if the light that had for all these days been a symbol of liberation for her and provided her sustenance, that very light was now attacking her, reducing her to utter nakedness, from which emerges a distressed wail: What does he want from me? Am I only a woman, a female body? Pieces of the future come in and become one with the present. She is lifted up and clothed in a red robe. She is marked out as the sacrificial offering to God and death. Gradually her body goes limp. The final piece of her clothing falls off. The body is exposed, blood, flesh, and bones. Both life and death come to receive her in the same hand.

Calcutta Dateline, 1982

Health for All by 2000

"We're in the same boat, brother."

An emaciated young wife
Newly come to this city to beg.
Only the few bones of her body left now.
A baby in her arms, another child held by the hand.
She could barely speak without a child's stutter—
She was supposed to light a lamp in her husband's
homestead in the evening, now—
Standing beneath the neon light on Jawaharlal Nehru
Road she gazes in astonishment at the wondrous and
captivating things
In the shops—and as she gazes, she wonders:
"All these things, so many things,
Why do people need them? What for?"
As her gaze falls on magazines with pictures
Of nude women laid out on the pavement
She pulls up the cloth over her breasts in modesty.

From her womb would Hari the hoodlum be born, begotten by a babu.

The unbearable length
Of the road named Jawaharlal Nehru would be left far behind. Every morning as I sip my tea, I run my eyes over the newspaper.
"45,000 die of hunger every day"

"45,000 die of hunger every day"

How expensive tea has become nowadays.
Would it be cheaper to drink coffee instead?

2000 Shaler Modhye Sokoler Jonyo Shastyo, 1985

লোভ আর স্বার্থ মিলে কী হাল করে রেখেছে এই পৃথিবীটার তাই যুদ্ধ চাই শান্তি নয় যুদ্ধ চাই যুদ্ধই একমাত্র যুদ্ধ ঠেকাতে পারে এই ভিক্ষমাংগা শান্তি নয় ব্রহ্ম-অস্ত্রের মতো শান্তি চাই যা শুধু যুদ্ধই দিতে পারে উপসাগরের তৈলস্রোত ক্রমশ ভেসে ভেসে আসবে ২০০ বছর ধরে যার জের শালা মানুষের বাচ্চা জানুয়ারির এই অবেলায় ফাটিয়ে অভিনয় করে যাচ্ছে সাদ্দাম হুসেন চাঁদনিচকে পোস্টার পড়ছে WE SALUTE LION OF THE ARAB NATION SADDAM HUSSAIN সাউন্ডট্রাকে কামানের গর্জন আর পয়রা গুড়ের মতো আলোর লালা গড়িয়ে পড়ছে এ-এ-এক-টানা নতুন রিক্রুটেরা ক্যাপ্টেনকে জিজ্ঞেস করছে অসহায় মানুষকে মারতে পারি তো স্বচ্ছন্দে পারো   দোকানে খেয়ে পয়সা না-দিয়ে গটমট করে চলে আসতে পারি তো স্বচ্ছন্দে পারো   নতুন ভর্তি হওয়া ছেলেদুটোর তখন কী ফুর্তি তখন   চল এখুনি চল যুদ্ধে যাই চল চল যুদ্ধে যাই চল যুদ্ধে   তারা পণ ঠিক করে নেয় আর যোগ দেয় লড়াইতে স্বপ্নের রসদ নিয়ে সে পার হয়ে যায় অবধারিত একটি গোটা জীবন সারা কলকাতা চষে বেড়িয়েও সে কোনো দোকানে এ্যান্টি-ডুরিং খুঁজে পায়নি পৃথিবী খোলস ছাড়ে মাটি বিস্তৃত করতে থাকে তার কোকদ্বার জাপটে ধরে প্রবেশ করিয়ে দেয় তার শেকড় জন্ম দেবে এক নতুন পৃথিবীর আর মানুষ তো এই মাটিরই সন্তান শেকড় অগ্রে গ্রহণ করে ক্লান্ত অহল্যাভূমি উর্বর হয়ে ওঠে নতুন প্রজন্মের হাওয়া ভেতরে এসে সবকিছু কাঁপিয়ে দিয়ে যায়

সত্য যে খোঁজে
সে সবসময় সাবধানীর কাছে হেরে যায়
সত্যের কখনো কোনো নিরাপত্তা নেই

A Perfect Picture of This Social System—Who's Responsible?

[A real incident in Sonagachi]

. . . the bloke's simply one of a kind
shoved a mango tree behind.

The film we shall discuss now, *Who's Responsible?*, is about those people in the world who always give but never receive anything. The film has as its focus a girl named Roma who is a victim of this social system, trapped in the flesh trade at the forbidden neighborhood. In that sense, this film holds up a mirror to society. Eventually, at the end of the film, Roma asks who is responsible for her plight: is it she, or society? It is this question that the director answers in the film, using powerful language.

The film, which has been scripted by the director himself, devotes considerable attention to the subject of Sonagachi. That the fallen women are human, that they whore in order to feed themselves, and that society compels them to do so—the story is about this burning problem. In order to realize his vision for the film, the director frequented the brothels in Sonagachi, night and day, for three years. After this he was convinced that if he shot right there, instead of using a studio, an exact reproduction of reality would emerge. He consummately presents the characters of the madams, pimps, middlemen, and babu clients in front of the camera. He had observed the lives of the prostitutes from up close—"I've even seen them washing their clothes at noon under the standpipe, wearing petticoats." No one else has ever observed this subject so closely.

Our knowledge of Sonagachi is not so scanty. Long ago, in the wake of Sarat-babu, Sonagachi created itself, and it did so overnight. Before making the film, the director went there with the entire film unit, including the hero and heroine, to find real-life stories. Where else but in Sonagachi could Sonagachi's lives be found!

The film's heroine is Roma. In her former life, she was Sita, a chaste girl, loved by her parents and siblings. All that is shown in flashback every now and then. By dint of her circumstances, Sita from the tea gardens becomes Roma Bai of Sonagachi. In fact, she even enjoys a few years of marital happiness. Her husband was an airline pilot. He dies suddenly in an accident. He kisses Roma goodbye as he is leaving, and never returns. Alas, the terrible mockery of fate! There is a song at this point, a sad song, to be sung in a very somber tone. Even the animals and birds of the forest weep at Sita's sorrow.

With a baby in her bosom, Sita has no other option. Driven by penury, the pilot's wife becomes a whore in a few days and finds shelter in Sonagachi. Her child is her very life, he is all she knows. In order to raise him, she does not balk even at selling her body every night. When the child grows up he becomes a doctor. Of course, when he understands his mother's real situation, he initially refuses to openly admit his mother's identity. But if the story had consisted only of this it would have been pedestrian. This is where the story takes a dramatic turn. The merit of the director-cum-author-cum-scriptwriter lies in the fact that he has projected modern consciousness onto the story.

An elder brother of Sita wanders around Sonagachi, searching for Sita at every door. The brother will eventually find his sister. Sita, aka Roma, will cry out, "Dada!" and embrace her brother. Hot tears will roll down her cheeks. But when the brother wants to take his sister back home, no one at home accepts her. How can they shelter a woman who had become a whore? At this juncture the son incarnates into a messenger from the gods. He is a doctor by now, a world-famous doctor. The storywriter had made him a Nobel Prize winner in medicine. At first he had misunderstood his mother, but now he returns for atonement. Toward the end of the film comes his forceful question. Having traveled the whole world, his eyes have been opened. He asks who was responsible for his mother becoming a prostitute. Who pulled and dragged her into this hellhole? No one is able to give a suitable reply to his question. The son proves that his mother is innocent. It is society that is to blame for everything. Mother, son, and uncle have a tearful reunion. Peace returns to the world.

In the film, in-between Sonagachi's daily rituals, one would see in flashback scenes of Sita and her pilot husband's blissful conjugal life. Amid mountains and snowy peaks, rivers, and streams, they would sing a duet and dance. It would be quite an exciting song, in the style of a Hindi film. A couple of intimate scenes, one or two exciting bedroom scenes would also be included—of course, only as much as Bengali cinema would permit. After all, every class of viewer had to be satisfied. Watching pornographic videos had become very popular nowadays. That too had to be reckoned with or else the cinematic arts would suffer. But when scenes from their conjugal life appear in flashback, the heroine's acting, for obvious reasons, is different. This is something that could easily be done by many actors. But the difference between the bedroom scenes in Sonagachi and those of normal conjugal life—at least the difference that we have been taught to believe exists—is brilliantly portrayed by the heroine under the director's instructions. The refined section of the audience does not have to be told that one is the routine kind of bodily surrender while the other is the key to worldly pleasure—divine union. Canned applause (naturally, in parenthesis).

On his visit to the prostitutes' quarter, the director had entered a woman's room. This was not a common alley whore but someone quite respected in the prostitutes' community, she was something of an aristocrat. The room looked different from the others too. Although small, it was a lot like a salon of the olden days, with thin mattresses laid out on the floor and cushions strewn about. The whore was also a singer. Afternoon turned to evening—what in Bengali is poetically called the "bride-seeing light." The director empathized with the plight of the prostitutes. Taking a deep breath, he thought about how no one came to this neighborhood to see a bride to make their daughter-in-law. Instead, here, society's sacrificial girls prepared to show themselves at this time of the day. It was time to lay out the merchandise. The darker it became, the more the fountains of frolic erupted. Reptilian desires emerged from the darkness within men. The director felt quite pleased to have thought of the phrase "reptilian desires"—what a fantastic phrase, really apt. Now it was time to lay out the sacred offerings to that desire. As evening descended, two uniform-clad schoolboys entered the room. The landlady-cum-madam explained: They go to school. Many of the girls here have children. But will you lot be able to bring all that into the story? Here, fourteen- or fifteen-year-old boys show customers the way and bring them to their mothers' rooms. It's perfectly normal. Very commonplace. Part of the daily routine. Can your film handle all this? Chewing her paan, the madam continued: You know what they say: *Don't eat shit 'coz it's too smelly and don't eat iron 'coz it's too hard!* Despite her age, she had painted her lips. Yes, she was quite a character. Hearing what she said, the director clicked his tongue. Oh god, all this doesn't work in a film! The audience will burn it! Is this an art film or what? The audience wants problems but they don't want complexity. A problem, play around a little with it, and then a sweet solution—that's it, only so far. No more. Changing the subject, he now threw a question of his own to the madam: Tell me, when a mehfil assembles here, when there's song and dance in the room—where do these boys and girls go? Jutting out her head by way of retort, the madam replied: Where else? All of us have maidservants. The children study in the evening. The tutor comes. After that, for as long as the session continues, they stay in the verandah.

Or they go up to the terrace. Alarmed, the director asked: What if people stay till one or two in the morning? Unperturbed, the madam replied: People stay all night too. If there's no other option, the boy lies down under the cot. Of course, the customer doesn't know. The business goes on above. A fourteen- or fifteen-year-old boy—doesn't he know his mother is a whore? Where will he go? Everyone has just one room—we have to make do somehow. She took a bite of another paan and asked the director for a 555. Turning the cigarette in her hand and examining it, she said, I know this cigarette. The big babu's cigarette. Lighting it and letting out a mouthful of smoke, she said: Lay out the money and then I'll tell you all about the women here. Fifteen-year-old boys who use foul words and abuse their mothers, call her "cunt's sister," and the mother too retorts in foul language and says, *Why should you be left out, I'm taking my clothes off, come and have a poke, you working cunt's son*—you haven't seen such scenes, haven't heard that language. You haven't heard someone say, *I went out, became a whore, destroyed my own family, and now this fucker who lives off me talks to me threateningly!* Of course, we don't dance like whores behind the veil of respectability like you decent folk . . .

To show all this in the film! As he sat perspiring under the fan, the director thought: That's the limit! They will skin me alive! In the wake of Saratchandra, a very sweet Sonagachi had been created in the Bengali market—bel flowers, tittering laughter, tears, Parvati, Devdas . . . The madam continued absent-mindedly: Here, those who can do so send their children away, put them in boarding school. They live in Darjeeling and grow up there. Of course, most of them rot and die in this hellhole. But no matter how many vile abuses we mouth to the babus' faces, as far as character goes, we're far better than decent folk. It's the decent women who snatch away our food. Don't they say, *there's shit bubbling on his bum, but the bugger professes austerities glum!*

Suddenly the madam grabbed the sleeve of the director's shirt and pulled him toward her: Have you done a girl anytime? A whore? The gentleman was dumbfounded. Not knowing what to say in front of so many people, he began to perspire. He had not been prepared for this sudden assault. The madam swayed her hips mockingly and burst out laughing: Oh, how well we know the male race! The pussycat says I won't eat fish, I won't touch bones, I'm going to Kashi! Why do you keep looking slyly at that fair-skinned girl, do you want to go to her room? Her rate is a bit steep. We don't have any caste . . . but the babu is like the insect that appears around Diwali. As soon as his business is done, he drives us away. After that, changing her tone somewhat, she said: Our real vulnerability lies elsewhere. Wherever we might be, the yearning for home and family remains, every woman wants to be a mother. As she spoke, a strange transformation came over her appearance.

In the film *Who's Responsible?*, the elder brother, Jatin Kumar, has a major role. He goes to Sonagachi in search of his lost sister. If you ask, why Sonagachi, you're likely to be disappointed. You have to assume that people go only to Sonagachi to search for lost sisters. A small boy doing his school homework in a corner asks Jatin-babu: Who are you looking for? A change comes over Jatin-babu's face. The audience can see infinite love gradually suffusing his face. He tries to get familiar with the boy—what's your name, which school do you go to, which class are you in. As soon as he asks about his family, from the other side the local hoodlum, played by Samit Bhanja, says: Stop! Don't ask. I know what you'll ask after this. About his father, isn't it? Here in Sonagachi, women become mothers, they give birth to babies. You'll find everything here, but you won't find any fathers. If you look too hard you'll end up getting fucked, it'll be a case of lantern in hand and bamboo up the ass.

The director has created some special moments in this film, ones that were sure to earn him the audience's applause. They just wouldn't be able to control their tears. One babu, unable to bear the suffering of the prostitutes, leaves behind a hundred-rupee note. The girl does not know. When she discovers the money, she angrily throws the note in his face and says: You have a lot of money, don't you? Take your money back! None of your coquetry, please. We've seen a lot of such money. Bhadralok! Don't we know bhadralok! *The wives of my husband's brothers and friends are my own, while that slut, my husband's sister, is a foe. When the slut of a mother-in-law pops it, I'll be independent and go!* With just a few words, the director clearly portrays their nobility of character. What Saratchandra, with all his fanfare, could not achieve, this director had done, and with such ease. When you think about it, you cannot help but be amazed. Oh, the audience would certainly love it.

Besides employing dialogue, the director has also used some significant symbols in the film. Every prostitute has a babu, and in this film the babu was Ranjan. Ranjan enjoys Roma. If she wasn't ready in time, he whipped her. He lashed her with a conch-fish whip. Whether or not such things existed now, they had to be retained in the film. It was a film about prostitutes, so however old-worldly it was for a whore to be lashed with a conch-fish whip, the film simply couldn't run if it weren't there. There were fights as well. In the prostitutes' quarter, the elder brother fights using his bare fists, flattens all the toughies and hoodlums with karate blows and returns unscathed. And when he goes back home with his lost sister, once again a symbol appears. The familiar world becomes alien, and the alien world familiar. Inside a car on a rainy day, the car's windshield becomes unclear, the wiper moves, and the familiar streets are visible once again, the familiar houses; once again a stream of falling rain—the symbol.

There are some prevalent notions about the prostitutes' quarters, like the beat of the tabla, the melody of the harmonium, the cry of the bel-flower seller, just as Sarat-babu and company had proclaimed. But there were some flats in Sonagachi that were completely different. Many people may have heard about Nandarani's flat. A small room, lots of appliances in it—a fridge, a TV, even a videocassette player. For sure, Hindi songs played on the tape deck, but foreign music played too. There were several different drinks in the fridge. A long verandah stood adjacent to the room. The rent for such a flat was about two thousand. Even after paying for everything from the pimp's commission to all his expenses, the babu could still afford to spend two thousand rupees on rent.

One girl had come down from the third floor to see the film shoot. She was fair-skinned, tall, and pretty, like a classical figurine. On hearing the story before the shooting began, the girl asked: Who's doing the elder brother's role in this film? The director asked: Who do you think would be good? The girl replied: One person could have done it—Uttam-da—but he's dead. The director asked: Can you think of anyone else? The girl mentioned the names of two middle-aged actors. The director asked: What if I did it? The girl pursed her lips, as if to say it wouldn't work. She watched the shooting for a long time. The karate scene, too. Later, after the shooting was over, the director asked the girl: How did you like it? The girl touched his feet in obeisance and said: Please don't use the formal "you" with me. You are indeed like an elder brother.

After the shooting was over and the director was in a more relaxed frame of mind, he asked the madam: Can you please tell me how you people entered this profession? The madam pursed her lips. Certainly not the way you lot show it in films. *Oh, dear husband's brother, is she her husband's brother's? Why doesn't your sister sleep with that husband of hers?* Is there any ill heath in your film? Do they have to take injections? Bad diseases are commonplace in a whorehouse. All the girls have to take penicillin. Once in a while every girl has trouble urinating. There's pus. The gift of decent folk like you. You call it VD or something like that. We don't talk of such things outside. If we did, the customers wouldn't come. Where deprivation is most acute, middlemen hover. The first vulture is this middleman. He entices you with the promise of employment in Calcutta. And then he deposits you here. A band of foxes and vultures descend to tear and devour the body. A feast session. Chew-suck-lick-drink. And thus begins the nose-ring ceremony, for entry into the oldest profession in the world. There is deprivation of every kind. Apart from the deprivation of food and clothing, there are other kinds of deprivation too. For instance, suddenly one finds the man of one's heart. There is an exchange of hearts. Unable to wait, they go and get married in Kalighat. And then he brings her to a house. After a few days he leaves, saying, I'll just be back—never to return. He takes whatever jewelry or money there was, all of it, everything. So now you die, you become a whore. Of course there's no shortage of people who drop into the profession. Do you know what "putting on the nose ring" means? Come here sometimes. Gradually you'll get to know. At first it's very difficult. Whatever one earns is taken away by the madam. Of course, one is provided with food and so on. If you are clever and intelligent, you find the right time and opportunity and ensnare some babu and grab all his money. After that, either you trip him, or else the babu himself becomes bankrupt while feeding his debauchery. Sometimes one has to say, don't try to act too smart or I'll tell the wife and then you'll be fucked. One does feel a bit bad, but it's the sons of these decent folk who brought us to the street in the name of marriage. I don't give a damn. At least one gets a room of one's own with the money. So many babus have come and gone. The sky's full of many kites. Cut them all, *bo-katta*! Make the string sharp—we learned this at the very beginning in this profession. Feel sad for the babus? Rubbish! Wash and wipe yourself and wring the towel and hang it out to dry. Don't talk to me about morals! *In shame I'm in the brothel and eat to still my stomach's woe, it's because I have shame that I choose to wear clothes and go.*

Scratching his head, the director said: My heroine came to this quarter driven by poverty. She is a victim of our social system. She can do no wrong. That she filches a babu's money—such a so-called reality does not work in this country. It's Saratchandra's land, moshai! The audience won't tolerate such things. She became a prostitute because of poverty—that's our eternal theme, a burning problem, created by Sarat-babu with his own hands. Without that, how can the public accept the film? I've concocted a fine punch by adding a progressive outlook to it. Absolutely twenty-first century. The son does not hate his whore mother. He accepts her! Takes her home. Society recognizes her. Completely modern thinking! The latest! It's bound to be a hit! So you just lap it up and I'll rake it in!

Ei Somajbyabostar Nikhunt Chitro—Dwayi Ke?, 1987

Will You Preserve Your Chastity, Aparna?

[For Jean-Luc Godard, of *First Name: Carmen*]

While Ma was alive—until about a year into my marriage—whenever it rained she would phone me in my office to ask: Tell me, which dal would you like me to make you khichudi with? Nowadays, if it rains and I mention that I'd like to eat khichudi, she gets irritated. And we haven't even been married five years. Neither of us expects anything from the other now.

Hold the PC muscle tight for two seconds. Hold it there. After two seconds, let go. And then relax. Hold it tight again. Keep it that way for two seconds. Let go. Do this again and again. Hold it. Let it go. Hold it. Let it go. You'll find that your capacity, what is known as retention capacity, has increased greatly.

I hate my mother, the girl said exasperatedly, shaking her bobbed hair, responding to the remote assault. I don't call her Ma, I say Mrs. Sanyal, Mrs. Aparna Sanyal. I find it disgusting to call her Ma. *She returns drunk every night*—she flirts with every one of Dad's friends. I smoke, I drink, I push drugs, heroin, smack—everything. Who cares? Why does Mrs. Sanyal poke her nose into my private life? A woman like that has no right to admonish or order me. I'll do whatever I want, I can share my bed with whoever I wish. *I am seventeen years old.* I'm old enough to know what's good for me and what's not. *I will do whatever I feel like.*

There are women who are unwilling to wait. Even while the party's on, she takes her companion where no one can see and pulls at his shirt buttons, kisses his neck, rubs her head on his chest, and when she is at the peak of excitement, begins to open his zipper with trembling fingers. Tchaikovsky begins to play behind the scenes, and sometimes Rachmaninoff. Twenty minutes are spent in this manner.

The girl began lying for no particular reason. She spends most of her time at home standing in the verandah. She speaks rudely, whether there's any justification or not. From her accumulated grievances I understood that the girl was simply coming of age. She had a kind of complex in her mind about me. She would get very happy if she saw me ill at ease. As if my discredit was to her credit. And she got annoyed if she discerned the slightest intimacy between her father and me.

One afternoon, her father and I were lying on the same bed. My daughter was in the next room. Thinking she was asleep, my husband got intimate with me. But my daughter had witnessed the whole thing. What fury thereafter! She wouldn't speak with me or her father. When I found out,

I explained to her that this was the way of the animal world. If she wished, she too could do all this with whoever she liked. With her father, too. After that day, if my daughter had any questions regarding sex, she would ask me straightaway.

The face should not be too dry or too moist. Many believe that for such things nymphomaniacs are more suitable. Open your lips a little, but not too much. When a man and a woman stand together, their heights should be about the same. If you have to do it by bending or craning your neck, often the neck, back, and spine ache. To find out if your height is all right, measure yourself so you don't have to strain your neck too much.

When I look back about ten years ago, to the time I reached adolescence, I realize I had felt a kind of jealousy within me regarding Ma. I felt that my mother was my rival. If someone called Ma beautiful—if they said, Aparna, you're looking great today—I felt it was a slight on my own appearance. I got angry when I heard anyone praise Ma, then again, I couldn't tolerate any denigration, either. I suffered from a narcissus complex. I would stand for hours in front of the mirror, and think I was far more beautiful than my mother. So why did Uncle Robi praise my mother and not me? I would find a reason to pick a quarrel and create an uproar.

It is girls who must accord chastity the greatest value. When it comes to boys, no one opens their mouths. On behalf of those of us who work outside the home, I speak openly—chastity and suchlike are a joke. Nowadays good contraceptives are available even in paan shops, they are sold openly. By giving men our company for an hour or an hour and a half, we get lots of opportunities and benefits that we can use for building our own careers. Is it wrong to build one's career?

For any girl, her mother is her ideal. It is from her mother that she intuits what her role in life will be in the future, as a woman. Consequently, there is always an intensity here—either a tendency to oppose or a desire to emulate. Whatever it may be, the mother's influence will always be there on the daughter. He had lost his virginity in a bizarre way. It happened in Bombay, with an elderly woman. The woman had a twenty-four or twenty-five-year-old daughter who studied at university. He was only fifteen then, and inexperienced. So it was the woman who had to be active. She asked him to undo the hook of her blouse, and it took him a very long time. He just couldn't do it. He didn't know anything at all then. You're an idiot, the woman said with a laugh. While removing her clothes in this way, he felt like he was peeling the whorls of an onion. As he removed her clothes, one by one, he was startled, and at the same time despondent. He could still remember, quite clearly, how awkwardly and erroneously he had lost his virginity.

> Exactly opposite the writing, an exhibition of
> porn films ran all night long.
> Long lines of people. Of the third world. Hun-
> gry and angry. Parallel to this,
> the writer wants to test the patience of the
> readers, to read something perverted. . . . I
> love him with my heart and soul and
> he wants my body. What shall I do—what
> shall I do, Aparna—tell me, what shall I do?

The female character in this story thinks her daughter should not have any inhibitions regarding sex. And translating this idea into practice was the most important thing for her. In the Victorian era, men used to get terribly excited if they saw a woman's ankles or a bit of lace on her tummy. Whether there's blazing heat or freezing cold or a night of pouring rain, entertain your loved one while wearing a silky nightie—and if there's some artistic naughtiness in it, just a little, there's nothing more to add. Yes, plainclothesmen keep watch everywhere. There are people from the security forces every few yards. And in the middle of this, two heroines, mother and daughter, naked, bathing next to each other, oh, splashing and frolicking around in the water! For most of the time, the camera gazes at the splashing water. Behind the camera, at first a hard-core film was played, and then two soft ones, one after another, and finally another hard-core. Sex-starved masses. Of the third world. They were head over heels. The camera catches them too. Does the camera alter even the reality of realism? At first, some kind of lubricant has to be applied inside yourself, and the rubber applicator attached to the vibrator also needs to be lubricated. The pain is reduced thereby, and the intensity of feeling is enhanced. But the whole thing is made of transparent plastic. Its length and thickness can be increased or decreased according to your preference. It is fitted with an electric motor. At the peak moment, or for that matter even midway, the velocity of the thrust can be increased. It is reported that the speedy rotation of the vibrator can bring about supreme ecstasy in a minute or less. A photographer from a local daily went to click a picture. His camera was snatched away.

Shirley Tomcuse, of the women's liberation movement

Men want us to wear lace and silk because apparently these arouse them tremendously.

Ms. Gloria Steinem, editor of New York's Ms. magazine

We don't want to show men our breasts. That's why we don't wear a brassiere, because it flagrantly increases the sex appeal. . . . In the next century, boys and girls will first establish sound physical relations, and marriages will be made according to their individual needs. What's actually needed in marriage is physical compatibility. All talk of meeting of minds and so on is rubbish, a sham. And remember, it's because of sexuality that human progress will never cease.

Subhas Roy, age thirty-two, married, college teacher

Only married men and women have a right to sex. Men and women are biologically very different. The male's desire for sex is much greater than the female's, this is why men can enjoy unhindered sex before marriage. But women should not do that. Because if a woman has a sexual experience before marriage, the experience after marriage might seem terribly monotonous to her. The man himself wants unrestrained sexual intercourse, but from the woman he demands virginity, because our social heritage has taught us to think this way. That is absolutely correct.

Shailendra Goyal, age twenty-six, film director

Most men love to boast about their sexual experiences before marriage. And women boast about their virginity.

If that's so, where did all these men get their sexual experiences? Either most of what men say is false, or else most of the girls are actually not virgins, however much they may boast about it.

Tripurari Ghosh, age thirty, married, stage artist

I wholeheartedly support the notion and existence of chastity. Because it strengthens the basis of mutual trust and understanding between husband and wife. Besides, if this remains intact, a woman would never get the opportunity to compare her husband with other men. And that's what's best for everyone. Women agree to premarital sex only to blackmail men.

Ambika Patel, age twenty-five, unmarried, reporter

The notion of chastity has not become as extinct as we think. The women who decry this loudly, especially unmarried women, actually accord this a lot of significance inwardly. Sometimes for fear that this might come in the way of a good marriage, and sometimes for fear of dishonor. After all, everyone wishes to get married into a respectable, aristocratic family. The more aristocratic they are, whatever they may profess outwardly, inwardly they are just as conservative.

Aparna

I value trustworthiness much more than chastity.

You're a writer, aren't you? No, just like that . . . that's what I thought as well. If that were not the case, no one would waste their time like this. The way she sat, with one leg lifted high, even the lace on her panties was visible. However much of a writer he might be, he belonged to the male species after all. He did not want to poke his nose into other people's affairs. He gazed in that direction every once in a while as he breathed in the fragrance of French perfume. Even though she knew I was looking at her, she didn't lower her leg. In the end she stated her views on chastity. I think the girl was Goan, it happened at night, on the train from Bombay to Goa.

A slender, doe-like body that should emit fire like Vesuvius when it gets down to business. She had to be extremely artful in bed—otherwise men, that is, the male species, could not be held onto. There is a class of women who, whether they are beautiful or not, are very self-assured. They quickly take off their clothes, without the slightest hesitation, get into bed, and call you.

Measure the depth of your love

(1) Tell me, do your husband's fondles and caresses still give you a tingling sensation, or is it just the opposite? (2) Do you think the sexual act is an expression of deep love or is it a duty of marital life? (3) When any other man lavishes praise on you, do you try to draw your husband's attention to the man's compliments? (4) When your husband jokes about you with his friends, or relates some intimate story about you, do you enjoy it or do you turn in your grave? (5) Did a situation ever arise when some matter or subject was disclosed to your husband that you didn't want him to know about, and you became terribly angry?

She wants to establish a sexual relation with the masses

The massacre has to take place as the night comes to a close, when dawn is breaking. All night long, the youth dithered. The character emerges from a *closely guarded train*. Actually it's a story about the physical relationship between man and woman. He wants to make myth and modern militarism stand face-to-face. He selects a woman from among the masses, one who wishes to establish a sexual relation with the masses . . . If you don't obey your dad, he'll give you such a bleeding fuck that—the mother says to her daughter, giggling as they frolic in the water.

Slip in the two blades together and spread the handles on the two sides. The two blades find place on the sides of the walls. With practice, you'll get a clear view, right up to the mouth of the distant womb. With a speculum—which looks a lot like kitchen tongs—you can see yourself well, on your own. You must try it out. At the time of insertion, the body should be as still as possible. It's a good idea to keep a mirror opposite, and direct the light from a table-lamp at the mirror—then you can see your insides in the mirror. Insert it slowly, gently, keep inserting it, the way a tampon is inserted, keeping the two blades of the specu-lum pressed together, very slowly. Never hurry in your excitement. If you like, you can also apply some lubricant. After insertion, if you move the two handles apart and lock them in that position, the two blades move to the two sides, giving you a good view of the inside. Now look, at the very end of the passage, the neck of the uterus, clearly visible. Dome-like, smooth, a brownish color, engorged— you'll be thrilled to see it, you will be astounded. And it's so near that simply by stretching your hand you can see the mouth of the uterus—the womb-hole.

I really liked his mouth-work on me. We split up in Delhi. Earlier, he had enticed me with the bait of a good job and called me to Delhi. He arrived one dawn, staggering. His daughter was with him. He smelled of whiskey. After a bitter quarrel, I returned to Calcutta. Perhaps women want to enjoy their sexuality while men only want to brag about it.

Want a gigolo? If a woman wants a gigolo, she can get one in today's marketplace for as little as a bottle of booze, a bite to eat and a few rupees. Women who set out to hunt prey can easily spot the gigolos. In a secret survey, it was found that in Bombay, at present, more married women engage in extramarital relations than their spouses do. The woman he was with told him that some of the gigolos might be quite ugly to look at but once you've downed two pegs of whiskey, all men are the same—life becomes colorful.

I caress her back first, I press her earlobes gently, and sometimes I kiss her straightaway. In this way, through hints and signs, I convey my feelings, purely through the language of the body, through glances, without talking at all, not a word even by mistake. Later, if I get the chance, I say: It would be nice to go somewhere and have a cup of coffee. Or: I feel like going back home, I don't like it here. Eight out of ten times, I don't have to make the effort to say these things, the woman comes up with the proposal on her own. To the extent that if she has come to the party with her husband or a male friend, she evades him most artfully. Initially there is some shyness and hesitation, and then they get excited and readily agree to novel means, and what's more, generously offer their body for enjoyment. Most of them like my first performance, and I push their face to my groin, some love to use their tongue or lips. Some turn artists and become unceasing inventors in bed. But if the girl is in a bad mood, she has to be handled carefully. Most importantly, one has to remain constantly alert to the minutiae of the girl's preferences. And of course, one must help her remove or put on her clothes, take her to the bathroom and bathe her, rubbing soap all over her body, wake up early and bring a cup of coffee to her face. Women are charmed by these little things. One needs to know what they want and when they want it—for instance, if you sense that the woman wants you to use force over her, do just that. You must always say, Don't call me, I'll call you, I'll phone you. At your place or somewhere else, it'll be difficult at my place. But never in your own house, for you could get into trouble at any time if you did that. For the rendezvous, it's best to make an arrangement in a known hotel or restaurant.

A handkerchief wound up lengthwise is held in the hand, with two or three knots on the upper end. It looks a lot like that. It indicates the size to the woman. Rich, lonely women love such gigolos.

Love rating in the estimation of husbands and wives

[In the blank cells of the table below, note down your estimated percentages. The figures provided by you will help to complete the story. Your active participation in the writing is vital.]

How much of a lover the husband ought to be to his wife (%)	How much of a lover the wife ought to be to her husband (%)	Appropriateness of the marital relationship
		Most ideal couple
		Ideal couple
		Average couple
		Marriage can continue
		Separation imminent

If you want a gigolo, go down to the coffee shop of a fancy hotel between midnight and three in the morning. Alone. After ordering a coffee, look around carefully to see whether there are any men sitting alone. One or two of them are bound to be gigolos. After a while, the man himself will come up to you. If nobody comes, you will have to advance on your own. If even this doesn't work, be aware that in every elite hotel there is a list of gigolos, just as there is a list of call girls. But in such matters, always bear in mind that nothing happens overtly. There's code language in all trades. You need to learn that, or at least a few terms. And learning these things is not at all difficult. Someone taught me—it was under him that I was an apprentice—that the first thing you need to know is how to get out of any situation you are caught in, especially at the very moment when you feel you ought to get out. Godard? Of course it's Godard. The one who imposes Van Gogh's yellow on hard-core.

> His protest is against sex-violence and he wants to protest through sex-violence.

Perhaps in this story Stefania Sandrelli could have acted in an important role, in the role of the mother, the one who openly offers her daughter to her own husband. Amanda Sandrelli could have played the role of the daughter. Amanda is Stefania's daughter in real life. Mario Soldati's *Lie* would have begun in this way. But Aparna, our Aparna, snatches away everything of the character. Whether chastity ought to be preserved or not, that becomes the issue. Through quarrels, fights and all kinds of action sequences, the rich man's daughter falls in love with the tonga-wallah hero. *Mard* enters *Lie*, wholly. While being screened, the film's reels somehow got mixed up, they kept getting mixed up, on and on. Such incidents occur in a few more spheres. Sex symbols emerge. But rather than sexual intercourse with the one who ought to be slept with, it is sexual intercourse with the one who ought not to be slept with that is more manifest. The camera keeps altering the reality. After a reel and a quarter, love blossoms, and as soon as the second reel begins, their song and dance routine starts. Aparna keeps saying coyly: Please put the hook on the blouse. The one she says it to is her son's friend. The hero and heroine stand in front of each other, he will sit down and shake his knees, and she, who is now sitting, will stand up. Then the two of them hug each other, a real-life kiss is a thousand times better than the kissing pose they adopt. Instead of that, as Subimal says, why doesn't he shove it in? *Love, love, and love—have a baby.*

In the middle of all this, in the midst of so much trouble, it is difficult to identify the PC muscle accurately because it is often confused with the sphincter muscle. But there is a way to find out. Sit on a stool and spread your legs apart as wide as you can. Now, don't be reluctant, start urinating. As soon as you start to pee, you have to hold back the flow of piss. The muscle you use to stop the flow is the PC muscle. Start pissing again, and then stop the pee the very next moment. In this way, for a few days in succession, if you hold your piss every time you urinate, you'll figure out how to tighten the PC muscle. In the first week, you should do this at least seven times, and then do it ten times before you go to bed, after removing your clothes. Do it about fifty times whenever you want, at any time of the day. The following week, increase the duration of the exercise until you are able to loosen and tighten it a few hundred times. Each time, you must hold tight for at least two seconds.

Parallel to this, as an epilogue to all the physical techniques and exercises, is the film *Sacrifice*. At the height of the threat of nuclear war, a perturbed Alexander makes a sacrifice by destroying his beautiful house. On the other hand, his infant son, Little Man, protects the environment by watering the plant that father and son had nurtured. They had watered it at the time of planting. *Sacrifice* was Tarkovsky's final film, he dedicated it to his son.

Sex for the sake of the son, or a son for the sake of sex?

Yes, so it was that until the end not an extra kiss was planted on his cheek.

After a point the camera, which deceives the writer on and on, begins to deceive reality too.

Word gets around that there is a strong dose of sex in *Love Me Physically*. What a boy actually does with a girl is shown openly. The tickets were to be sold from nine in the morning, but there was a line from noon the previous day. Fuck, what hot stuff, must see it! Great turmoil on the day of the show. Stones rained down on the hall. The police were unable to control the situation. Paramilitary forces were called in. The assembled masses demanded: We must be permitted to see this film. Such a hot film had never before come to this city. A cigar in his mouth, Godard of *First Name: Carmen* smiles wryly with lips askew. He wants to protest against sex-violence and he wants to do that with sex-violence itself. *Unseen, unsaid.* The real becomes unreal, reality embraces the unreal. Someone secretly smears butter-acid on the screen. When the projection begins, the screen erupts in flames. The screen keeps burning, and Godard lets it burn. What sex would the masses like to see—they sit agape as the naked niece swaggers, spanning the entire screen. The sex-starved masses of the third world are left astounded by such a presentation of the naked female body, in such Van Goghian yellow. The screen keeps burning, not because of butter-acid, but with Godard's sex. He flings sex at our faces, at the open-mouthed faces of eunuchs. Sex comes down like a whip—sex, whoosh, whoosh. It fiercely scorches the skin of those of us who secretly, furtively, watch hard-core.

And then, together with the camera's realism, you keep testing yourself to observe whether or not you have been able to correctly learn how to tighten the PC muscle by yourself. Unknown to you, the hand goes . . . yes, it goes there, in a most suspect way. If there's any doubt, shove it in, inside your thing, insert a finger and then tighten your PC muscle and see if you can feel the force of the contraction. Every day, before going to bed, do it for a few minutes. The biggest benefit of doing this is that once you are used to it, you can do it whenever and wherever you want. Even if you initially feel somewhat ashamed, eventually you won't have any reservations. Father and son will gleefully go hand in hand to watch hard-core, and it will be called progress.

A cigar in his mouth, Godard smiles wryly, his lips askew. He is the one who wants to question the notion of progress in today's civilization, the biggest lie of all.

If only you can slip your finger in there, it's done. Whether you're lying in bed or reading the *Anandabazar Patrika* or watching television, or for that matter even when you're sitting on the pot, you can shove your finger into that part of progress, at your ease.

Lots of excerpts have been taken from popular women's magazines. I acknowledge my debt for informational assistance from two books: *My Secret Garden: Women's Sexual Fantasies* by Nancy Friday and *Human Sexual Response* by Dr. William H. Masters and Dr. Virginia Johnson.

Sotityo Ki Rakhbe, Aparna?, 1987

Here's How We Wring a Quarter of Lime

[For Kamalkumar Majumdar]

As a new traveler, what his role in society was,
what he ought to have started at that age, he wasn't
permitted to follow. Consequently, in many matters
he becomes a renegade, and being outside the mainstream, he remains a singular being, and doesn't even
possess the magic wand to return . . .

The bed rolled up rapidly and tried to wrap us up. Strange
and mysterious sounds emanated from within the room.
The doors and windows banged shut and blew open, as
though caught in a gust of wind. Chhoto Mama and I lay
in bed. Unable to fathom what was happening, we tried to
break free of the bed and sit up. With all our strength we
tried to push and throw off the rolled-up mattress. The
next moment it rose again and enveloped us. At the same
time the two pillows began to jump up and down noisily.

As if someone were juggling a pair of balls in his hands. Our studies were going well. Chhoto Mama was five months younger than me. We were in the same class in school. He was stellar in academics, the best student in the school. The teachers said he was sure to get a scholarship for higher studies. It was obvious that he would secure high marks in math, English, and life science. They said he might even secure a rank in the district. He was the pride of the school. Chhoto Mama always had his face stuck in a book. As they say, humming at one and reading at two . . . I had to study all by myself at home. When I visited my mother's paternal home, I began discussing the school subjects with Chhoto Mama. At first, Chhoto Mama used to do all my homework. To tell you the truth, I was never into studying. I preferred cinema and secretly, furtively, I went through the pages of film magazines. My friends called me a Hindi cinema addict. Mithun was my hot favorite. I kept track of all his latest films. There was always a color picture postcard of Mithun hidden inside my book. From time to time I kissed him on his lips. I had a group of friends, and we would slip out of school during the lunch break and go to the newly opened video parlor a short distance away. If my father ever heard about it, he would scold me mildly. Instead of studying you're going around doing all this! That's all. But after he took a second wife, he never bothered to do even that. Where did he have the time to bother? But once I was in my mama's house, there was no one to oversee me. I saw as many videos as I liked. If Chhoto Mama scolded me, I ignored him. One day he said something awful and I lost my temper. Why don't you go and tell my father, I don't give a damn! I was possessed by something. I decided that one day, if I ever got the chance, I would expose just how "virtuous" he really was. Come what may, I would destroy his pride. After all, how long could boys restrain themselves? I laughed inwardly. I had become quite precocious by then, influenced by all the movies that I had watched. Anyway, Chhoto Mama didn't say more. Meanwhile, the selection examinations got over. The list of those who would sit the school final exam was put up. Chhoto Mama came first with over 87 percent marks. My name wasn't there. But I was not worried. Thanks to my father's clout, I was included in the second list as a special case. Immediately after, special classes commenced in school, with the teachers coaching the exam students. The classes were sometimes held in the morning and sometimes in the evening. It was compulsory for everyone to attend the coaching classes. Chhoto Mama and I used to set out for the evening class as soon as it was dusk, taking a lantern with us. The two of us returned together after the class got over, at about nine at night. There was nothing to be scared of on the road between mama's house and the school. A wide embankment meandered its way into the village. On one side lay the dry riverbed and on the other side was a hyacinth jungle. Every now and then, here and there, a couple of small thatched huts. The river had run dry long ago, not much water flowed during the rainy season either. Skirting the dry riverbed was the embankment, and across the embankment was mama's house. We used to walk across the river bed. Although it was desolate, there was really nothing to be worried about. *Yes, my dear, the other day, the chairman of the school had come. The saga of Vidya-sundar is to be performed on the puja mandap.* The house was empty. It was getting dark. Then it became completely dark. Father was a panchayat pradhan. He had to do everything from distributing land to preparing the sharecroppers' list. As a personal indulgence, he taught at a local primary school. His other duties took up much more of his time than school teaching did. Of course, he didn't take his salary, he donated it among the poor and destitute in the village. He was also the president of our secondary school. Despite the abolition of zamindari, he had a huge amount of property in his own name, and benami property as well. With his farm and livestock and so on, he had a large establishment. He had gotten a tractor recently. It was the age of science, after all, it wouldn't do to remain stuck in old-fashioned ways of thinking. The country had to be lifted up to the twenty-first century. Those were my father's words. Two Jersey cows yielded about three buckets of milk, morning and evening. And he had four pairs of English white mice. Keeping these English mice was my father's only hobby. He fed them tender blades of fresh green grass twice a day, with his own hands. This opulence was not viewed favorably by all. But my father had tremendous clout in the area, hence people feared saying anything to his face. I had gathered that when a panchayat in a particular region was ruled by a particular political party, the party's dominance in the region was established. Thereafter, nothing could go against the wishes and reservations of the panchayat head. I was my father's younger daughter. My sister had married a long time ago. Father always had a soft spot for me. Because I loved to eat cake, every month cakes were bought for me from Kathleen in Calcutta. The latest styles of salwar-kameez came from New Market. Father's only sorrow was that he had no son. If there wasn't a son, who would perform his last rites?

Who would look after his affairs and all the property? After he became panchayat pradhan, Father always wore a silk punjabi and a very fine dhuti from Finlay Mills. Haru's Ma, our maidservant, folded and pleated it beautifully. He wore a thin gold chain around his neck. And then, all of a sudden, I found him obsessed with applying attar, morning and evening. The house was always redolent with the fragrance. After a few days I heard that our new mother was going to arrive. The days sped by. After the wedding, Father had no time for us. But to be honest, he did not leave any wish of his daughter unfulfilled. And that's why, ever since I was a child, I never bothered about studies. Before I knew it I was in class ten. I felt a strange trembling in my body, and my mind was always restless. Once or twice a week, I went to the cinema hall near our house to watch movies. Although it was only a tent-hall, Shri Krishna Talkies showed the latest Hindi films every week. Father was busy with our new mother, besides, there were thousands of tasks in the panchayat. My own mother stayed at home all day, grieving, covered in jewelry, praying before a picture of Anukul Thakur. The road from our house to the school was not so safe for girls. The distance was about two miles. The road wound through paddy fields and there were dense thickets here and there. My new mother didn't think it was proper for me, at my age, to walk down this road every day. Eventually we found a way out. My mama's house was near the school. Mama's family circumstances were not too good. Chhoto Mama lived in the house with my grandfather and grandmother, who were both old and feeble. But the school was just a fifteen-minute walk from mama's house and there would be no problem if I stayed there. It was an old zamindar house but it was in a poor state for not having been maintained for so long. I studied till the eighth standard at the junior high school near my house. I managed to get through the ninth standard somehow, putting up with the difficulty of walking the two miles to the senior school. The pressure of studies mounted as soon as I came up to the tenth. Three or four months went by, with me staying sometimes at mama's house and sometimes at my own house and making the long journey. After that I remained at mama's house. I didn't like studying at all. Thanks to my father's reputation, somehow or the other, with much prodding, I had reached class ten. But now I knew I'd fail if I didn't study properly. And then it was discovered that every night one horse from the king's stable was devoured by an ogress. Only some scattered bones remained. One night the king lay in bed, pretending to be asleep, intent on watching over the stable late into the night. Suddenly he realized that the queen had gotten out of bed and furtively left the dark chamber. Curious, the king followed her. From his hiding place, he saw, to his surprise and astonishment, that the ogress in his beloved stable was none other than the queen herself. Holding up a whole horse, she was biting into the flesh, chewing and devouring it. Within minutes, she had polished off a white horse. Then, wiping her mouth on her anchal, she went back to bed like a good little girl and lay down. Right then, the mattress began to roll up and wind around the body. The two pillows began jumping up and down noisily. A stormy wind descended from somewhere and began to race through the room. The doors and windows banged open and shut. And so it went on. We walked to the coaching classes for a few days. Until now we were still mama and niece. After that whatever had to happen happened. I remember the first day's incident well. After the coaching class was over, Chhoto Mama and I were returning home, like we did every day. The road was desolate. Most of the villagers in these parts were farm laborers. They did back-breaking labor all day and by eight or nine at night they finished eating and went to bed. Like every day, that day too the two of us were talking as we walked along. Suddenly I sensed something pass by in front of us. For a long time I had been looking for a cue. *Oh my god, what's that!* I hugged Chhoto Mama firmly. Raising the lantern in his hand, Chhoto Mama looked around carefully. A jackal. Chhoto Mama's muscular body. He was a bit startled at being hugged so suddenly. Even after I knew that the fleeing animal was a jackal, I continued to clasp Chhoto Mama. To tell you the truth, it wasn't as if I had never experienced the male touch before, but that day it was as though a secret desire had wiped away all ties of blood. I deliberately held mama's well-built, masculine body firmly for a long time. I was in a state of intoxication. I laughed inwardly as I recalled something. About three minutes in all, that day. After that, as each day went by, the intoxication of the feel of that firm, capable, powerful, masculine body seized me even more. I observed that the trivial incident that day had not left any impact on mama's mind. That made me all the more obstinate. Chhoto Mama may have been a very good boy, with his face buried in books all day long, but to disregard a beautiful, modern girl like me? I, who was supposed to drive people crazy! My friends often told me that. They said I looked like Mandakini. The village boys certainly, and even the young history teacher in school gaped at me covertly. I had seen *Ram Teri Ganga Maili* thirty-one times. With a lot of difficulty I had obtained Mithun Chakraborty's address in Bombay and written him a letter, asking him to help me get into films. For this I was even willing to be his maidservant. Perhaps the reply would come soon. So, to disregard me! For quite some time we had occupied two adjacent rooms on the desolate terrace of my mama's house. It was true I was precocious, but because he was my own mother's brother, I did not want to deliberately nurture any bad thoughts in my mind. Besides, Chhoto Mama was truly a good boy. But I just had to smash his conceit about being a good boy. It was all I ever thought about. After that day, I began to look for excuses to touch mama. On holidays, after meals, when mama lay down to rest, I used to go and sit on his bed. In the course of conversation, I would touch him on various pretexts. Sometimes it was a piece of straw in his hair. Sometimes I discovered a mole on his bare body or relieved his prickly heat. The more I touched him, the more my lust grew. I would do all this whenever I got the time and opportunity. I was a precocious girl and it was not possible for any man of flesh and blood to stay away from such an attraction in a desolate room. I had understood this long ago. And eventually, I won. Suddenly there was loud banging on the house's worn-out, ancient twin doors. The courtyard was covered in weeds, clumps of bushes, and a jungle of wild flowers. The old mansion's rat burrows were a den of poisonous snakes. At first the unearthly sound came from the direction of the doors. Thereafter it flew around the house, spinning around like a stormy wind. Suddenly the wind hit the window. At once the twin casements blew open with a bang. The wind rushed down upon the study table. The forbidden books concealed among the pile of books crashed to the floor. The stormy wind sped out and entered the adjacent bathroom. The bathroom door was latched from outside, but it sounded as though someone was kicking the door from inside. As though someone had put an enraged bull in the bathroom and shut the pair of doors. Chhoto Mama ran up and unfastened the chain latch. There was nobody inside. The bathroom was completely empty. Then we saw the bed. The whole mattress rolled up and bound us within it. I tried to free myself with all my strength, but once again it rolled up and wrapped us up. On that bed, in the dead of night, the two of us began to perspire. Sin never remains concealed. At first the boys and girls in our class saw this simply as an expression of affection between uncle and niece, but by and by they got suspicious. By now the relationship of blood was immaterial to us. The yearning for flesh had surpassed everything. Meanwhile, my friends had somehow found out. Perhaps I myself had given some indication of it in order to dispel mama's good boy image. The final examinations had come to an end now. Mama did badly in all the subjects. On the day of the mathematics paper, he gave in his answer sheet an hour early and left. Apparently his mind had gone blank. Juicy stories about us began to spread, and we were spoken about in whispers. The youths of the neighborhood began to pass lewd comments openly. Respected elders were thinking about getting people together and taking appropriate steps. Mama didn't associate with anyone. He had no friends to speak of and had no idea what he should do. One day he pleadingly mentioned the subject of a registry marriage. I remained silent. Finally he proposed: Let's run away and go somewhere far away and live together. I just smiled wryly. This was exactly the sort of thing I had wanted to hear this good boy utter. I knew my father. He would rescue me, come what may. After all, he had the strength of money. Anything was possible if one had money. He would let nothing destroy his family's honor. Besides, I didn't have the slightest interest in running away with mama. There was a dead man lying inside the dry well, clear signs of injury near the back of his head. He lay in the sediment at the bottom of the well. A synthetic red had been injected inside which would drain the blood from his body. And yet he wouldn't be alive. On all four sides, white borders had been drawn. And there were knotted cloth barriers to prevent his unholy soul from exiting his body and entering another person's body. The dead person was not yet an adult. The way the body lay, one would think he wasn't dead, merely sleeping. In the next century, this renegade solitary being would be discovered among a heap of skeletons. The next incident was of an extremely summary nature. Some members of the action squad of Father's party whisked Chhoto Mama away to some unknown person's house, in a faraway village. There he was thrashed and subjected to physical and mental torture. Father had for long nursed an animosity against his in-laws, add to that this dirty affair. Mama was beaten again and again with plastic bottles filled with water. They were poor, besides, they did not have any party affiliations. There was no one to intervene on their behalf, by scheming. That he could scheme and seek refuge and obtain shelter from some party—mama couldn't even think along these lines. He never mingled with anyone in the village. And the police and so on were entirely under Father's control. I believe one of his eyes was gouged out. The thumb on his right hand was cut off with a sharp cleaver. And other things were done to him by the people in Father's party. I did not want to hear everything. I had gotten up and walked away when I heard about it. On the other hand, it wouldn't be wrong to say that I received no punishment at all, a mild scolding, on account of my father's mighty rage. He said that I was getting worse by the day, that I had destroyed the family honor. Everyone thought Chhoto Mama was principally to blame. Having found himself in a desolate house, he had used force and brought me to this pass. But I knew myself. I knew the provocation and vengefulness I was capable of. Mama had kept himself in check for a long time. Perhaps the oppression on him went too far. But what could I do about that? I believe he was laid up in bed for six months. I don't know what happened after that. The pace of my life became frantic after that. My new mother did not bear any children. And so my father went around in despair, wearing talismans and charms. Without a son, who would look after all his worldly property, who would conduct his funeral rites? Father had a strong hold over the party, he did not let word of the scandal spread. He sent me to Calcutta and arranged for the termination of my three-month pregnancy. His henchmen took care of everything secretly. After that Father got me married. In this country, if one had money there was no shortage of good suitors, and my father was enormously wealthy. He paid a dowry of fifty thousand rupees and gave three hundred grams of gold. A refrigerator, a color TV set, and a shining red Hero Honda motorcycle for his son-in-law. He even bought me an imported videocassette player from Fancy Market in Khidirpur, since I was fond of watching films. In the name of his daughter and new son-in-law, he paid for first refusal on a plot of land of about six kathas in the district headquarters where his son-in-law worked. The wedding was a grand affair. He invited and fed people from four villages. Word of my doings had gotten around, but no one said a word openly. They feasted until their bellies were full of fried rice, fried fish, mutton, rossogolla, and sandesh served by the famous Bijoli Grill caterer from Calcutta, and returned home burping. I moved to another district town as a well-paid engineer's wife. Everything was forgotten within ten days or so. I set up home blissfully. I had children. Suddenly one day, in the dead of night, we heard doors banging, as if they were about to fall apart. A gust of wind blew into the room. And then I saw our mattress rolling up toward us. It moved swiftly and tried to wrap my husband and me within its folds. My husband was paralyzed with astonishment at what he saw. I tried for the life of me to straighten out the mattress. I kept trying to straighten out our beloved mattress with all the strength in my body. But it kept rolling itself up with me and my husband. It folded up and wrapped us in its folds. I was panting. It was as if my arms and legs would collapse into my stomach. As if I would suffocate. The two pillows began to jump up and down like soccer balls. There was a terrible banging from inside the adjacent bathroom, as though an enraged bull had been let loose inside. The doors and windows banged open and shut loudly. I remembered a night just like this one, about a year and a half ago. And for the first time in my life, I was frightened.

Ei Amader Shiki Lebu Ningrani, 1989

Translator's Acknowledgements

It is an honor for me to be translating Subimal Misra, and I am grateful to have received his permission, encouragement, and inputs, but also more than that, his friendship. I have had the privilege of gaining Misra's affection and trust, which means a lot to me. This brings with it considerable responsibility, and I hope I have been able to do justice to that.

This volume would not have gotten off the ground but for the Sangam House writers' residency, in Nrityagram, Bangalore, in January 2011. The volume also includes stories translated while I was in the Ledig House writers' residency, in the USA, in April 2013. Such residencies are any writer's dream, and I am deeply indebted to Sangam House and Ledig House for providing me the opportunity. I also wish to thank: Toto Funds the Arts, for the readings in Bangalore in January 2011; Hudson Wine Merchants, for the readings hosted by them on behalf of OMI International Arts Center in April 2013; and Sangam House, for the readings during the Lekhana literary weekend in Bangalore in January 2015.

This project has benefited from the inputs and contributions of many people. That has also been a privilege and a source of satisfaction. I am grateful for that.

Dr. Mrinal Bose, who first introduced me to the name of Subimal Misra, continued his active interest in my translations and never failed to respond immediately with comments. For me, he is like a colleague in my ongoing Misra translation project, and I remain grateful for his intellectual and creative comradeship. I have benefited greatly from discussions with Nilotpal Roy—scholar, teacher, and writer. The selection of stories in this volume would not have been possible but for his valuable guidance. Procheta Ghosh has also been a colleague throughout my work for this volume, and also contributed a note for the *P. S. Section*, together with Tapas Ghosh, his co-editor for *Jari Bobajudhyo*. My thanks go to them.

I was fortunate to receive the timely assistance of Sangita Roy, an exceptional young woman, which helped greatly in sustaining the translation momentum.

It has been my good fortune to have as a close friend, Janam Mukherjee, historian of wartime Bengal, whose own enthusiasm about my translation project and insightful comments served to vindicate my commitment. He has contributed a note about this collection, which appears in the *P. S. Section*. I have also benefited from Nilanjan Bhattacharya's interest and enthusiasm about Subimal Misra's work. He too has contributed a piece about Misra for the

P. S. *Section*, as has artist Sumitro Basak. My thanks to both of them.

Kenneth Slawenski, writer and biographer, has been a generous source of critical affirmation. Vivek Narayanan, poet and translator, has been a huge source of encouragement and inspiration. I would also like to thank Ruchir Joshi, Sharanya Manivannan, Kushanava Ghosh, and Sibaji Pratim Basu for their encouragement. The continuing assistance of my colleague Tapas Ghosh must also be acknowledged. As this book went to press, I learned of the tragic death of Colie Hoffman, poet, who was a fellow-resident in Sangam House and Ledig House and had been warmly appreciative of my work.

It has been a pleasure to work with Karthika V. K. and Shantanu Ray Chaudhuri of HarperCollins India. Sk. Jan Mohammad lent his masterly skills for the original cover design.

Several of the stories have appeared in journals and e-zines. These include: *Nether, Metamorphoses, Almost Island, The Four Quarters Magazine, Open Road Review, Northeastern Review, Earthen Lamp Journal, AntiSerious, Out of Print,* and *Caesurae.* One story appears in the anthology, *Other Places,* published by Sangam House, and a text collage that includes excerpts from several of the stories in this collection appears in *Strangely Beloved: The City of Calcutta,* edited by Nilanjana Gupta. I am grateful to the editors of these publications for carrying the stories. Gaurav Jain, of *Tehelka,* interviewed Subimal Misra in 2010, in the wake of the publication of *The Golden Gandhi Statue from America.* The full version of the interview is included in *P. S. Section* of this volume.

Subimal Misra's short fiction is now being translated into Malayalam and Farsi, and I am grateful to Cecily Joyce, Anuradha Sarang and Mustafa Raziee for their initiative in this regard.

My grandfather, T. V. Ramaswamy, came to Calcutta in 1930 to take up a job and lived here for the next fifty years. My father lived in this city all his life; he would have been eighty-five now. But for them, I would not be here today.

Kolkata was their home, as it has been for me. My translation project is a small contribution, in gratitude, to Kolkata and Bengal, and to the Bangla language, on behalf of my Tamil family.

V. Ramaswamy

ADDITIONAL RESOURCES

SUBIMAL MISRA ON READING HIS WRITING

AN INTERVIEW WITH SUBIMAL MISRA

SUBIMAL MISRA,
THE CRYPTO-REVOLUTIONARY

Subimal Misra on Reading His Writing

"In the capitalist system, artists and litterateurs have to survive by being amicable sometimes, and sometimes by wrestling . . . he stands on the left side, left of everyone . . . I do not want my writing to be converted into a commodity, or be capable of being digested in the intestines of middle-class babudom. I want to make writing into a weapon against repressive civilization."

". . . Given that which takes place flagrantly all day, the mentality of avoiding that and escaping is idiotic. If the perspective of social conflict does not emerge—if that is not elaborated upon—it's nothing but a ploy to make money from the business of bright topics. If sexual titillation is the only objective—a rape scene, if it remains just a rape scene; if the conflict-ridden process behind the rape is not indicated, if it's not saturated with the economic backwardness—if upon reading it, hatred toward the social system does not arise in the readers' mind, if it does not make one aware about the terrifying nature of the capitalist scheme of things . . . The fundamental thing is the point of view, from which angle it's being shown. Just as the writer who denies reality is dead, again, the writer who merely writes admitting the reality, is also just as dead, for the same reason."

". . . Not merely left or right politics, my battle's against anything connected with every kind of establishment—which suppresses people, and does not let them be fully human."

—From the anti-novel, *This Could Have Become Ramayan Chamar's Tale* (1982)

"The needs of the reader who makes an effort to become one with the times are not met merely by the popular stream of stories and novels. For him the story has to say many more things beside the story. And it is through these many more things that the real character of the writer can be discerned. Consider all the information and statistics pertaining to a country or a society, which are easily available in books and are published in newspapers. Some truths are contained ever more clearly in the many more things of a story, the effort is made to make it contain that. It's because of the credibility of the writer's effort that a piece of text is simultaneously story, history, proclamation, and personal diary. The carrying capacity of the text can be stretched as far as man's thinking and imagination can reach and ascend. And in the normal course of things, in the eyes of the unpracticed reader, it may well appear complex and entirely doomed. A story or a novel is not merely a form of art, it is also a medium of expression of a personality. On the other hand, the writer is not merely a social theorist or sophisticated political thinker. The conscience of the independent writer submits only to truth and truth alone. And in that sense, it is the task of a writer to raise all kinds of questions, of all sides . . . and to always evaluate the possibility of alternative realities. Let us be able to recognize our own likes outside of the likes imposed on us."

". . . I don't know whether my writing is Marxist or not, but I do know that my fundamental inclination is to investigate. Until now, it is the search, rather than reaching a decision on anything, that I'm more enthusiastic about. I am always aware of my sense of incompleteness, and the inclination to search arises from this sense of incompleteness. I look at two broad strata in society (the arrangement of strata is however not so easy and simple, rather it is quite complex and this is not the place for a discussion on that): a certain class is content with the progress of a few people, while most people, ordinary laboring folk, are merely a means for the progress of the few people. Today there is an effort to build a society where the progress of the majority of people takes place. There is no end to artful analyses or opinions about this, and to the division into levels as well, but it is clear that my writing and the attempt of my writing is against those who in earlier times had the sole right over culture, and in favor of the excluded people."

—From the anti-novel, *When Color is a Warning Sign* (1984)

An Interview with Subimal Misra

Caveat

I give very few interviews, and when I do, it is only for literary magazines. Prior to this one, I never thought it necessary to give answers to any other periodical or newspaper. I never went to the media. Hence, owing to my unfamiliarity, I don't know how useful it is. But I can't make it any easier or simpler, even if I tried to.

Translator adds: Subimal Misra does not like to converse in any language other than his mother tongue. This is extremely difficult to translate, especially in a manner that conveys its precise literary flavor. I have tried my best to render his answers into English.

Gaurav Jain, 4 August 2010, translated by V. Ramaswamy, *Tehelka*, online edition, 9 September 2010.

Gaurav Jain: *What have been the major changes in your stories since these stories from the 1960s* (referring to the book *The Golden Gandhi Statue from America*—Trs.)?

Subimal Misra: There have been many phases in my writing over the past few decades. Getting out, and then getting away from montage, collage, and cut-up, I tried to make my voice more pinpointed, so that even without seeing the writer's name people could know for certain that this was Subimal Misra's writing. (There are both positive and negative aspects to this.) In my writing, I have used the form of the story, my own secret diary, reportage, excerpts from advertisements, pornography, slang—even a series of interviews with dacoits from south Bengal. Everything was mixed up, to became a unified whole. I walk along my own path through all this, whether this has been a progress or not I don't know. I am unable to say how much of it is story, and how much simply text.

In my writing, and especially in my current writing, there is a conscious tendency to abandon "meta-narrative." There need not be a definite, fixed meaning of all the words, all the time. One may discover that the same words may have been used in diametrically opposite ways in the same text. Or one may find that the text is broken up and thus deconstructed and made interpenetrating and interdependent. In the sequential flow of the narrative, "yes" and "no" become mutually interdependent.

What I sense now is that if a person continuously and consistently wants to rebel, at a certain juncture he also has to become a rebel against his own rebellion. Finally the business of deconstruction has itself to be deconstructed.

GJ: *After the initial experiments of these stories and all your subsequent work, what are your conclusions today about using montage in literature?*

SM: Where's the montage? There was just one montage-based title, *Haran Majhir Bidhoba Bouer Mora Ba Shonar Gandhimurti* (Haran Majhi's Widow's Corpse or the Golden Gandhi Statue). Two sentences of completely opposite forms were taken and imprinted on the consciousness of the reader (something thought of by Eisenstein, but here my own conception). As a shortcut, that was shortened, apparently because such a long and unconventional name could not be gulped by readers. This is the unfortunate plight of an independent writer who wants to reach the public. Abandoning montage, abandoning the phase of anti-stories and anti-novels, abandoning personal story-writing—involving story and text, a very personal kind of prose—I have been carrying on, with constant enlargement, from the late '60s.

GJ: *The characters in these stories often have no history, and minimum social context—they are very cinematic in that way. When you read them today do you find them too thin, or do you consider cinematic characters to be valid in literature?*

SM: Unless one reads the writing in the original Bengali, one cannot reach the various dimensions. To put it differently—a scholar and doctor like Isak Borg (portrayed by Victor Sjöström) was so selfish, and yet Bergman did not see any purpose in elaborating that social context in a so-called realistic manner. A desolate city road, mid-afternoon, a clock without hands, the sound of the hooves of a horse, one of whose eyes is blinkered, and from that ramshackle horse-carriage there falls a coffin—from within which a dead man's hand is outstretched, and held captive in its closed fist is Borg's pale, ancient hand. That extremely dramatic revelation is a terrifying scene. Was the dead man actually Borg himself? Was this his soul's corpse, which he was carrying on his body? Shadow-free light over the entire surroundings. The use of sound and camera is astounding. And lying there, like something rejected, is the sleeping Borg, who is supposed to receive the most important honor of his life in the city the next day. Watching *Wild Strawberries* is like encountering a fragment of a poem communicating an endless, powerful, impenetrable secret. No, Bergman did not see any point in elaborating Borg's real social context in one of the world's greatest, human documents.

GJ: *There seems very little happiness in these stories, little joy of being alive. One of the main charms of the young Godard was his enthusiasm for life's small joys. Did you disagree with him on that?*

SM: Godard taught a new form of the thought process of argument, which is seemingly not a process at all. But I do not imitate Godard's method. One can go very deep into that subject, but that would not be fitting here. And "joy?" There are multiple levels and dimensions in my writing. People take something from my writing based on how capable they are. How many people get "joy" from Faiyaz Khan-Baba Alauddin-Amir Khan, or from Beethoven-Mozart-Bach? How many people can claim to possess the musical awareness to listen patiently to Indian classical music's supreme form, Dhrupad? How many people are happy reading Dante-Proust-Joyce? These things, all of these, occupy a marginal space, and are for very few people. To put it differently, people derive great "joy" watching Hindi films, yet they have not heard the name of Mani Kaul. I do not consider such people to be "educated." "Joy" cannot be simply obtained, it has to be earned.

GJ: *How can artists like you and Godard today be effective critics of mainstream culture if you remain so cut away from it?*

SM: My short reply is, definitely yes, I did do that, and I will be able to do it. By actually staying far away from the media-fed, glamor-debased world, Subimal Misra wants to reach his readers by writing in little magazines which print only two or three hundred copies in Bengali. He wants to be tested thus. He wants to be judged by his writing alone, and not by media publicity. Here, in such matters, two lines of Rabindrasangeet inspire his work:

"না হয় তোমার যা হয়েছে তাই হল
আরো কিছু নাই হল – নাই হল।"

Na hoy tomar ja hoyeche taiyi holo
aro kichu nayii holo—nayii holo

What this means is:

You may not have gotten what you sought,
but what you did get is enough,
So what if you did not get anything more?

One more point I'd like to add here is that you can be sure that I cannot be made to accept any award or prize—small, big, middling, whatever be its stature—which has become cheaper than even a "sack of potatoes" now—awards which only serve to identify mediocrity, not genius. When the Nobel Prize was instituted, Tolstoy was alive, as was Joyce. Their genius was beyond the imagination of those who decided on the awards. And Sartre's refusal of the Nobel Prize is of course legend.

GJ: *What has been your main goal in your writing? Do you feel hope for it today, after all the years of rejection and marginalization?*

SM: I do not have any goal, in the commonly under-stood sense, in my writing. While watching *Sholay*, I only wanted to know the name of Gabbar Singh's horse.

There is a notion of an average in the mainstream. Average knowledge, average taste, average entertainment, even though in reality things are not so easy or simple. What you consider rejection or marginalization actually challenges a linear and one-dimensional notion of prog-ress. In my view, what Foucault calls "disciplinary power" is only one part of the establishment, of the mainstream. The hidden, unseen threads of power are spread all over, and are constantly at play in different forms or garbs.

Some people think that mainstream culture yields only hollow pleasure, but on the opposite side, we argue, we make people think, compel them to think about their situ-ation, about their surroundings. From the time of Socrates, to Rousseau, to Nietzsche, all of them, at one time or the other, in one form or the other, saw this mainstream culture in a negative light. Some people realize greater joy not from the mainstream but from the opposite side, even though they are only a minuscule part of the whole population. It is because they are there on the opposite side that the mainstream is also in existence. But I also feel that there are gaps in such thinking on my part, things can't be drawn in such an easy, simple way.

No conception is complete by itself, independent of others. But on the other hand, this may also not be so.

GJ: *What gives you hope today?*

SM: Everything, and also nothing whatsoever. Whatever exists in this world bears the shadow of everything else.

GJ: *What do you think of the major Bengali writers that remain popular today, from Tagore to Amitav Ghosh?*

SM: From whatever little I have read of Amitav Ghosh, I don't think he has been able to develop something distinctive. He hasn't even learned how to render an ambiguous sentence! Rabindranath's pictures and his songs are more dear to me than his literature.

Only one book written in recent times in English, just one, could agitate me somewhat, that's *Satanic Verses*. Yes, Rushdie is capable. And although out of context, I would like to say that my favorite film director in India is not Satyajit Ray, but Ritwik Kumar Ghatak.

GJ: *Which contemporary writers do you enjoy reading today? Why?*

SM: Even now, ultimately I turn only to *Finnegans Wake*. I try to read it again in one form or another. Even in 2010, I consider this to be the most modern book. However many rimes I read this, somehow, new meanings and dimensions emerge, I discover new word constructions.

Postscript

Subimal Misra has not taken any of your questions lightly, the way a journalist's questions are treated casually. Rather he has tried to answer the questions seriously, which is why the answers have become a bit lengthy. He has said that his response should not be edited under any circumstances, and should either be reproduced verbatim, or rejected.

Subimal Misra,
the Crypto-Revolutionary

Janam Mukherjee

Although a "Mukherjee" by birth, I am no Bengali. My father fled Bengal, in fact, long before I came into this world. What he had left behind remained scarcely discernible, except in the moans of his nightmares and in the few truncated stories he told me of his impossible youth. After coming to America he married a woman of European descent; the daughter of a "rounder," half-Irish and half-Hungarian. My rough-living Irish grandfather (my mother's father) rode the rails in the 1920s, leaving Chicago at the age of thirteen and traveling—rough—back and forth across America for the next several decades—a real-life hobo; drinking, fighting, loving, *living,* and even, occasionally, working. Back in Chicago, he lost a few

Janam Mukherjee is the author of *Hungry Bengal: War, Famine, Riots and the End of Empire* fingers in a machine press, probably either half-drunk or fully hungover, when the steel punch came down across his hand. If I remember correctly, it was the middle finger that was cut off at the knuckle, and the ring finger that was cut at the cuticle. From that cuticle a hardened, twisted yellow nail used to grow—"shorty and the claw" he used to call the pair of them. Though not formally educated past the age of thirteen, he read three newspapers a day and commanded the respect of even the likes of university professors (such as my father), who would defer to his wit, super-sharp "common sense," and unflinching honesty.

Well into my twenties, my grandfather remained my hero and role model. Accordingly, as soon as I could, I left home and began to travel—rough—like him. By the time I was thirty, I too had clocked tens of thousands of miles on the open roads of America, had ridden freight trains, slept beneath overpasses, spent nights in jails, and days under the scorching desert sun of the southwestern United States, waiting for an improbable ride. At times I lived on whiskey fumes and stale pizza, at other times, on the kindness of strangers. In any dicey situation, I channeled my grandfather, and his spirit would see me through. By and by, I thought, I was growing tough and wise, just like him. Unlike him, however, I meant to *document* the passage. While my grandfather was an inestimable raconteur who could hold any given audience rapt, I would be a writer—a great American writer. But aside from being a bum and an occasional manual laborer, in order to write, I knew, I would also have to *read*. And so I read, and read: Faulkner, Miller, Bukowski, Fante, Beckett, Hamsun, Stoppard, O'Neil, Sartre, Camus, Dostoevsky, Baldwin, Cleaver—anything and everything that I understood to be anti-establishment, pro-rebellion, iconoclastic, debauched—*free*.

To cut a long story short, after many thousands of miles, and as many packs of cigarettes, I began to wonder about my methods. I was working hard to generate stories, to accumulate "experience," to hone my perception and to concoct a style to cleverly impart my hard-won "wisdom." At times—in those halcyon days—I even sometimes imagined that I was succeeding. But overall, there seemed something terribly artificial in the exercise. The commotion, displacement, irony, and slapstick that defined my own life—and prose—was almost entirely of my own invention, and as such could never really escape being ultimately contrived. Meanwhile, there were still those haunting stories —*real* stories—of my father's—of a life far away, stories of a world where corpses of starvation victims got stacked like chord wood in the streets, a world of riots and bombings, of madness, cruel indifference, fierce resolutions, and fear. There was no joy in the telling of such stories and very little artifice, but, nevertheless, they remained powerful and profound. Most often they were told in a low and sad voice. Sometimes after telling them my father would cry. But what could such stories mean to me? At school in New York I was called a "spic" and a "nigger." If I protested that I was, in fact, half "Indian," that only drew the predictable howls and jokes about head-feathers and teepees. And to be truthful, the idea of any "Indian"—no less Bengali—identity meant scarcely little more to me. I had cut my teeth—quite literally—on Marlboro boxes. My secret ambition was to play basketball in the NBA. Henry David Thoreau, more than any other thinker, informs my political sensibilities, and

Charles Bukowski remains my favorite poet. I knew not a word of Bengali, and cared nothing about my supposed "roots." But those stories of my father's . . . a writer *needs* stories.

So, having run the gamut of American life, I traveled for the first time to Calcutta, in search of stories. In particular, I was interested in the Calcutta riots of 1946, the "Great Calcutta Killings," that had left my family, along with so many others, refugees. I had heard it so many times: the attack on the house, the bloodcurdling cries, my father's sister bludgeoned, her husband's family slaughtered, the fire, the fear, the shots from a rusty rifle, the escape . . . And then the years of uncertainty, compounding misfortune; sorrow, uncertainty, loneliness. Though without any substantial knowledge of Bengal, by the time I left for Calcutta in 1999, I could almost feel the riots in my very bones. The riots had driven my father across the sea and by now they had become firmly lodged inside of me. My aim was to excavate those riots, about which I could find almost nothing written, and thus reconstruct the story of my father's childhood in war-torn Calcutta.

But as I began my investigations on the riots, at the frayed end of each and every lead that I followed, what I was repeatedly confronted with, was *famine*. What I came to realize was that in as much as the riots emerged from a specific sociopolitical context, the most salient factor impacting the lives of the vast majority of the population of Bengal during this entire period was *hunger*. And so, in the end, what began as a personally motivated investigation of the Calcutta riots quickly developed into a multifaceted investigation of the catastrophic event called the Bengal Famine of 1943.

That first visit I spent two years in the city of my father's birth, learning Bengali, struggling to come to an understanding of the complex and chaotic culture of Calcutta, renamed Kolkata during my stay, and talking to anyone I could find who had survived the 1940s in Bengal and wished to share their stories. Ten more years of intensive research, as a Fulbright Scholar and doctoral student in Anthropology and History has finally culminated in a historical monograph, *Hungry Bengal*, that details this period of violence and despair in great depth. In my analysis I conclude that famine in Bengal cannot merely be seen as the "collateral damage" of war, nor simply as the crystallization of the monstrous structural violence of colonialism, but it must also be understood in relation to a shocking proliferation of local venalities: the rapaciousness of the middle class, the cruel expediency of extortionary intermediaries, and the mute complicities of an increasingly callous society at large, increasingly inured to death, becoming increasingly more indifferent, month after month, and then year after year. It is also the story of a mushrooming and pervasive moral bankruptcy that stems from the burden of a thousand banal decisions made in the face of increasing despair.

Over these years of research in Kolkata, I was inevitably concerned not only with the historical landscape of pre-independent Bengal, but also remained deeply immersed in the project of coming to terms with the seething city around me—endlessly fascinated by the complexities, ironies, outrages and eruptions that characterize Kolkata even today. Meanwhile, my perspective remained that of the grandson of a hobo, the son of a refugee, a child of foreign sensibilities, deeply influenced not by Saratchandra or Rabindrasangeet, but by Jack Kerouac and Allen Ginsberg, Flannery O'Connor, and Tennessee Williams. From these angles, I looked into every crevice and corner, ventured into every back alley, and peeled my eyes to every encounter with adamant openness. There was much that was new, moving, shocking, enlightening—even beautiful—but there was also much that was dark, contemptible and infuriating; cruelty, violence, outrage; scenes and scenarios that one wishes one had turned away from, rather than stared down intently. Steeped as I was in the history of famine and riots, moreover, what was perhaps most disorienting of all was a sense of dizzying simultaneity between the city at large and the history of it that I was delving deeper into. Hunger *still* seemed to be everywhere, haunting the shadows, moaning in dingy corners, undoing the faces of young children on street corners, gnawing at the spines of middle-aged sweepers, and silently ravaging the collective consciousness of society at large, an ongoing instigation to yet further violence, yet further indifference, yet further merciless competition for resources, for space, for human dignity. At length there arose a burning question in my mind—which still burns today—did the Bengal Famine ever really come to an "end"?

But there was yet another aspect to my meditations that was just as disconcerting; namely, that they were my own and seemed to be shared by few others. My interlocutors in Kolkata were almost exclusively middle class, educated, Hindu, housed. Many were shocked when I recounted the scenes that I had witnessed on the streets of *their* city. What violence? What hunger? And how could that be? Surely *someone* must have done something about it! (Perhaps it was that a ten-year-old girl had been dragged through the street by her hair for failing to fold an uncle's punjabi shirt properly . . .) "How is it that you are always turning up such things?" At times, in conversation with my genteel contacts, I felt that perhaps I had gone slightly mad, that my immersion in history was corrupting my clarity, and that the hunger and violence that I found haunting the sidewalks and alleys of Calcutta were merely figments of my imagination, hallucinations of an overwrought historical imagination that hears echoes of a clamorous past everywhere. "You seem to be too focused on these things, Janam, there is much more to Bengali culture than all that. We all remember the famine, the famine is with us still, but not in the way you seem to think. We have come a long way . . ." And yet, still the emaciated figures prostrate on doorsteps, and still the nose-holding "Babu," who has nothing to share with the skeletal old widow, and still the sharp-kneed "Party Worker," who gives one to the groin of the half-starved potato farmer on the local train just to let that wretch know who the boss is.

It was not until I met the translator of these stories, V. Ramaswamy, that I was able to conclude with any certainty that I was, in fact, still in my right mind. It was he who confirmed for me that these visions were actual, and that there exists a vast conspiracy of *not seeing* that renders many of the moneyed classes in Bengal almost completely ignorant about the more brutal aspects of the social reality that surrounds them—and which they, in fact, willfully, if blindly, reproduce. It was, moreover, my introduction (again through Ramaswamy) to the prose of Subimal Misra that confirmed for me that not only were these sights real, but that they are *meaningful* and despite inclinations otherwise, one *should never look away.*

Everywhere in Misra's stories one finds the stark ravages of a hunger that is impossible to ignore, a mute but irrepressible destitution that nags every plot and that pricks at the conscience of the reader. In the title story, "Wild Animals Prohibited," it is the haunting materiality of hunger—in the body of a beggar girl—that spoils the mindless hedonism of a middle-class sex club, as in the more poetic "Health for all by 2000," it is a headline announcing the death by starvation of forty-five thousand Indians a day that interrupts the writer's morning tea. Such juxtapositions of want and excess underwrite the jarring candor of Subimal's prose and reveal enormous amounts about the craven dynamics of entrenched inequality and structural violence: the middle-class girl in "Spot Eczematous" who dreams of making lice fried rice the "food of the proletariat"; the "elderly revolutionaries," in "How a Horse Becomes a Donkey," who "afflicted by constipation, enunciate the objective condition of the nation, spewing Marx–Lenin"; while, as in "Drumstick Flowers Make a Fine Chochchori" the little children of Radhanath, a beedi-worker, "stay at home and make beedis instead of going to school . . . [and] never get the opportunity to hear about the International Year of the Child."

In all the stories in this volume, in fact, Misra examples a truly rare form of prose that probes into the dark recesses of human society and consciousness, revealing the hunger, craven desire, cruelty and absurdity of uninspected lives. In this aspect, Misra's writing represents a mission that he himself (in one of his inventive flights of meta-narrative) describes as "shock therapy." Hunger and power intermingle at random in the cauldron of characters that Misra stews, and while it is always power that puts the boot down across the neck of the hungry, an almost inexplicable inkling of humanity silently accrues to the downtrodden, and all at once—in a word, or a gesture, or even in a stench (as in the case of Misra's story "Golden Gandhi Statue from America")—breaks through to starkly reveal the vanity and diabolic arrogance of power. In his undaunted attention to dark detail, in his penchant for describing the depravity of the rich, the indifference of the bourgeoisie and the malignancy of the sociopolitical order, Misra might be compared to Faulkner, or Celine, or Elfriede Jelinek. But in the irreducible material *presence* (and in many cases it *is* sheer physical presence alone) of the poor and the downtrodden, Misra identifies an immanent critique to power and impunity. It is not that Misra "champions" the poor, and in no sense does he promote any particular social agenda, instead, he extremely artfully demonstrates that for all the jockeying and chicanery, for all of the *will* to snuff them out, or push them aside, or smite them—either through violence or indifference—the wretched of the earth still *remain*, and in their mere *existence* lies proof that power is both inhumane *and* incomplete. In this double revelation, Misra might be understood as a crypto-revolutionary, pointing not only to the human wreckage that power and social hierarchy leave in their wake, but also to the weakness in power that allows for such human refuse to *still* disrupt its morning tea.

Between Subimal Misra's "anti-stories" and my own historical work on Bengal in the 1940s, I see a strange affinity. A central aim in my empirical account of famine in Bengal was to expose the intimate (and obscene) relationship between power and hunger, and to narrate the extent to which the fulfilment of the craven desires of some is *dependent* on the abject immiseration of others. Moreover, I wanted to capture the way that clamorous greed silences human sorrow. During famine it was the din of power—in its depraved pursuit for money, resources, recognition, "security," and even sex—that provided cover for the annihilation of the poor masses, while in the "middle"—between "power" and destitution—morals failed, fear prevailed, and a grotesque callousness deepened to the point of inhumanity. Hunger, in this sense, provides a singular hermeneutic to examine a very sick society. It was not, however, the plight of the destitute and dying that I aimed to capture in my work, but rather the broader effects on "civilization" at large, of brutal inequality. I also wanted to detail the multiplying moral hazards of passively upholding structures that guarantee human extermination, and the particular kind of heartlessness this entails. Famine is just as much a story about human cruelty, self-interest, vanity, insatiability, and vindictiveness as it is about starvation. Subimal Misra's work confronts similar themes and supports my contention that *famine in Bengal has never ended*. Throughout his work, hunger continues to haunt the landscape—hunger as the foil against which all plots unfold, and hunger as the hermeneutic that belies the vain gesticulations of disappointed lives. He himself draws the historical link to the Bengal famine in "Calcutta Dateline": "A dog stands over a dead body, tears out and eats the flesh. It wouldn't have been proper to show this scene too clearly. Why does the moon cast so much light on the dry riverbed on the night after the new moon? Bit by bit, the past arrives and becomes meshed with the present."

The famine, again, and again—forever reappearing in violence done to the bodies of the poor and the willed ignorance of the self-contented. Though "it would not be proper," Misra always shows the scene, all too clearly—without apology or pause. *"A dog stands over a dead body, tears out and eats the flesh."* This same unflinching frankness is perhaps why I began this note by mentioning my own Irish grandfather. Subimal Misra's writing, like his life, always reminds me that if there is redemption to be found at all, it can only be found in a street-fighting sense of honesty. In the fight against brutal inequality, it is not a question of change, but a question of justice—the most universal question of all—and justice demands breaking through the deathly silence of "proper" lives. Wild animals not prohibited.

Toronto
July 2014

SUBIMAL MISRA is a Bengali novelist, short story writer, and essayist. He's considered by many to be one of most important, and experimental, Bengali writers of all time. Heavily influenced by Jean-Luc Godard and William S. Burroughs, Subimal Misra uses various cinematic techniques, like montage, jump-cut, etc., in his literary works. The author of more than a dozen books, *Wild Animals Prohibited* is his second collection to appear in the United States.

V. RAMASWAMY is a nonfiction writer and translator based in Kolkata, India. As an activist working for the rights of the laboring poor, Ramaswamy has written about workers, squatters, slums, poverty, housing, and resettlement, and has been at the forefront of efforts to envision and initiate the rebuilding of his city from the grassroots. Since 2005, he has been translating the short fiction of the Bengali anti-establishment experimental writer, Subimal Misra, whose critical eye examines the society, politics, and culture of his time.